LITTLE SCARLET

WALTER MOSLEY

LITTLE SCARLET

Weidenfeld & Nicolson

LONDON

First published in Great Britain in 2005
by Weidenfeld & Nicolson, a division of
the Orion Publishing Group Ltd
Orion House
5 Upper Saint Martin's Lane
London
WC2H 9EA

1 3 5 7 9 10 8 6 4 2

A CIP catalogue record for this book
is available from the British Library

ISBN 0 297 848283

Printed and bound by Butler & Tanner Ltd,
Frome and London

www.orionbooks.co.uk

For Gregory Hines

LITTLE SCARLET

1

The morning air still smelled of smoke. Wood ash mainly but there was also the acrid stench of burnt plastic and paint. And even though I knew it couldn't be true, I thought I caught a whiff of putrid flesh from under the rubble across the street. The hardware store and Bernard's Stationery Store were both completely gutted. The Gonzalez Market had been looted but only a part of its roof had been scorched. The corner building, however, Lucky Dime Liquors, had been burned to the ground. Manny Massman was down in the rubble with his two sons, kicking the metal fixtures. At one point the middle-aged store owner lowered his head and cried. His sons put their hands on his shoulders.

I understood how he felt. He had everything in that liquor store. His whole life. And now, after a five-day eruption of rage that had been simmering for centuries, he was penniless and destitute.

In his mind he hadn't done a thing wrong to anyone down in Watts. He had never even thought about calling someone a nigger or boy. But the men and women down around Central and Eighty-sixth Place took everything of Manny's that they could carry, then smashed and burned the rest.

Four young black men passed in front of the liquor lot. One of them shouted something at the white men.

Manny barked back.

The youths stopped.

The Massman sons stepped forward with their chests out and their mouths full of angry sounds.

It's starting all over again, I thought. Maybe we'll be rioting a whole year. Maybe it won't ever end.

The black men crossed the threshold of the Lucky Dime's property line.

Stephen Massman bent down to pick up a piece of metal that had once been attached to their counter.

One of the angry youths shoved Martin.

I held my breath.

"Halt!" a man shouted through a megaphone.

A dozen or more soldiers appeared out of nowhere. A black soldier wearing a helmet and camouflage khakis talked to the black men while four white soldiers stood in an arc in front of the store owners. The rest of the troop stood across the property line cutting off the ravaged lot from the street.

Most of the National Guardsmen brandished rifles. A crowd was gathering. My hands clenched into fists so tight that my right forearm went into a spasm.

While I massaged out the knot of pain, the black soldier, a

sergeant, calmed the four youths. I could hear his voice but my fourth-story window was too far away for me to make out the words.

I turned away from the scene and fell into the plush blue chair that sat at my desk. For the next hour I just sat there, hearing the sounds of people in the street but not daring to look down.

It had been like that for the past five days: me holding myself in check while South Los Angeles went up in the flames of a race riot; while stores were looted and snipers fired and while men, women, and children cried "Burn, baby, burn!" and "Get whitey!" on every corner familiar to me.

I stayed shut up in my home, in peaceful West L.A., not drinking and not going out with a trunk full of Molotov cocktails.

WHEN I FINALLY roused myself the street down below was full of black people, some venturing out of their homes for the first time since the first night of rioting. Most of them looked stunned.

I went to my office door and out into the hall.

There was the smell of smoke in the building too, but not much. Steinman's Shoe Repair was the only store that had been torched. That was on the first night, when the fire trucks still braved the hails of sniper bullets. The flames were put out before they could spread.

I went to the far stairwell from my office and down the three flights to Steinman's side entrance. There was a burnt timber blocking the way. I would have turned around if it weren't for the voices.

"What the hell you mean you don't have my shoes, white man?"

"Everything is burned up," a frail voice replied in a mild German accent.

"That's not my fault, man," the angry voice said. "I give you my shoes, I expect to get them back."

"They are all burned."

"And do you think if this was my store that I could tell you I didn't have nuthin' for ya?" the customer said. "Do you think a black man could just say his store done burned down so he don't have to make good on his responsibilities?"

"I don't have your shoes."

I shoved the timber out of the way, smudging the palms of my hands with sooty charcoal. When I came into the burned-out room, both occupants turned to look at me.

Theodore was a short, powerfully built white man with little hair and big hands. The irate customer was much larger, with a wide chest and a big face that would have been beautiful on a woman.

"Hey, Theodore," I said.

"Wait your turn, man," the Negro customer warned. "I got business to take care of first."

He swiveled his head back to the cobbler and said, "Those shoes costed me thirty-six dollars and if you can't give 'em up right now I want to see some money across this here hand."

I took a quick breath and then another. There was an electric tingle over my right cheekbone and for a moment the room was tinged in red.

"Brother," I said. "You got to go."

"Are you talkin' to me, niggah?"

"You heard me," I said in a tone that you can't make up. "I been in the house for some time now, trying not to break out and start doin' wrong. I've been patient and treadin' softly. But if you say one more word to my friend here I will break you like a matchstick and throw you out in the street."

"I want my shoes," the big beautiful man said with tears in his voice. "He owe it to me. It don't matter what they did."

I heard his cracked tone. I knew that he was just as crazy as I was at that moment. We were both black men filled with a passionate rage that was too big to be held in. I didn't want to fight but I knew that once I started, the only thing that would stop me would be his lifeless throat crushed by my hand.

"Here you are, sir," Theodore said.

He was handing over a ten-dollar bill.

"Your shoes were old, you know," the shoemaker said. "And they both needed soles. It was a good make and I would have bought them for seven dollars. So here's ten."

The burly man stared at the note a moment. Then he looked up at me.

"Forget it," he said.

He turned around so quickly that he lost his balance for a moment and had to reach out for a broken, charred timber for support.

"Ow!" he shouted, probably because of a splinter, but I can't say for sure because he blundered out, tearing the front door off of its last hinge as he went.

There was a sleek antique riding saddle on the floor, under a shattered wooden chair. I moved away the kindling and picked up the saddle. Theodore had received it from his uncle who was a riding master in Munich before World War I. I'd always admired the leatherwork.

Setting the riding gear on a fairly stable part of his ruined worktable, I said, "You didn't have to pay him, Mr. Steinman."

"He was hurting," the small man replied. "He wanted justice."

"That's not your job."

"It is all of our job," he said, staring at me with blue eyes. "You cannot forget that."

"Ezekiel Rawlins?"

It was a question asked in a voice filled with authority. It was a white man's voice. Putting those bits of information together, I knew that I was being addressed by the police.

2

He wore a rumpled green suit and a white shirt that had yellowed from too many launderings. He didn't wear a hat but it was already almost eighty degrees and too hot for the kind of hat that unkempt white man would own. His tie was like a muddy creek bed with a few murky jewels showing through.

"Are you Ezekiel Rawlins?" he asked. "I was up at your office. A man across the hall said you'd gone downstairs."

I waited for him to say more.

"Detective Melvin Suggs," the man said.

He held out a hand.

I looked at it. Not many policemen had offered to shake hands with me. Outstretched hands of the law held wooden batons and pistols, handcuffs and warrants but rarely a welcome and never an offer of equality.

"What is it you want, Detective?"

Melvin Suggs first closed his hand and then opened it to rub his fingertips together. His smile held little friendliness and that was fine by me. I didn't need a friendly white cop right then. Enough of my world had already been turned inside out.

"Are you here about the damage to the building, officer?" Theodore Steinman asked.

I could have told my friend that the policeman hadn't come for our structural troubles. The cop was there for me. He needed me to help him — that's what I thought at the time.

"No sir," Suggs said. "There will be a unit here later in the week to investigate every act of arson and looting. But right now I have to speak to Mr. Rawlins."

"That's too bad," I said, "because right now I have to help my friend clean up what's left of his store."

"This is important," the policeman said, again in that tone of authority.

"People got problems all up and down the street, Officer. Every doorway got some kinda mark on it. People lost their businesses, their jobs. Some little old ladies got to take a bus five miles just to find a store to buy a quarter pound of margarine."

"But only thirty-four people lost their lives," he said.

"Radio said this morning that it was thirty-three dead," I said, feeling the need to contradict him.

"One went unreported," the policeman replied. "It's a special case and we would like you to take a look at it."

"Excuse me, Officer, but you must be mistaking me for some other Ezekiel Rawlins. I'm just a custodian for the board of education, down at Sojourner Truth Junior High School. I don't have any official capacity whatsoever."

"No. I have the right man."

Suggs had brilliant taupe-colored eyes that somehow fit his grubby appearance. He just stood there, staring at me.

For my part I turned to assess the destroyed cobbler's shop. All he had left was the burnt and broken worktable surrounded by a couple hundred pairs of scorched shoes. Why would somebody want to burn shoes? Other than with footwear, the floor was covered with things turned out of Theodore Steinman's drawers, shelves, and filing cabinet. There was a bone-handled pocketknife, a yellow package of Juicy Fruit chewing gum, a fat pink eraser, and maybe a thousand rubber bands. There were index cards marked by the footprints of looters and firemen, and the torn and crumpled leaves of a Bible written in German. Under a broken oak chair I saw a small shattered pane of glass within the loose confines of a splintered wood frame. I knelt down and shook the slivers of glass from a portrait-like photograph of Sylvie — Theodore's muse and wife.

"Oh my," the shoemaker said when I handed him the scraped and punctured picture.

He cradled it in both hands as if holding a baby.

"Mr. Rawlins," Detective Suggs said.

I had forgotten he was there.

"What?"

"Go, Ezekiel," Theodore Steinman said. "He needs you."

"I can't leave you here like this, Theodore. Suppose somebody else comes for his shoes like that guy?"

"I will talk to him."

I already knew that Theodore had blue eyes. I had been bringing my shoes to the man for nearly twenty years. I see things, things that other people overlook. That's why the sign on my office door reads EASY RAWLINS — RESEARCH AND DELIVERY. But there was something about the quality in Theodore's eyes that I had never seen before. It was as if the violence of the past few days had given me the power to look deeper, or maybe it was that the people around me had changed — Theodore and his angry customer and maybe even Melvin Suggs, the cop that approached me with his hand proffered in greeting.

DETECTIVE SUGGS AND I left through the now doorless doorway of the shoe shop. That took us out onto Central. There were dozens of people wandering the street. This was unusual because in L.A. even poor people got around by car. But in the aftermath of the riots, the smoke in the air brought people out by foot to investigate the aftermath of a race war.

Suggs drove a Rambler Marlin. It was roomy and equipped with seat belts.

"I never use the damn things," the cop told me. "It's my ex. She says I can't take the kids unless I have 'em."

We had been driving for quite some time when I asked, "So what do you want from me, Officer?"

"I got a case that needs solving outside of the public eye."

"You?"

"The LAPD," he said. "Chief Parker, Mayor Yorty."

Suggs didn't look at me while he talked. He didn't seem like the kind of driver who needed to keep his eyes on the road, so I guessed he was a little embarrassed by needing my help. This was both a good and a bad thing. If you were a black man in L.A. at that time (or at any time) it always helped to have a leg up on the authorities. But you didn't want to have it too far up; because the higher you get, the further you have to fall.

"What case?" I asked.

"You'll see when we get there."

"No I will not."

"What?"

"Either you tell me where we're going and what it is you plan to get me involved in or when you stop this car I will go find a bus to take me home."

Suggs took a sideways glance in my direction. He muttered something that sounded like "funny papers cabbage head."

We were on the southern end of La Cienega Boulevard by then.

He pulled to the curb, yanked on the parking brake lever, and turned toward me. It was then I noticed that the man had no smell. No kind of body odor or cologne. He was a self-contained unit, with no scent or any kind of style — the perfect package for a hunter.

"You ever hear of a woman named Nola Payne?" he asked.

I had not and shook my head to say so.

"What about her?" I asked.

"She's victim number thirty-four."

"And what does that have to do with me?"

"The circumstances around her death are a little confusing and possibly a problem if they make it to the press before we have a handle on the case."

"You not tellin' me anything, man."

"I don't want to tell you about how we found her until you get where we're going, Rawlins. But I can tell you that we need your help because a white policeman looking into anything down in Watts right now will only draw attention to something we need kept quiet."

"And why would I want to help you?" I asked, unable to resist kicking the man when he was down.

"What does that sign on your office door mean?" he asked in way of reply.

"It means what it says."

"No," Suggs said. "It means that you're down there playing like you're a private detective when you don't have a license. That could pull down jail time if somebody wanted to prosecute. I'm sure if I went around and talked to a few of your clients I could build a pretty good case."

I wasn't so sure. Most of the work I'd done wasn't anything to get me in trouble. I never misrepresented myself as a private detective. And Suggs was more right than he knew about white cops in black L.A. — no one would talk to them after the riots, or before.

But I said, "All right, Officer. I'll go where you're taking me. But I'll tell you this right now. If I don't like the way things smell I'm walkin' away."

Suggs nodded, released the brake, and cruised out into the boulevard. His easy manner accepting my conditions made me think that this simple ride in a policeman's car was going to take me down a much longer journey than I had planned on when I rolled out of bed that morning.

3

The Miller Neurological Sanatorium was a long, flat bungalow off of La Cienega just above Wilshire. If you drove by it you would have thought that it was a motel or maybe a factory for light manufacturing. The entrance was at the end of a long driveway and the bronze sign announcing its name was half the size of a sheet of notebook paper.

Suggs parked his car so close along a high white fence that I had to scoot across the seat to get out on the driver's side.

A few steps ahead of me, he opened the door to the clinic and walked in. I followed cautiously.

A young white woman in a nurse's uniform sat behind the desk in the reception area. She had a delicate face that was more red than white with thousands of freckles crowded around enormous brown eyes. Those eyes got bigger when we walked through the door.

"May I help you?" she asked the white man.

"We're going to room G-sixteen," Suggs told her.

We had taken two steps toward the double swinging doors behind the reception desk when the freckled fawn stood to block our way.

"I'm sorry but I can't let you back there."

Suggs frowned at the plucky youngster. I could imagine the bile roiling in his gut. First he had to explain himself to a Negro and now a mere woman was trying to block his way.

But he took it pretty well. The white man's burden, I suppose.

He held out a worn leather wallet that had his detective's badge on one side and his identity card on the other. The woman looked very closely at the wallet and mouthed the name.

I realized then that I hadn't asked Suggs for his I.D. I was too well trained, knowing that asking for a cop's badge might well expose you to manacles and blackjacks and a night of deep bruising.

"And who is he?" the nurse asked.

"Who are you?" Suggs asked back.

"Why . . . I'm not the one being identified," she said.

"Neither is he," Suggs said.

We went through the double doors, all three of us. Suggs led the way, I followed him, and she took up the rear.

The floor of the hallway was paved with shiny white tiles. The ceiling and walls were white too. There wasn't a smudge or a streak anywhere along the way. It was by far the cleanest medical facility I had ever seen.

We got to the end of one hall and turned right onto another. Halfway down this corridor we came to a door marked G-16. Suggs reached for the knob but the nurse got in front of him again.

"I'm not supposed to let anyone in without first identifying them at the desk," she said.

"Honey," Suggs said, "this is way beyond you. I showed you the badge, so get out of the way before I twist your pretty wrist."

"I will not."

I wondered if the riots were just one symptom of a disease that had silently infected the city; a virus that made people suddenly unafraid of the consequences of standing up for themselves. For almost a week I had seen groups of angry black men and women go up against armed policemen and soldiers with nothing but rocks and bottles for weapons. Now this eighty-seven-pound girl-child was standing up to a gruff cop who outweighed her three to one.

"Ezekiel Rawlins, ma'am," I said.

"What?" For the first time she looked directly at me.

"My name. It's Ezekiel Rawlins. I'm here as a consultant to the police. If you had asked me I would have told you my name."

"Oh," she said, realizing that maybe she was the one that had been discourteous. "Rawlings?"

"No 'g,' " I said.

"Oh."

"Can we go in now?" Suggs asked.

The nurse stood aside, looking down.

I remember that moment very clearly. The white walls and floors, even the doorknobs were painted that colorless hue. And that brave young woman made shy by simple honesty. The cop who was the first piece of solid evidence I had that the white man's grip on my throat was losing strength. All of that brought me to a doorway that I didn't really want to go through. I should have turned away right then. I wanted to turn away. But it was as if there was a strong wind at my back. I had resisted it all through the riots: the angry voice in my heart that urged me to go out and fight after all of the hangings I had seen, after all of the times I had been called nigger and all of the doors that had been slammed in my face. I spent my whole early life at the back of buses and in the segregated balconies at theaters. I had been arrested for walking in the wrong part of town and threatened for looking a man in the eye. And when I went to war to fight for freedom, I found myself in a segregated army, treated with less respect than they treated German POWs. I had seen people who looked like me jeered on TV and in the movies. I had had enough and I wasn't about to turn back, even though I wanted to.

The door opened and the wind blew me through.

The room we came into was bright. Three men were standing around a silver table that held the nude corpse of a Negro woman.

The men had on white smocks. Almost everything in this room was white. The walls and floor, the counters and the ceiling. Two of the men had on white shoes.

Just one pair of black dress shoes and Nola Payne brought any color into that lifeless room. And the shoes and Nola were just so much dead flesh.

"Yes, Detective Suggs," a bald white man with a trim gray mustache said.

"This is the man I told you about, sir. Ezekiel Rawlins."

"Why did you bring him here?"

"I thought he should see what we saw, Captain. I mean he *is* going to go out investigating."

The bald man turned his eyes to me. He started at the floor and worked his way up. I knew what he saw. I had on brown-red leather shoes, gray slacks, and a square-cut charcoal shirt.

I had gone casual down into SouthCentral, not expecting an interview with a white man standing in a black man's hell.

"Investigate?" he said to me.

"And your name is?" I replied.

The captain looked over at Suggs. The detective had no response.

"I'm the one in charge here," the captain said.

I made the mistake then of glancing at the corpse. She wasn't young — thirty-three or -four. I couldn't tell if she'd been pretty. Her hair had a reddish tint that some midwestern Negroes were prone to. One of her eyes was gone, probably due to a gunshot, and her tongue was sticking out of her mouth from her having been strangled, no doubt. The thing that caught my eye was the trickle of red blood that had started from somewhere above her lip, crossed over her teeth, and dribbled down her cheek. It was as if she died with her lips whispering vermilion secrets.

"Well if you're in charge, then may I be excused?" I asked the arrogant white man.

"What is this, Melvin?" the captain asked. "A joke?"

"No sir," Suggs said.

"What's your name again?" the captain asked me.

"I haven't got yours the first time yet."

"Enough of this, Lee," the other as yet unnamed white man said.

He was a head taller than the captain or Suggs, my height. He looked familiar but I didn't remember where it was that I had seen him. His face was slender and hard. He had tight black eyes and black hair, no lips to speak of, and a tiny red mark under his right eye.

"I'm Captain Fleck," the bald cop said. "And I asked you a question."

"No sir, Captain, you did not. You said the word 'investigate' in an interrogative tone. But tone alone does not a question make."

The third white man snickered. I appreciated the audience.

"Let's get out of here," the tall white man who was really in charge said.

I had no argument with that.

4

The tall man led Captain Fleck and me into an office that had a sign on it saying DR. TURNER, M.D. We left the third white man and Suggs in the colorless hallway.

Turner's office was a welcome relief. There was an orange-and-blue carpet, a brown desk, and four splashy landscapes on the wall.

And there was a test there for us. The room had three chairs: one behind the desk and two in front. The tall man went to the guest chair on the left. Captain Fleck turned toward the doctor's chair, but I was closer. I cut him off, taking the padded swivel chair for myself.

Fleck stood over me and stared down, waiting for me to give up the preferred seat.

· It was crazy. All of it. I never did anything like that when involved with the intricate dance necessary to keep out of trouble with the law. I rarely spoke around white men with authority. I never willingly said anything intelligent. And to go so far as to tease a cop — that wasn't even me.

But there I was, sitting back in the head man's chair with Captain Fleck staring death down on my head.

"Sit down, Lee," the tall white man said.

For a moment Fleck remained motionless.

"Lee."

He faltered and I smiled. If we were alone he would have drawn his pistol, I'm sure. But all he could do was obey his master's call. It's no wonder I always order sweet and sour when I go to a Chinese restaurant. You can't enjoy the pleasures of one without at least the presence of the other.

When we were all seated and comfortable the tall white man said, "It's a pleasure to meet you, Mr. Rawlins. My name is Jordan, Gerald Jordan."

"You're the deputy chief," I said, remembering at last, "the one in charge of the curfew."

"That's right. But the curfew has been lifted. Everybody can go where they want when they want as long as they obey the law."

Deputy Commissioner Jordan was a terror on the TV. He called the rioters thugs and criminals who had no respect for property and no reason to riot other than their own immoral desires to loot and destroy. Jordan's inflammatory words had probably caused the violence to last a day longer than it would have. On television he always wore a black dress uniform with medals across the left breast. That's why I hadn't recognized him in the makeshift morgue.

"Well, Deputy Commissioner, what is it you want from me?"

"I'm not here, Mr. Rawlins," he said.

"No? Am I here?"

22

"Not with me. As far as any records are concerned, we had you come down to identify Nola Payne. You failed to do so and were taken home."

"And who brought me here?"

"Detective Suggs brought you, and Captain Fleck debriefed you."

"I see."

Jordan smiled. I liked him. I liked him the way a slave learns to love his master or a prisoner develops an affinity with his warden. Gerald Jordan was the white man in charge. He was the closest I had ever come to the source of our problems. I wondered if I killed him right then, would the problems of my people become that much lighter? Of course the idea was ridiculous. Realizing the impotence of my fantasy, I laughed.

"Something funny, Mr. Rawlins?" Jordan asked.

"Not you, sir."

"Let's get down to business, shall we?"

"It's your show."

"Lee?" Jordan said.

The bald captain cleared his throat.

"Nola Payne was found by her aunt in the living room of her third-floor apartment on Grape Street earlier today," the sour captain reported.

"Not to me, Lee," the deputy commissioner said. "Mr. Rawlins is the one who will need this information."

Fleck would have much rather spit in my face but he controlled himself. He did a quarter turn in the visitor's chair and fixed his gaze on my forehead.

"She was strangled to death and then shot —"

"Was she raped?" I asked.

"She had intercourse within six hours of her death. It might have been rape but there are no bruises, cuts, or tears to back that up."

He twitched his mustache as if to ask, Anything else?

I shook my head.

"Miss Landry," he continued, "that's Miss Payne's aunt, called the police immediately but it took a while for anyone to come because of the problems in that area. When the patrolmen finally arrived they found Miss Landry in a hysterical state. She was screaming that a white man had murdered her niece. No matter how much they tried to calm her she kept shouting that a white man had raped and killed her niece. The officers took her into custody because they were afraid her ranting would incite another riot."

"So they arrested her?" I asked.

"No, Mr. Rawlins," Gerald Jordan said. "She was distraught. The officers were directed to bring Miss Landry here, where the doctors could sedate her, ease her pain."

Whenever Jordan smiled I wanted to slap his skinny face. The riots were still going on in my chest.

"You drugged her?"

"Would you rather I let her start up the riots again?"

"Where is she?"

"Down the hall," Fleck said. "She won't be awake until the morning."

"We need to know what happened down there, Mr. Rawlins," Jordan said, pretending to care.

"Why?"

"Because we want L.A. to get back to normal."

"You mean you want businessmen back at their desks, the shoppers to go back to the stores, and tourists buying mouse ears at Disneyland."

"This is no joke, Rawlins." That was Fleck. "The LAPD needs your help and if you know what's good for you you will cooperate."

"What is it you want me to do exactly?"

"Talk to Miss Landry when she awakens," Jordan said. "Go down to Grape Street and find out the circumstances of Miss Payne's death if you can."

"I don't get it. Why are you so worried about a dead black woman? You're not doin' this for every Negro killed."

The captain and his boss shared glances. Jordan shrugged.

"On the second day of the riots we had a report that a white man was dragged from his car down on Grape Street. He was harassed and beaten but finally managed to escape. No one has heard about him since. Under any other circumstance we could ignore the report. Maybe the man got away and went home. But a story about a black woman being murdered by a white man across the street from where a white man fled could cause rumors that might flare up into something ugly."

Like Nola Payne, I thought.

"So you want me to find the white man?" I asked.

"We want you to find out anything you can," Jordan said.

"And what will you do with what I find?"

"Try to keep a lid on the flow of information."

"What if a white man did kill her?"

Jordan and Fleck shared glances again.

"We don't want a murderer going free," Jordan said. "No matter his color. In this case if it came out that a white man killed Miss Payne and we put that man up on trial, then the people will see that we mean to maintain the balance of justice."

His words might have been an ad for cigarettes or whiskey. He didn't care about justice. He didn't care about a dead black woman or her killer. The only way that either one of them could ever bother him was if someone came around and held him accountable for the consequences of their actions.

"Okay," I said.

"What does that mean?" Captain Fleck asked.

"I'll do it. I'll go down there and ask around. I'll try and see what happened."

Jordan might have been smiling. I couldn't quite tell. His lips moved about an eighth of an inch and the flesh around his eyes eased up a bit.

"Thank you," he said.

"But I'm going to need something in order to get this done."

"And what is that?"

"There's a white man in this someplace. That might mean that I'll have to go around in white neighborhoods. In order to do that I'll need some kind of identification from the police department."

"Once you find out anything you come to me," Captain Fleck said. "You don't have any business in a white neighborhood."

"Then forget it," I said.

I stood up from the comfortable doctor's chair and took three steps toward the door.

"Wait outside, will you, Mr. Rawlins?" Jordan asked. "I'll see about what you need."

I passed through the door and waited around for a few moments. But I didn't like that, so I wandered down the hallway, pretending that I wasn't waiting on the policemen's whims.

5

The corridors of the clinic were a maze. I turned a few times before passing a wide white door that had a glass portal. Inside I could see a black woman in bed under a thin white sheet. From where I stood she seemed to have no arms.

When I pushed the door open I could hear her moans. She was in a straitjacket, saying things I didn't understand. Her head was flailing back and forth. Drool covered her jaw. When I reached out to touch her face, her eyes came open and fastened onto me just like the women used to do down in New Iberia when I was a child doing something wrong.

"Where am I, Roger?" she asked me.

"In the hospital," I said.

"Am I sick? Am I dyin'?" she asked in a distraught tone.

"No ma'am. I think you had a shock and the policemen brought you here to the doctor."

"Yes," she said in a very knowing way. "I have seen terrible things. Things you wouldn't ever want to see, Roger."

I thought about what it must have been like for her to come upon the corpse of Nola Payne, a woman she had probably known since Nola was a child.

"Why am I tied up?"

"Because the doctors thought you might hurt yourself."

"It wasn't that white man, was it?" she asked over my reply.

"What white man?"

"The one with Nola. The one that choked her and shot her and ran."

"What white man?" I asked again.

I had learned over the years that when someone is in shock you can ask them the same question again and again, getting a different answer each time — every answer bringing you closer to the truth.

"The one in her house. The one she tried to save. All them white men wanna do is beat you and stick their things in your behind like you was a whore."

"Who did she try and save?"

The woman closed her eyes and moaned.

"They were tryin' to kill him, the people. And he runned and Nola took him in. He was bleedin' and bloody. She didn't know about white men. I never told her and now she's dead."

"What was his name?" I whispered.

She sighed and then passed back into the stupor the doctors had induced. I sat with her a bit just to be some company. I wondered where Nola's story ended and her aunt's began.

After a while I left the sleeping, tortured prisoner and made my way back toward Dr. Turner's office.

THEY WERE WANDERING the halls, looking for me. Both Fleck and Jordan had removed their borrowed doctor's smocks. Fleck wore a dark blue uniform and Jordan had on a cream-colored suit.

"Where are you coming from?" Fleck asked me.

If he had been a brother or a young beatnik I would have thought he was talking in slang. But I knew it was just that the language he spoke and hipster talk sometimes overlapped.

"Out lookin' for a place to smoke," I said. "I got lost in these damn white halls."

I was trying to sound down-home, half ignorant — but it was too late for that now. I had already talked to the white man in his own tongue and he would know from that day forth that his bastion had been breached.

"Here you go," Jordan said, handing me a folded sheet of paper.

I unfolded the white sheet and read it silently.

It was a letter composed on the typewriter.

```
August 18, 1965
To Whom It May Concern:
The bearer of this letter, Mr. Ezekiel Rawlins,
is hereby empowered by the writer, Deputy Com-
missioner of Police Gerald Jordan, to be given
free access by the police and any other security
employee as he is conducting private consulta-
tions for the Los Angeles Police Department.
```

If there are any questions as to his authority
you should contact the central office of the
police department and inquire at the desk con-
cerning the police commissioner's business.

Gerald Jordan
Deputy Commissioner Gerald Jordan

"This is enough?" I asked.

"It should be," Jordan said.

"And when does it go into effect?"

Past the deputy commissioner's shoulder I could see Suggs and the third white-man-in-white coming down the hall.

"Right now, Mr. Rawlins. I called it in before coming to find you."

I refolded the letter and put it in my shirt pocket.

"I have to leave, Mr. Rawlins," Jordan said. "Is there anything else you need?"

"No sir."

"What about remuneration?"

"I don't usually take on white clients, Mr. Jordan."

"So you want a higher fee?"

"I don't want no fee whatsoever," I said. "I'll do this thing but not for you. I'll do it for the people I care about."

For one instant Gerald Jordan's smug, superior attitude wavered. Behind the mask of sophistication was a face that made Nola Payne's death mask look benign.

But then he was the politician again. Smiling and nodding at me.

"The city appreciates your goodwill, Mr. Rawlins. It's too bad that your community doesn't have more citizens with such a sense of civic responsibility."

Before I could come up with a fitting reply Jordan was walking away, with Fleck scuttling behind.

"I'll give you a ride back to your office," Suggs said to me.

"No thanks. I think I'll stick around here for a while. Maybe Miss Landry will come to. And I'd like to talk to the doctor."

"That's me," the third white-man-in-white said. "Dr. Dommer."

He put out a hand and I shook it.

"I don't really have very much time, Mr. . . . ?"

"Rawlins. People call me Easy."

"Well, Easy, I can give you a few minutes but I have to prepare for surgery this afternoon."

"I'll be quick." I turned to Suggs and asked, "How do I get in touch with you, Detective Suggs?"

"The Seventy-seventh Precinct will be my home until this is finished."

"You got it," I said.

Suggs looked at me a moment, and then he realized that he was being dismissed. At that moment I realized the same thing. The world was changing so quickly that I was worried about making a misstep in the new terrain.

"Okay," Suggs said. "You call me when you got anything."

He hesitated a moment more and then turned away.

Before he was out of sight in the long white hall Dr. Dommer asked, "How can I help you, Easy?"

"How did she die?"

Dommer wasn't a large man. His chest was concave and his brown eyebrows were bushy. His lips were normal size but flaccid and his brown eyes were on the way to becoming yellow. He had hands like a woman, long and slender, soft and tapered.

"Strangled."

"Then why did he shoot her?"

"I can't tell you that, Easy. Maybe he wanted to make sure that she was dead."

"Was there anything else you found?"

"I didn't do an autopsy. That's the coroner's job. But I'd say that she was knocked around quite a bit before she was killed."

"Was she raped?"

"She had sex with someone," the doctor said. "But considering the way she was beaten I doubt if he raped her too. There was no trauma in the vaginal area at all. This guy wouldn't have been a gentle lover."

"What about Miss Landry?" I asked.

"What about her?"

"Why do you have her all trussed up in that straitjacket?"

"How do you . . . ? The commissioner asked us to keep her sedated and secured."

"Isn't there some law against that?"

"Not if we believe that she's a danger to herself or others."

"Do you?"

"Is that all, Mr. Rawlins?"

"I'm coming back here tomorrow, Dr. Dommer. Please try and have Miss Landry out of those restraints."

The doctor and I made eye contact. When I was sure that we understood each other I turned away and walked down the white maze.

6

I wandered up and down the halls until I found my way back to the reception desk. The freckled girl glanced up at me when I emerged from the swinging doors. I made it all the way to the exit before she spoke.

"Excuse me," she said to my back.

"Yes?" I turned my head to be halfway civil.

"I'm sorry . . . about before."

"About what?" I knew what she meant but I asked anyway.

"I'm from Memphis," she said.

With the emphasis on the last word her Tennessee drawl took control. Her origins explained why she looked at Suggs and not me when she asked for our names. Where she came from, a white woman didn't address a black man directly. I wasn't supposed to speak in her presence or even look in her general direction.

"Yeah," I said, turning back to the door.

I reached for the knob.

"Mr. Rawlings."

"No 'g.' "

"I'm sorry. Mr. Rawlins."

I turned all the way around and went to her desk. "That's okay. No blood drawn."

"Are you related to those poor women?" she asked.

"Yes I am," I said. And I didn't feel that I was lying. Over the past few days, I came to feel a new connection between myself and the people caught up in the throes of violence. It was as if I had adopted Nola Payne as my blood sister.

"They brought them in in the early morning," the receptionist-nurse said.

"What's your name?" I asked.

A tremor went through her and she looked around, maybe for the Klansmen that would hang us both if she answered.

"Marianne," she said softly. "Marianne Plump."

We both smiled.

"What were you saying, Marianne?"

"I have a girlfriend, a colored girl that has the graveyard shift. She told me that Miss Landry said that they were killing poor black people."

"Who?"

"She just said that it was a white man."

"Did she say anything else?" I asked.

"Maybe," Marianne said. "I don't know."

"What's your friend's name?"

"Tina Monroe."

"Do you have a pencil and some paper, Marianne?"

She pointed at a pad on the edge of her desk and handed me

a yellow number two. When I took the pencil our fingers touched. I think we both got a shock. It wasn't a sexual thing but the breaking of a taboo that had governed her people and mine for hundreds of years.

"This is my number," I said as I wrote. "I'd really appreciate knowing anything about what happened to Nola, anything that Miss Landry said. So if she can I'd like Tina to call me."

Miss Plump nodded solemnly, taking the flimsy slip of paper.

WALKING DOWN La Cienega I thought about Marianne Plump and the shock we both felt when we touched. It wasn't that I'd never made physical contact with a white woman before. I had been through World War II. I had had many French and English and even German lovers. I had known American white women too. But this was different. Marianne and I were cut from the same rag. We spoke the same language. And though I couldn't explain how, I knew that the riots had broken down the barriers between us.

I WALKED SOUTH to Wilshire and then headed east.

It was a beautiful day. In the eighties and nearly clear because of a slight breeze. Wilshire was a nice street in those days. Small businesses and a few nondescript office buildings. I was walking at a brisk pace, steeling myself for the second test that day.

After I'd crossed to Fairfax Avenue the police car pulled to the curb beside me. Two tall white policemen got out as a team. Really I should call them policeboys because both of their ages put together wouldn't have added up to my forty-five years.

"Hold it right there," one cop said. He had a button nose, pale skin, and small, stunned-looking eyes.

His partner was a few inches shorter and six shades darker.

They both wore hats, so I couldn't say what color hair they had.

"What are you doing here?" the taller, paler cop asked.

"Walkin' home."

"Where do you live?"

I gave him my address on Genesee Avenue, a few blocks away.

Without asking permission the interrogator started patting my sides and pockets. The darker white cop stood a few paces away with his hand on the butt of his gun.

"Where are you coming from?" the pale cop asked, still frisking me.

"May I give you something, Officer?" I replied.

"What?"

"A document that will explain my presence here."

"Did you hear that, Mike?" the pale boy asked the dark one.

"What, Gil?"

"He wants to give me a document that will explain why he's here."

Mike got a quizzical look on his face and his partner went over to him. They discussed my unusual request for over a minute. Meanwhile pedestrians and shop owners had come to see what was going on. Everybody in L.A. was on alert. At the height of the riots angry black crowds had threatened to leave the ghetto and bring the violence into the white neighborhoods. Who knew when the Molotov cocktails would start exploding in Beverly Hills?

Mike came up to me.

"What is it you want to show us?"

I took Gerald Jordan's letter from my shirt pocket and handed it to him.

The Mediterranean-looking boy took enough time to have read the note six or seven times. Either Mike was slow or he was surprised by the content and signature. He looked up at me with dark Hellenic eyes.

"Is this a joke? I mean, do you think you can get away with this?"

"No joke, Officer," I said. "And yes, I do expect to walk away if not get away."

Mike went back to the police car and made a radio call while his partner kept an eye on me.

More and more people had gathered across the street in front of the May Company department store. My mind stayed calm but my body was reacting to the situation. I could feel the blood racing and my muscles getting tense. I could have run a quarter-mile sprint but instead I took out a new low-tar cigarette and lit it up.

Cigarettes would kill me one day, I was sure of that, but inhaling that smoke right then probably saved my life. Without the calming effect of the tobacco I might have taken a run at that pale child calling himself the law.

Mike got out of the patrol car and went up to his partner. They discussed the letter, glancing at me from time to time. People across the street were pointing at me and talking about me too. There wasn't one dark face on the corner of Wilshire and Fairfax.

I took another deep drag on my cigarette, wishing that it were a filterless Pall Mall.

Finally the cops approached me.

"Break out some I.D.," Mike ordered.

I took out my wallet, pulled my driver's license from its sleeve, and handed it over.

They eyed the name on the letter and compared it to the license.

"Are you Ezekiel Rawlins?"

"Yes I am."

"What are you working on for the commissioner?"

"That's none of your business."

"What did you say to me, son?" Mike asked.

That brought a smile to my face. The letter worked. The police were impotent and that made them mad.

"May I go now, Officer?"

"I asked you a question."

"Ask Deputy Commissioner Gerald Jordan," I said. "Because I'm reporting directly to his office — son."

Mike stared hard at me, committing my face to memory. He wanted me to know that one day he'd see me again, when I wasn't protected by his bosses.

It was a serious threat but I didn't care. I was having my own rebellion against the power structure. I was making a stand right there in West L.A. under the scrutiny of three dozen white people.

"Go on," Mike said. "Get out of here."

The police returned to their car. They went east on Wilshire so I decided to walk down Fairfax to Pico.

"We're not gonna put up with that crazy mess around here, nigger," a man's voice said.

I turned and saw a white man, with a white woman at his side — both of them staring hate at me.

"Are you talkin' to me?" I asked him.

"Yeah."

He was all loose. His casual clothing, his skin, his drooping jaw.

I took a step in his direction and he scooted away with his girlfriend in tow. After five steps he turned to see if I was running him down. I took another step, and he and his girlfriend took off at a gallop.

"He is a fool," another white man said. This one had a European accent.

When I turned I expected to see him talking to someone about me but he was alone. A short man wearing wire-rimmed glasses. He wasn't old, maybe fifty-five.

"He is afraid, and frightened men are almost always fools," the small man said to me.

"I'm not too much better," I said, "puffin' up like that."

"You can't help but to stand up for yourself," he said. "Even if you struck him, it would have been okay. Maybe he would learn something."

"That's a hard school you talkin' about there," I said.

The little man in the gray suit smiled. "I am Henry Berg," he said. "I own a watch shop up a block from here, on the east side of the street. If you need a timepiece fixed bring it to me."

We shook hands and I walked away thinking that I had to keep the lid on. Because if I didn't all hell might boil over.

7

Even if I had had my car I wouldn't have been able to put it in the garage because there was a sailboat in the driveway. Bonnie Shay's new pink Rambler was parked in the street in front of the house. From behind the boat I could hear the monotonous, back and forth rasping of a sandpaper block on wood.

"That you, Juice?" I called.

Jesus stood up from behind the boat and smiled. He'd taken his single sail out every day for three months before the riots. I made him stay home while the curfew was on, though. He took the time to fix any damage the craft had suffered.

"Hey, Dad," he said in a voice made strong by the sea. "Bonnie's home."

He wasn't very tall, five six in his deck shoes. His skin was the color of brown eggshell. His eyes were dark and almond shaped and he was fluent in English, Spanish, and French. The latter he picked up from Bonnie as easily as some people acquire an accent by moving to a different part of the country.

When Jesus came to live with me he was five and had never spoken a word. He didn't speak for many years because of abuse that he was exposed to at a very early age. And even after he did start talking, it was seldom and soft.

But then he decided to drop out of high school and build himself a boat. I allowed him to do it, even though everyone told me it was a mistake. Jesus had promise in school. His grades were just average, but he excelled as a long-distance runner. UCLA had been talking to the track coach about Jesus, but then I let him drop out to build his boat and take reading lessons with me at night.

The sea made him stand taller and speak out loud. He was the master of his own fate when he no longer had to deal with anyone he didn't want to, like all of the teachers who didn't believe that little Mexican kids were worth the seats they sat in.

"How's it goin', boy?" I asked.

"Daddy!" Feather yelled. She came running out of the front door with her thick blond-brown hair bouncing behind her. She'd shot up in the few months that Jesus was sailing. In just a few years she'd be taller than the brother of her heart. She was light skinned, even lighter than Jesus, but definitely American Negro — that's black mixed in with something else. Her mother was a white stripper who died and her father was someone like me. She came to live in my home before she was eight months old. I was the only father she knew.

She ran right into me and hugged me as hard as she could.

"Are you all right?" she asked, whining.

"Sure I am, baby girl. Were you worried?"

"Juice said that you were going down to your office. Where the black people are shooting up everybody they see."

"Juice didn't say that part about the black people, did he, honey?"

"No. Graham did."

"That little boy with the green eyes?"

Feather was still holding me. She looked up and nodded.

I kissed her forehead and carried her to the short stack of concrete stairs that led to our front door. When I sat down she twisted so that she was sitting in my lap. It was a dance step we'd developed over the nine years she'd been my girl.

She'd left the front door open. Her little yellow dog, Frenchie, came to the door and bared his sharp teeth. He hated me, dreamt every night, I was sure, about ripping out my throat. But we both loved Feather and so kept an uneasy truce.

"I don't care what they say around here or over at Carthay Circle, honey, but black people aren't running around crazy, shooting at people."

"That's what they say on the news," she said.

"I know they do. But they don't talk about why people are mad. They don't talk about all the bad things that have happened to our people. You see, sometimes people get so mad that they just have to do something. Later on they might wish that they didn't but by then it's too late."

"Is that why you were crying, Daddy?"

"When was I crying?"

"The other night when you were looking at the news and I was supposed to be in bed."

"Oh." I remembered. It was late and Bonnie had been stranded in Europe because of a series of thunderstorms around Paris. I was watching images of the rioters on the late news with the volume turned off, witnessing those poor souls out in the street fighting against an enemy that I recognized just as well as they. I had read the newspapers and heard the commentaries from the white newscasters. But my point of view was never aired. I didn't want the violence but I was tired of policemen stopping me just for walking down the street. I hated the destruction of property and life, but what good was law and order if it meant I was supposed to ignore the fact that our children were treated like little hoodlums and whores? My patience was as thin as a Liberty dime, but still I stayed in my house to protect my makeshift family. That's what brought me to tears. But how could I say all of that to a ten-year-old girl?

"I was sad because the people didn't understand each other," I said. "That's why people fight."

"Why?" Feather asked. She leaned her head against my jaw and all the pain released.

"Because they don't know what it's like to be in the other man's skin," I said.

"I'm hungry, Daddy," Feather said, and I knew I had found the right words.

"Hi, baby," Bonnie Shay said.

I leaned back and looked up, like a child, and saw her upside-down image. She looked down on us with eyes that took me away from America to a place where music was part of talking and walking and even breath.

Her skin was as dark as mine and her smile knew a happiness I craved. She squatted down and put her arms around Feather and me. Bonnie was the only woman I had known in my adult-hood who could make me feel like a child in the presence of maternal love. I leaned back against her and closed my eyes. I'm a big man, weighing one ninety, but her work as a stewardess had prepared her to deal with heavy objects.

Feather sighed and Jesus came over to beam down on us like the sun on his own ancient homeland. For a moment there I almost forgot about the smoldering slums and Nola Payne's cold body laid up in a white room under lock and key.

BONNIE AND I had a deal that I'd always make dinner on the day she returned from a transatlantic flight. I made glazed oxtails and collard greens with cornbread and tapioca pudding. It took fifty-seven minutes for me to do it all from scratch. That's how you can tell who's a good cook: by his speed and timing. There are a lot of men, both white and black, who call themselves gourmet cooks. They only work once a month or so and then they make only one dish. Those men have no idea what the real art of cooking is.

A real cook comes home not knowing what's in the icebox because he doesn't know who has eaten what since the last time he looked. You have to be fast on your feet making a balanced meal that has got to be on the table no more than five minutes after your brood gets hungry. And everything should be ready at the same time. I'd like to see these weekend gourmets come up with something new and tasty five days a week on a budget that some housewives get.

I didn't get any complaints at the dinner table. It was nice to have everybody there. Bonnie was gone at least one week out of four on her European and African routes with Air France. Jesus spent all day every day either working at the Captain's Reef supermarket in Venice or sailing along the coast. Most nights he spent with friends on the shore. To have all four of us there together felt like a blessing, even though I am not a religious man.

"Dad?" Jesus said.

"Uh-huh."

"What is Vietnam?"

"It's a country."

"But who's fighting them?"

"They're having an internal disagreement," I said. "People in the north want to have it one way and the people in the south want it another."

"Which one is right?"

When Jesus dropped out of school I made him promise to read every day and then to talk to me about what he'd read. That carried over into us discussing newspaper articles almost every morning. We had skipped that morning because I left for the office early, so he kept his discussion for the dinner table.

"Johnson says it's the south that's right. I really couldn't say."

"Does Juice have to go over there and fight the Veemanams, Daddy?" Feather asked.

"I hope not, honey. I really do hope not."

8

Jesus and Feather were both in bed by eight. She because it was her bedtime and he because he worked so hard. Bonnie and I stretched out on the couch in front of the TV and got reacquainted.

"It sounds so terrible," she was saying. She had her back against the arm of the sofa and her bare feet in my lap.

"What?"

"The fighting and the violence," she said.

"I guess."

"What do you mean, you guess?"

"It's hot and people are mad," I said. "They've been mad since they were babies."

"But it's stupid to attack just anybody because of their skin."

"Yeah," I said. "It sure is."

"Then why don't you think it's terrible? I was so frightened for you and the children when I was away."

I began to massage the joint under her big toe. She always relaxed when I did that.

But Bonnie pulled the foot away.

"Talk to me, Easy. I want to know what you mean."

"I missed you every night," I said. "I wanted you in the bed with me. I kept thinkin' that if you were there, then things would be better."

"I wanted to be. You know that."

"Yeah."

Some months earlier Bonnie had met an African prince and spent a holiday with him on the isle of Madagascar. After I found out she told me that they hadn't made love, but there were questions we both had afterwards — questions we didn't have before.

"Pain has a memory of its own," I said, thinking of Joguye Cham, the African prince, and Nola Payne.

"What do you mean, honey?" Bonnie asked.

"If I was to hit you right now," I said. "Haul off with my fist and crack you upside your head it would be on your mind for the rest of your life."

I balled my fist as I spoke. Bonnie leaned down and kissed the big knuckle, then licked it.

"Every day," I continued, "you'd wonder why I did it and when I might do it again. You'd wonder if you'd done something wrong. You'd hate me but you'd be angry at yourself too."

"Why would I be angry at myself if you attacked me?"

"If you hit me back, you'd worry that it wasn't enough or maybe too much. You'd worry that maybe I had a reason to hit you and you just didn't know what it was. If you didn't hit me back, you'd feel like a coward or a fool. The pain of that one blow would worm around in your gut and change everything you did from that moment on."

Bonnie had had her own share of pain in life, I knew that. I didn't want to bring it up but I felt compelled to explain myself.

"But even if something happens to me," she said, feeling the hurt as she spoke, "does that make anything I do right? Shouldn't we decide at some time to let it go and move on?"

"You can't ever leave something like that behind. You go to sleep with it and you wake up with it too." I was looking her in the eye then. She wanted to turn away but would not.

"But it's worse than that," I said. "For most people the pain they experience is just inside them. I hit you in the head but that's you and me. You could leave, find another man. You could go to work and none of the other women got a big knot on their heads. But if you come from down in Watts or Fifth Ward or Harlem, every soul you come upon has been threatened and beaten and jailed. If you have kids they will be beaten. And no matter how far back you remember, there's a beatin' there waiting for you. And so when you see some man stopped by the cops and some poor mother cryin' for his release it speaks to you. You don't know that woman, you don't know if the man bein' arrested has done something wrong. But it doesn't matter. Because you been there before. And everybody around you has been there before. And it's hot, and you're broke, and people have been doin' this to you because of your skin for more years than your mother's mother can remember."

There were tears in my voice if not in my eyes and Bonnie was crying too. She put her hands on my forearms letting her heat sink into my skin. We didn't talk for a long time after that.

"THE POLICE CAME to see me down at the office today,"
I said.

We were both undressing for bed.

"What did they want?"

"They want to hire me."

"No. Why?"

I told her everything from Theodore Steinman's story to Nola
Payne to the cops stopping me and the watchmaker asking for
my business.

"Are you going back down there?" she asked when I was
through.

"What else can I do? Nobody else can do it."

"It might be dangerous. You have children."

I leaned over and kissed her right nipple. She made a sound
that told me that she hadn't realized how much her nipple
missed that kiss.

We didn't talk any more about the LAPD or Nola Payne. Our
only words were sweet promises about a world made up of two.

9

I was up before five. After donning my day's costume I shook Bonnie out of bed. She wrapped herself in a housecoat without complaint. She didn't even stop to make a cup of coffee, just staggered out to her pink Rambler and turned over the engine.

Neither Feather nor Jesus would be up before seven. By then Bonnie would be back in her bed.

On the ride to my office Bonnie and I said very little. She was slow to wake up the first day after coming back from Europe. But she wouldn't let me take a taxi.

The sun was rising but not risen. The streets were fairly empty until we crossed Florence. After that we came across the occasional army Jeep. Two trucks full of armed soldiers sped past us at one point. There were groups of soldiers on a few major corners. But the main thing we saw was the wreckage left by the riots.

Bonnie gasped and sighed with every new ruin we passed.

On Avalon and Central and Hooper the burned buildings outnumbered the ones still intact. There was at least one torched car hunkered down at the curb on almost every block. Debris was strewn along the sidewalks and streets. Smoke still rose here and there from the wreckage. Furtive shadows could be seen sifting through the debris, searching for anything of value that had been overlooked.

City buses were running and the police made their presence felt. They were still riding four to a car, some wearing riot helmets or holding shotguns upright in their laps. They were still jumpy from days and nights when the Negro population rose up and fought back.

Bonnie let me off in front of my building. She kissed me and told me to be careful and then she kissed me again.

"Call if you're going to be late, honey," she said. "You know Feather will be worried."

I kissed her and then walked off to my car.

TRINI'S CREOLE CAFÉ on 105th and Central was just an open-air coffee stand with a fancy name. All Trini had were a counter and six stools under a dirty yellow awning.

"You opened the minute they called the curfew off, huh, Trini?" I said to the open-air restaurateur.

"I been open every day, Mr. Rawlins," Trini replied.

"With all this riotin' and snipin' goin' on?" I asked.

"Dollar don't make itself, brother."

He had straight black hair from his Mexican father and the chocolate brown face and flat nose of his mother, who worked in the kitchen.

"Didn't they give you any trouble?" I asked after enjoying the first real laugh I'd had in a week.

"Most of your serious riotin' was done at nighttime. I'm mainly a breakfast place. I had looters, rioters, even cops and soldiers buyin' coffee and jelly doughnuts."

"Cops and looters at the same counter?"

"Oh yeah. You know the cops come six and eight at a time, and so it wasn't too much to worry about. But mostly it was just neighborhood peoples comin' out for to see what had been burnt down and tryin' to feel a little normal."

"Weren't you supposed to be closed?" I asked.

"Oh yeah. They come by and told me to shut down a time or two but what was they gonna do, book me with the bombs goin' off around their heads?"

I laughed again. Trini was about my age. He held himself like an elder, though. Wisdom was his crutch. He never worried about anything because he could explain it all away with a few sage words.

"So I guess you know all the dirt, huh?" I asked.

"So much I got to wash my hands every ten minutes."

I smiled. "Lemme have another one'a those lemon-filled doughnuts, will ya?"

The sun was up and the streets were halfway normal. While Trini got my doughnut, I turned over a question in my mind.

The stock-and-trade of wise men was to educate. That meant they always had to feel they knew something you didn't know. So when asking a question of a wise man it was always best to ask it in the wrong way.

Trini brought my doughnut on a thick tan plate.

"You hear about some white dude got dragged outta his car

and killed down on Grape Street?" I asked when he set the plate down.

"You ain't got that one quite right, Easy," he replied.

"No? Why not?"

"There was a boy drivin' 'round lookin' at the play when a couple'a the brothers saw him and drug him out for a dustin'."

"They didn't kill him?"

"Nope. Just a citizen that some'a our boys beat on. They say he run off so quick that nobody could catch him. Nobody said nuthin' about no body."

"I ain't read about that at all."

"That's street talk, brother. You know what it's like."

"So you sayin' a white boy come down here in his car and gets dragged out and beaten and the papers don't even cover it?" I shook my head as if to say that that just couldn't be true.

"Oh yeah, Easy. Yes sir. Bobby Grant told me himself and he live right around the corner from there."

I sucked the lemon custard out of its pastry pocket. I liked Trini's mother's lemon filling because she didn't add so much sugar that the lemon lost its tang.

"You got some cigarettes back there, Trini?"

"What's your brand this week?" he asked.

"I'm gonna need a man's cigarette down around here," I said. "How about Chesterfields or Pall Malls."

"I only got Lucky Strike in the filterless, Easy."

"Gimme one'a them then . . . no, no. Gimme two packs."

I COULD HAVE asked Trini for Bobby Grant's address or phone number — if I wanted everybody who came into his shop for the next three days to know about it. The reason so many people braved the violent streets to come to Trini's café was that they knew all the information of the neighborhood filtered through him. Anything he heard he repeated. And Trini had a piercing voice, so he could be talking to a man at one end of the counter and you heard every word six stools away.

Bobby Grant wasn't in the phone book but that was no surprise. Back in 1965 a good half of your poor people didn't have phones. They used one in the hall or maybe a relative's line across the street.

WHEN RAYMOND "MOUSE" Alexander first moved to L.A., he gave Information his name to go along with my number. I still remember the look he gave me when I told him that I had his listing removed.

Mouse was a serious man who had killing in his blood. Telling him no was as dangerous a task as moving nitroglycerine in a truck with no shock absorbers.

"What you say, Easy?" the little gray-eyed killer asked. I remember that he was wearing an outrageous orange suit and a brown porkpie hat.

"It's either that or you gonna have to shoot me," I said.

"Huh?"

"Ray," I said, "you got women callin' me on the line day and night. 'Where's Raymond? Do you know how I can find Mouse? What's your name, honey? You sound nice.' I know you don't like nobody messin' with your women but it's a little confusin' when they wake you out of a deep sleep and there you are all alone in the bed."

The evil stare turned into a grin and a shrug.

"Easy, you a fool, you know that?"

"Not me, Raymond. Not me."

I PARKED THREE blocks from Nola Payne's address and walked the rest of the way to her block. There was a group of men, and a few women, standing around on the corner of Grape and 114th. These were working people who got paid a dollar fifteen an hour, when there was a job to be had. But most of their potential employers had gone up in flames over the past five days.

In order to fit in with that working-class crowd I was wearing faded blue jeans and a T-shirt with a few small tears and paint stains on it. My brown leather shoes were cracked and stained too.

The men were for the most part loud and blustering, laughing about their adventures and the exploits of their friends.

"Cops chased Marlon Jones up into the White Front Department Store on Central," one man was saying when I got there. "They run him up against the back of the store and told him to lay down or die. But you know he out on parole and so he jumped up on a shelf, climbed to the top and popped right out the window before they could catch a bead on his ass."

The crowd broke out into loud laughter. His audience didn't ask why the storyteller wasn't arrested instead of Marlon Jones. They didn't want proof. All they asked for was a good laugh in the face of the hard times coming up the line.

"Lonnie Beakman is dead," an older man said. "Shot him in the back while he was runnin' down Avalon."

That sobered the group.

A skinny young man wearing overalls and no shirt said, "Lonnie? He was engaged to my cousin a while last year."

"How is she takin' it?" a young woman asked.

"I'ont know," the youth replied. "She broke it off with him after she found him down the hall with her sister three weeks ago."

No one laughed at the story but that opened up the floor for a new line of talk.

"Meany got about a thousand pint cans of forty-weight oil," somebody said. "He sellin 'em for five cents a can."

"Motherfucker," a squat dark man said. "Motherfuckers killed Lonnie B and all Meany thinkin' about is nickels. It ain't funny, you know. It ain't funny at all. Cops come down here and murder us and we track through the blood to make a pocket full'a change."

On cue a police cruiser turned the corner.

As the cops drove past us one lowered his window and said, "No congregating on the street. Move along."

Almost as if it were choreographed, every one of the dozen people standing there started moving in a different direction. We each made it about a dozen feet or so, just far enough for the cops to have driven out of sight. Then we drifted back to the corner.

"Who are you?" the angry man asked me when I sidled up against the lamppost.

The police had broken the friendly mood, so I was seen for what I was — a stranger and possible threat.

"Easy Rawlins," I said.

"What you doin' sneakin' around the sidelines?"

"Just hangin' around, brother. I'm lookin' for somebody and I was waitin' for a break in the conversation."

The man wasn't really squat, that was an illusion caused by his unusually broad shoulders. He was nearly six feet. Less than two inches shorter than me. Other than his shoulders his most noticeable features were his big hands and yellow teeth, which he showed without smiling — like a feral dog or a wolf.

"I ain't never seen you before."

I could see that we were going down the road to war and I wondered how to make a truce without fighting first.

"That's Easy Rawlins," a woman in a blue-checkered dress said. She looked like a well-stacked pile of black pears held in place by a farmer's tablecloth.

"I never heard'a no Easy Rawlins live around here," the skinny youth said.

"That's Raymond Alexander's best friend, Newell," the woman said to the angry, broad-shouldered man. "Him and Ray been friends since Texas. Ain't that right, mister?"

I nodded.

"Yeah," another woman said. "I seen him wit' Mouse, down at EttaMae Harris's place. They was havin' a barbecue."

Newell raised his chin a bit then. Everybody knew about Mouse. He was one of the most dangerous men in L.A. No one but a fool would jump on his friend.

"Newell? That your name?" I asked.

"Yeah."

"I'm just lookin' for a guy I heard live around here. A guy name of Bobby Grant."

"What you want wit' Bobby?" Newell asked. He was just as afraid of Raymond as everybody else but Ray wasn't there and Newell didn't want to be seen as a coward.

"A woman I met, a Miss Landry, wanted me to ask him a question."

"You know Geneva?" the woman in blue asked.

"Met her."

"How do I know that?" Newell asked angrily. "You could just be a lyin' motherfucker out here."

"Why he wanna lie about Bobby and Geneva, Newell?" the older man asked reasonably. "You know Bobby live two doors away from her niece."

"All I know is that the motherfucker could be lyin'," Newell countered.

"Why the hell I wanna lie to some fool standin' on the corner?" I said.

That was the only choice I had. Either we were going to fight or we weren't. If we went at it either he was going to win or I was. That was the way it was on the street corners in Watts in 1965 — riot or no riot.

"He live in that gray buildin' across the street, Mr. Rawlins," the third woman said quickly, trying to head off the conflict.

I cut my eye to catch a glance at her. Then I turned my head. The young woman wore a one-piece dress made from a stretchy fabric. It was composed of horizontal yellow and white lines that hugged her figure like a second skin. My heart had been beating fast in preparation for a possible fight with Newell but the anger turned to excitement when I saw her.

Her eyes watched mine and she flashed an appreciative smile.

"On the fourth floor," she said.

"You live there too?" I asked. I didn't mean to. I had no intention of following her to her door. But the question popped out of my mouth of its own accord.

"No," she said. "I live next door in the blue buildin'."

"What's your name?"

"Juanda with 'j-u' instead of a 'w.'"

"That's a nice name."

"Watch it now!" the older man cried.

I could see Newell moving from the corner of my eye. He might have blindsided me if it weren't for the warning and the readiness of my blood.

I took a step backward, causing the broad-shouldered Newell to miss and step out of balance. Then I stepped forward with a nearly perfect uppercut to his midsection. I followed that up with three more blows, not to inflict added pain but to make sure Newell was put out of the fight.

He went down and two of his friends rushed to his side. My unexpected blows knocked the wind out of him and it was time for me to go.

In my youth that would have been the moment for me to say something insulting about Newell's manhood but I was past that kind of behavior. I just turned and walked across the street, hoping that I could finish my business with Bobby Grant before Newell asked for a rematch.

I turned when I got to the opposite curb to make sure that no one was coming after me. Everyone had their attention on their fallen friend. Everyone except Juanda. Her eyes were on me.

10

Robert Grant didn't get any checks in the mail. No one in the five-floor gray building did. The mailbox was two wooden crates, each of which once contained six one-gallon bottles of milk. The crates were hung side by side on the wall with names and apartment numbers scrawled over each square in red ink.

Bobby's number was 4-D.

With all the strength tapped in my blood I ran up the three flights without breathing hard.

The stairs and wall, floors, and ceiling had once been painted white but most of that had worn away years before. Now the color was pitted, dirty pine.

"Who is it?" a man called when I knocked.

"Easy Rawlins."

The apartment doors on either side of his came open. An old man stuck his head out of one side and a child peered from the shadows of the other. Both of them looked frightened.

I could imagine how they felt with buildings going up in flames around them and wild, angry voices shouting up and down the street. People were being shot dead in front of their homes and the law was helpless to keep the violence in check. Old people and children, working men and women, and any other peaceful soul had to hunker down in their living rooms and hope that the fires wouldn't spread to their walls.

"What?"

The door had come open on a sand-colored man with hair that wasn't much darker. He was slight but tall, young but already he had the slouching shoulders of someone who has been defeated by life.

Maybe he read the judgment in my expression because he stood a little straighter and cocked his head with bravado.

"Who are you?"

"Easy Rawlins," I said. "I'm here about Geneva Landry. The police got her and I'd like to help out if I could."

"The police got Miss Landry? What for?"

"I don't know for sure," I said. "But I bet it's got something to do with Nola Payne."

All Bobby had on was a pair of briefs. His sallow chest and knobby knees meant that any lover he had would have to be there because of the inner man — or a twenty-dollar bill.

"Nola's Geneva's niece. What do the cops think an auntie gonna do to her own blood?" he asked.

"I don't know what it is exactly," I said. "But from the sounds of it Nola's missing and the cops think that Miss Landry had somethin' to do with it. She don't know neither, so I told her that I'd come down and ask around."

"So what you want with me?"

"Can I come in?" I asked. "I mean, we don't really need everybody in the buildin' to know this stuff."

Grant studied me for a moment. He slouched down again and the sour taste came back into his mouth.

"Yeah. Okay," he said. "I guess."

I followed him into the one-room apartment. There was no real home furniture in evidence. The only thing his three chairs had in common was that they were all made from wood. The bed was a mattress on box springs on the floor and his curtain was a sheet that should have been shredded for rags.

In the corner, away from the window, he had six crates of new dishes, three model-train box sets, and a dozen or more pairs of green work pants.

He saw me looking and asked, "You wanna buy some dishes?"

"Not right now."

I sat on a whitewashed wooden chair and Bobby followed suit.

Despite his boy's body Grant held himself like an old man. Bent over, rubbing his hands together as if he could never get warm.

"What you got to do with Miss Landry?" he asked.

"She called me from jail and asked for help."

"I never heard'a you before," he said.

"I got an office over on Central. I help people out now and then. She told me her problem and I said that I'd ask around. A couple'a people mentioned that you been talking about a white man that got pulled outta his car and got the shit beat outta him. I just wanted to see if you knew who it was."

"Who said?" Bobby wanted to know.

"I didn't get no names," I said, using language that made us both feel at home. "I just heard about you and went around tryin' to look you up."

"I'd like to help Geneva out, man, but I don't know nuthin'."

"You know that a white man got pult outta his car and messed," I suggested.

"What's that got to do with anything?"

"Geneva said that Nola said on the phone that she had seen a white man runnin' around her buildin'."

I could see in Bobby Grant's eyes that I had hold of some facts.

"I — I don't know nuthin' about that," Bobby said. "All I know is that she was in the buildin' where he ran to after, um, after they beat on him."

"Who was that?"

"Just some guys. You know it was Friday night and he was drivin' down around here. They was pullin' every white person they found outta their cars. Beatin' 'em an' shit."

"Who was?" I asked again.

"What's that got to do with Nola and Geneva?"

"What kind of car was he drivin'?" I shifted gears easily.

"Red."

"Was it a Ford or a Chevy?"

"I'ont know, man. It was a car. A nice car. They pult him out and beat on his ass and then somebody drove it off."

"Did the white man know Nola?" I asked.

"Naw, man. That motherfucker was just lost, tryin' to get his ass back to Hollywood or wherever. Did Geneva say that that white man they beat on went to Nola's?"

"Like I said, all she knew was that that white man was run-nin' around Nola's place. So if you don't mind I'd like to know if Nola knew the white man you boys beat on."

"What you mean by that?" Bobby asked, his face now filled with fear.

"I see what you got here, man," I said, pointing at his pitiful pile of loot. "And what you ain't got. You was out there that night when your boys pulled that white man outta his car. Either that or you were up here twiddlin' your thumbs figurin' out what chair to sit in. You were out there. Maybe you didn't get a lick in. Maybe not. But you saw him and you saw where he went too."

It was all guesswork. He was a looter and young. He was black in America, transplanted from the South, and all alone in a room hot enough to brew tea.

Bobby stared at me with anxious, calculating eyes. He wanted to steer clear of trouble and he was wondering if a lie or the truth would accomplish that end.

"I don't know nuthin' about what happened to Nola," he said at last. "I haven't even seen her since before the riotin' started. All I know is some men pult that white man outta the red car and beat him. He ran away an' after that I don't know nuthin'."

It could have been true.

"So you didn't see Nola since the riots started?" I asked.

"No sir."

"Did anybody around here see her?"

"Nobody I know."

The police had put a muzzle on the murder. It hadn't hap-pened — yet.

"I need to know two things, Robert," I said.

"What's that?"

"Where does Nola live exactly and who stole the white man's car?"

"What do I get out of it?"

"For starters I won't throw you out the window."

"You think I'm scared'a you, old man?" the youth asked me.

"You should be, son. You should be."

Grant had a weak jaw. When his mouth hung open he looked pathetic, though I'm sure he thought he was looking mean.

When he saw I wasn't buying it he broke into a half-hearted laugh.

"I'm just fuckin' wit' you, man. Yeah, sure I'll tell ya. Nola live over on the right over here on the third floor, apartment three. And it was Loverboy stoled that man's car."

"Loverboy?"

"Uh-huh. He famous around here. He steals cars for a livin'. One boy tried to set that white man's car on fire but Loverboy an' this other dude pushed him down an' stoled that mothah-fuckah."

"You know his real name?" I asked.

Bobby Grant shook his head.

I couldn't think of anything else to ask so I left him with his train sets, work pants, and his stacks of empty dishes.

11

When I got back out on the street the crowd on the corner was gone. That was either a good or a bad thing. Maybe Newell went home to lick his wounds or maybe to get his pistol. But either way, there was no turning back for me then. I went to the apartment building where Nola lived. It was next to a small grocery that had been gutted and torched.

Across the street the Gaynor Furniture store was just a gaping hole flanked by three walls. There was devastation up and down the block and for miles around. For a moment the enormity of what had happened got to me. On TV they had aerial views of this part of the city. It looked like Germany did when we marched in at the end of the war.

It was like a war, I thought. A war being fought under the skin of America. The soldiers were all unwilling conscripts who had no idea of why they were fighting or what victory might mean.

NOLA'S DOOR WAS locked but I had a slender metal slat in a comb sleeve in my pocket. That slat could crack most simple locks and latches. I also had a letter in my pocket that would get me out of jail if it came to that.

The apartment seemed together. There was no overturned furniture or open, tossed drawers. Nola Payne had been a neat woman. Her bed was made and the floors were swept. The dishes were stacked on the kitchen counter because there were no shelves installed. She had a two-burner black wrought-iron stove.

In her bedroom there was a small photograph in a silver frame set upon a two-drawer cabinet. Nola was in the foreground backed up by a tall brown man with a grin on his lips and his arms wrapped around her waist.

In the trash can in the bathroom there were three bloody rags torn from a sheet like the one Bobby used for a curtain.

I couldn't find another drop of blood anywhere. Then I remembered that she was shot after being murdered.

Nola's window looked down on Grape Street. The youth in the overalls was back on the corner with three or four others. Juanda wasn't there. I was angry at myself for noticing her absence. I wasn't looking for a woman to play around with. Bonnie was my woman. We nearly broke up over her African prince but then we'd decided to stay together.

I intended to honor that decision.

There was no address book among Nola's things. That was odd. Such a neat and organized woman would have a place where she kept her phone numbers and addresses. I found her purse. She had a wallet with eight dollars and a silver chain with a broken clasp.

I searched for an address book for ten minutes. No one, especially a stranger, would have taken it, so I thought that it must be someplace obvious — staring me in the face. Finally I gave up. Maybe Nola was a loner and didn't have to jot down the few numbers she called regularly.

As I walked out of Nola's apartment I was thinking about Juanda's yellow-and-white dress. It fit her figure perfectly. I speculated that she was in her early twenties and unmarried. Her skin was dark and she had big nostrils. Her face had an animal quality, like a fairy-tale fox.

I shook my head, dislodging the image. But when I walked into the hallway, there she was.

"Mr. Rawlins?"

"Yes, Juanda, what is it?"

"Um." She was looking at me with hungry eyes. She expected me to embrace her. I was feeling it too but I didn't give in.

"Yeah?"

"Newell went to get some'a his friends. They drivin' around now lookin' for you."

"How did you find me?"

"I went to ask Bobby."

"Why didn't Newell ask him?"

"'Cause I told him that I'd go over and ask and when I told him Bobby didn't know he believed me."

I couldn't seem to take a satisfying breath. The clamor of new love was rattling around in my chest in spite of my intentions.

I knew it was an effect of the riots, that the passion of release had let something go in me. And Juanda was a black woman looking out for me, taking chances for me. She was a poor man's dream. And I was still, and always would be, a poor man in my heart.

"Why'd you do that?" I asked.

"I don't know. I like you, I guess."

"I'm parked over on Graham," I said. "What's the best way for me to get there without having to kick Newell's ass again?"

My brave words thrilled Juanda.

"Down out the back way. We could go on a Hundred and Thirteenth Street across Willow Brook and over to Graham."

"You comin' with me?" I asked.

"Maybe, if you don't mind. I need a ride to my auntie's over on Florence."

I gestured for her to lead the way and she smiled. Everything we did seemed to be important. I knew that any step I took, either toward her or away, I would regret in the morning.

"WHAT'S NEWELL'S PROBLEM with people?" I asked as we crossed Willow Brook. "I mean, I didn't start this thing with him."

"He just jealous."

"Of me? He don't even know me."

"Naw, it's me," Juanda said. "He think if he say I'm his girl enough times, it'a wind up bein' true. But you know I might have other ideas."

"But what do I have to do with you?"

"You stood up to him and he got embarrassed, that's all." Juanda gave me a sidelong glance that made my heart flutter.

I led her to my car.

"This new car is yours?" she asked.

"Yeah. Jump in."

She squealed and hopped in. For the next few minutes her talk followed a meandering line starting with how her uncle had a car like mine. Her uncle was a plumber for the city, he'd married her mother's sister twenty years before when Aunt Lovey (whose house we were going to) was only seventeen. Everybody thought it was scandalous for a thirty-eight-year-old man to wed a teenager but Juanda thought that it was okay. She liked older men. But not men like Newell. Newell was always complaining about how people did him wrong, white people mainly, but he didn't like black bosses, ministers, store owners, or policemen either. When a man got older, she said, he should feel comfortable with the world and not mad because things didn't go his way. That's why she liked me. I stood up for myself but still didn't lord it over people when I had the upper hand. For instance, I could have kicked Newell when he was down but I didn't. I could have told everybody that I was a friend of Raymond Alexander's but I didn't. That's because I was sure of myself and Juanda liked that, she liked it very much.

It may sound like I'm making light of the young woman in the tight yellow dress but I'm not. I remembered every word she said. They were burned in my memory.

"Do you know Nola Payne?" I asked during a lull in her narrative.

"Yeah. Why?"

"Her aunt Geneva is in some trouble. Nola might be too."

"Bobby said that Geneva was in jail and that Nola was missin'," Juanda said.

She crossed her legs and I resisted laying my hand on her bare knee.

"Did Nola have a white boyfriend?"

"Not that I know about," Juanda said. "I mean, Nola's a friendly girl and she don't hate nobody. If she met a nice white man she would go out with him I bet."

"What about a guy named Loverboy? You know him?"

"Uh-huh. He around. He wear nice clothes and have a nice car but you know he's a thief and a thief always wind up in jail or another woman's bed." It was clear that Juanda judged every man on his prospects as a boyfriend or more. But I didn't hold that against her. She was a young woman ready to make her nest. A man would have to be an important part of her plans.

"What do you do, Mr. Rawlins?"

She inched over on the seat and I held my breath.

We were driving on Central toward Florence.

Juanda touched my thigh with three fingers.

"You gonna tell me?"

"I own a couple'a apartment buildings here and there," I answered her honestly, as far as it went.

I was a property owner but I didn't want to tell her about my job at Sojourner Truth or my little office on Eighty-sixth and Central. I worried that if I opened up that far I'd never be able to close the door on her.

"That's nice," she was saying. "My daddy always says that real estate is your best investment because rent is always part of your salary."

"You know where Loverboy lives?" I asked.

"No. Why?"

"I think I might need to talk to him."

"That's my auntie's house right up there," she said.

I pulled to the curb. A large, light-colored woman was sitting on the front porch. She frowned at my car, obviously not expecting her niece to be inside.

"I got a pencil and paper in the glove compartment," I said.

"Yeah?"

"Why don't you write down your number. I might need to ask you some more questions about Loverboy and Nola."

Juanda's grin was victorious. She jotted down the number and put it on the dashboard.

"Don't forget to call me now," she said.

"I sure won't."

12

I did a U-turn on Florence even though there was a National
Guard bivouac across the street. I wanted to see if the
Guard were enforcing traffic laws — they were not.

Three blocks from Juanda's aunt, on the opposite side of the
street, was an unscathed two-story building that had a large
white tarp hanging from the second-floor window. The red
letters spray painted on the tarp read SOUL BROTHER. Sitting on
the front porch of the barbershop-turned-bookstore was Paris
Minton, the sole proprietor of Florence Avenue Bookshop.

I pulled up to the curb and jumped out. The exuberance I
felt over Juanda now fastened onto my joy that Paris's book-
store was saved.

The little bookworm rose to greet me.

"Hey, Easy," he said. I could hear the exhaustion in his voice.

Paris was short and had a slight build. His skin was the same dark brown as mine.

"Paris. What you doin' outside?"

"Been sittin' out here for six days and nights, man. Me an' Fearless tryin' to keep people from bustin' up my store."

"Damn. You didn't get any sleep?"

"Not too much," Paris said ruefully. "Every hour or so some new mob come by and wanna set a torch to my walls. But Fearless stood 'em all down."

Paris's friend, Fearless Jones, had his name right up there next to Mouse as being the most dangerous man in L.A. Fearless had been a commando in World War II. I had heard about him when I was in France. They said that he and one general made up for a whole battalion. The general, Thompkins, would point Fearless at the enemy and then pull the trigger. Both of them came out of the war with more medals than they could wear.

"Where is Mr. Jones?" I asked Paris.

"He left me last night," Paris said. "Him and this girl Brenda went down to San Diego for a few days."

Paris sat back down on his wooden stairs and I leaned against the banister.

The avenue before us was well traveled by National Guardsmen and cops and lined with burned-out, gutted structures.

"So what you think, Paris?"

"Ain't had much time to think, Easy. I had to do some fast talkin' to keep my store here. They burnt down the market next door. I had to keep that side of the house soaked with a hose to keep the flames off."

"You talk to many of the white people owned these stores?" I asked.

"A few came back yesterday," he said. "Some more today. They're like in shock. I mean, they don't know why it happened. They don't see how it is that black people could be so mad at them. One guy own the hardware store up the block said that if he didn't put his store in, then there wouldn't be no hardware store. He said that the people who live around here don't want to own a business."

"What'd you say to that?" I asked.

"What can I say, Easy? Mr. Pirelli works hard as a motherfucker out here. He don't know how hard it is to be black. He can't even imagine somethin' harder than what he doin'. I could tell him but he wouldn't believe it."

I liked Paris. He was a very intelligent man. But he was a pessimist when it came to human nature. He didn't think that he might teach that hardware store owner anything, so he just nodded at the man's ignorance and let it ride.

Who knows? Maybe Paris was right.

WHEN I LEFT Florence Avenue Bookshop I was a little lost. There were a few places I could go but I wasn't sure which one I should try first. With no other choice in mind I drove over to Sojourner Truth Junior High School, where I held the position of supervising senior head custodian.

The main building on the upper campus showed some signs of the rioting. There was a blackened window or two and a great many more that had their panes smashed. The front door was open and a Negro National Guardsman stood sentry there, stepping aside now and again for men in uniform coming in and out.

The sentry was brown; actually, he was little more than tan. He was holding a machine gun and staring out into space as if

75

maybe he were standing guard at the great expanse in front of the Pearly Gates.

"Halt!" he cried when I had only set one foot upon the concrete stairway.

I kept on walking.

"I said stay where you are," he said loudly, hefting the machine gun but not exactly pointing it at me.

"I work here, brother."

"School's closed. National Guard using it as a base."

"I'm the building supervisor. I want to see what damage there's been."

"Mr. Rawlins," a woman's voice called.

I looked to my right and saw Mrs. Masters, the school principal, waving at me from her office window, about a hundred feet down the salmon-colored plaster wall.

"I'm so glad you're here," she shouted. "Things are terrible."

"Are you okay?" I asked.

"I'm fine but our poor school . . . Come to my office."

"I'd like to," I said. "But the general here has orders to keep me out."

"It's all right to let him in, sir," the small woman said.

"No ma'am." He kept his eye on me. "I have orders that only the military and police can get in here."

"What rank is she?" I asked the sentinel.

He didn't dignify the joke with a reply.

"At ease, soldier," a white man in a colonel's uniform said from just inside the wide double doors. "This man works here."

"But sir —," the guard began.

He really didn't like me. He was willing to argue with his superior officer over orders that would allow a smart-mouthed Negro like myself into the compound.

"That's enough, soldier. This man is allowed in."

I smiled at my brother. He scowled at me before standing aside.

And there I was again, caught in the contradictions brought to the surface by the riots.

The sentry took his job seriously. Who was the enemy? Black people. Even though he was colored himself it was his job to bar our entry and he intended to keep us out. Even though I didn't know it at the time, that was the beginning of the breakup of our community. It was the first time you could see that there was another side to be on. If you identified with white people, you had a place where you were welcomed in.

I walked past him and nodded to the officer.

The white man merely watched my passage. As soon as he saw that I was headed in the right direction he turned on his heel and marched off, leaving the sentry and me at the opposite ends of a struggle that neither one of us had asked for.

"OH, MR. RAWLINS," Ada Masters cried.

We were on the third floor of the main building. Almost every door had been broken open and furniture was strewn in the halls. Here and there you could see where someone attempted to start a fire. But school buildings don't burn easily. The wood was thick and the walls were as much stone and brick and plaster as they were anything else.

The damage looked bad but it wouldn't take long to put everything back in order. I'd need painters and glazers, probably a carpenter or two, but I figured that the whole plant would be back to full capacity in two weeks' time.

I told the principal this.

"It's not just that, Mr. Rawlins," she said. "It's what they tried to do. Why would people want to burn and destroy their own community?"

She began to tremble and cry.

I folded the small white woman in my arms.

"It's okay," I crooned as if talking to a child.

"How can you say that? This is as much your neighborhood as the one you live in."

"That's just why I can say it," I said.

"I don't get what you mean."

I let her go and sat two chairs upright for us. When she was comfortable and a little more relaxed, I said those things that I wished Paris had said to the hardware store owner.

"This is a tough place, Ada. You got working men and women all fenced in together, brooding about what they see and what they can't have. Almost every one of them works for a white man. Every child is brought up thinking that only white people make things, rule countries, have history. They all come from the South. They all come from racism so bad that they don't even know what it's like to walk around with your head held high. They get nervous when the police drive by. They get angry when their children are dragged off in chains.

"Almost every black man, woman, and child you meet feels that anger. But they never let on, so you've never known. This riot was sayin' it out loud for the first time. That's all. Now it's said and nothing will ever be the same. That's good for us, no matter what we lost. And it could be good for white people too. But they have to understand just what happened here."

Ada Masters had a look of both awe and terror on her face. It was as if she were seeing me for the first time.

At the far end of the hall I saw a soldier come up the stairs. When he saw us he waited around to watch.

"I'm going to have to be off the next few days, Mrs. Masters," I said. "The police asked me to help them look into something."

"The police?"

"Yeah. I'll be here Monday. But if you need anything before then, call my house."

I stood up but she remained in her chair.

"You coming?" I asked.

"Not right now," she said. "I have to think, think about what's happened and, and about what you said."

13

Cox Bar was in a back alley off of Hooper. It was no more than a ramshackle hut but that was the place you would most likely find Raymond Alexander. Big Ginny Wright, the proprietor, was standing behind a high table used for a bar. She stood under a murky lamp that seemed to spread darkness instead of light. There was a pool table in the corner and a few chairs set around the room.

There were electric fans blowing from every side but it was still hot in there.

A small woman sat on a high stool at the far end of the table-bar, nursing a beer and staring off into space.

"Easy," Ginny said. "How you, baby?"

"I've been better."

Ginny laughed. "Me too. With these fools runnin' the streets

I been thinkin' of movin' back down to Texas. At least there you know what to expect."

"Mr. Rawlins?" The young woman who had been drinking the beer had come up to me. She was slight and medium brown, the same color as Ginny.

"Yeah?"

"You remember me?" she asked. "I'm Benita, Benita Flag."

I realized that I had met her before — with Mouse. She was beautiful then, wearing a little pink dress and red heels. Her hair, I remembered, was done up like a complex sculpture made of seashells. Now the hair was coarse and unkempt. She wore jeans and a stained white blouse that had been buttoned wrong.

"You seen Raymond?" she asked me.

"No."

"'Cause he ain't called me in two weeks and I'm worried he got hurt in all that's happened. You know Ray wouldn't just sit inside. I'm worried that maybe he got shot again."

Mouse had been shot a few times in his life but the last wound was because he was helping me. For a long while I thought that he'd died and that I was the cause of his death.

"Can you help me find him?" Benita asked.

Ginny's impatient sigh told me that Benita was just one more girlfriend that Mouse had let slide.

"I haven't seen 'im in weeks, Benita. Really."

She stared in my face, looking for a map to her boyfriend.

"I told her that even his wife don't know where he is," Ginny said. "But she just sit there drinkin' beer and hopin' he gonna walk in."

Benita ignored Ginny's barbs.

"Tell him to call me if you see him, Easy. I got to see him."

"Excuse me, Benita," Ginny said, "but Easy come in here to see me. I know that 'cause he don't drink, so he must have somethin' on his mind."

Benita didn't like being dismissed. She gave Ginny a hard look but then moved back to her lonely stool and flat beer.

"Raymond be lucky if that one don't shoot 'im," Ginny said in a low voice.

The comment unsettled me. It reminded me that the life we lived had always been perched at the edge of violence. That violence was Newell and Mouse and whoever killed Nola Payne. It was a constant threat eating away at happiness and any feeling of well-being.

"Do you know where Mouse is?" I asked, also in a soft voice.

Ginny studied me then. She scratched the mole at the left side of her mouth and snuffled.

"I could get him to call you," she said. "But that's all. Raymond's workin'."

Work for Mouse was never legal. The only time he ever held a real job was when he worked for me at Truth.

"That's fine, Miss Wright. Tell him I need his help."

"I'll tell 'im but you know he's busy and he ain't got no time to be helpin' you."

Ginny wasn't one of Mouse's girlfriends but that didn't matter. She was past sixty, three hundred pounds, and rough as lava stone, but she had a soft spot for Mouse just like Benita did. She believed, as did most of Raymond's women, that she had the last word on him.

"All he has to do is call," I said.

"All right."

"Maybe you could help me too, Gin."

"How's that?"

"You ever hear of a man name of Loverboy?"

"Oh yeah," Ginny said. "He's what they call a prime suspect if ever your car is gone from its garage."

"You wouldn't happen to know where he work at?" I asked.

I knew she'd have the answer. Ginny had a mind like a steel trap. Nothing ever escaped her notice or her memory. She was so good at counting cards that Raymond was the only one I knew that would gamble with her. And when it came to her customers she knew every one of their histories all the way back to Africa — almost.

"He in Watts over near Menlo and Hoover. You know the junkyard over there?"

"Sure do."

"It's a house with a green roof across the street from there. It's got a double garage in back. That's where Loverboy and Craig Reynolds make over the cars for sale."

"What's Loverboy's real name?"

"Nate Shelby," Ginny said. "It sure is. But be careful, Easy. 'Cause you know Nate don't play."

Ginny's last words stayed with me in the car. I rode with them all the way to West L.A., thinking that I wouldn't go up against the car thief until I was sure of my footing.

MARIANNE PLUMP WAS sitting at her post behind the reception desk at the Miller Neurological Sanatorium. It was about two in the afternoon. A young white man and an older woman were sitting on a small blue sofa set against the wall directly across from her. They both eyed me with fear.

"Miss Plump," I said.

"Good afternoon, Mr. Rawlins," she said with certainty.

She met my eye and even smiled. Overnight she had thought about our conversation and the morning brought on a resolution to live life the way she saw it.

That's what I surmised anyway.

"May I see Miss Landry?" I asked.

"She's in H-twelve. Dr. Dommer said that it was fine."

As I moved toward the swinging door, the young man piped up.

"Excuse me, miss, but we've been waiting here for over half an hour."

"The doctor is still with a patient," Marianne said, not in an unfriendly tone.

"Then why is he going in?" the young man replied.

"Listen, friend," I said. "You don't want to go where I'm going. Believe that."

He looked away from me and I laughed.

"You might turn your head, man, but I'll still be here."

Marianne Plump covered her mouth to stifle her grin.

I pushed open the door and never saw the young man or old woman again.

14

Geneva Landry was staring at the wall in front of her, wrapped in a cotton robe, and seated in a chair beside the high hospital bed. Whatever it was she saw, it had nothing to do with that room. The chair was made from chrome and blue padding. Sparrows chattered in a tree outside the window. Sunlight flooded the room without heating it. That was because of the air-conditioning.

Geneva hadn't turned when I opened her door.

"Miss Landry."

"Yes?" she asked, keeping her eye on the bare wall.

"My name is Easy Rawlins," I said, moving into her line of vision.

When I blocked her view of the wall she winced.

"Hello."

"I see they took you out of that straitjacket."

She nodded and crossed her chest with her arms, caressing her shoulders with weak, ashen fingers.

"Why they got me in here, Mr. Rawlins?"

"May I sit down, ma'am?"

"Yes."

I sat at the foot of the mattress.

"Do you remember what happened to Nola?"

I regretted the question when grief knotted up in her face.

"Yes."

"The police are worried that if a white man killed her, the riots will start up again."

"He did kill her," she said. "And there's nothin' they can do about that."

She glanced at me and then looked away.

"Did you see him do it, ma'am?"

"Are you the law, Mr. Rawlins?"

"No ma'am. I'm just tryin' to find the man killed your niece."

"But you not a policeman?"

"No. Why?"

"Because that's what that sloppy cop asked me this morning. He kept askin' if I saw her get killed. I told him that if I did he wouldn't have to be lookin' for the man 'cause I woulda kilt him myself."

Her hands were pulling at the shiny arms of the chair.

"That was Detective Suggs?" I asked.

"I guess it was."

"He's the one wanted me to talk to you and to ask around about who it was that hurt Nola."

"Killed her," the distraught woman said. "He killed her. Shot Li'l Scarlet in her eye."

"What did you call her?" I asked.

86

"Li'l Scarlet," Geneva said. "Her daddy, my brother, called her that because'a her red hair. When she was a child she was just a peanut and so everybody called her Li'l Scarlet. Li'l Scarlet Payne."

I nodded and smiled. I placed my hand on hers but she pulled away.

"Did Nola have a gun, Miss Landry?"

"No. Of course not. She wasn't that kind'a girl. She went to church and praised Jesus. It was a sin to kill her."

"Did she keep an address book?"

"She had a small green tin I gave her when she came here from Mississippi. It was for a little holiday whiskey cake. It was just the right size for the note cards she kept. That way she said if somebody's numbers changed she could just write up a new card and not have to scratch it out. She was very clean, Mr. Rawlins."

"I know she was."

"Are you gonna find that white man?"

"Yes I am. Do you want me to talk to the doctor about taking you home?"

"I don't know."

"Are you afraid to go home?"

"I don't know. I mean I don't think so, not afraid of nobody but . . . when I'm alone . . ."

"Do you have a husband or some family? Maybe I could tell them that you're okay. Maybe they can come and see you."

"My husband had a heart attack and Nola was my family after that," she said. "It's just that I get lost when there's nobody around, like I don't know where I am. There's a nice colored nurse at night who sits with me."

"So you want to stay here for a while?"

"I don't know," she said.

"Did Nola have a boyfriend?" I asked.

"A piece'a one," she said. "I mean Toby wasn't around too much and she broke up with him about every other week."

"Where does this Toby live?"

"In the big gray slum."

I knew the building. It was a block down from the Imperial Highway. An empty lot that some real estate syndicate turned into a series of five twelve-story apartment buildings. The quality of the building was substandard and the rents were too much for our neighborhood. Between the high turnover and the crumbling walls the place became known as the big gray slum.

"What's Toby's last name?"

"McDaniels."

I hesitated to ask the next question.

"Did you talk to your niece when the riots were going on, Miss Landry?"

"Every day and every night. We didn't see each other 'cause I was too scared to go out and she was nursin' that white man she saved."

"How did she save him?"

"Rioters beat on him and he ran. He ran past Nola's front door and she called to him . . . called to him. She took him upstairs and tended to his wounds and then he killed her."

"Did she tell you his name?"

"Pete. All she ever called him was Pete."

Geneva Landry turned back to the wall, looking for a way back to Nola. Her hands gripped the arms of her chair and big veins stood out on her dark temples.

"I should have told her about them white men," she said. "I shoulda told her."

"Told her what?" I asked.

"Never mind," Geneva Landry said. "It doesn't matter now."

I wanted to ask her more but she seemed so vulnerable in her chair. It was as if she were wasting away as she sat there staring at the wall and regretting words she never spoke.

MELVIN SUGGS WAS waiting for me in the white hall.

"So whataya think?" he asked me.

"She says that Nola didn't own a gun."

"Yeah."

"Nobody saw the white man go into Nola's apartment," I added. "And Geneva didn't see her niece get killed."

"You think she's makin' it up?" Suggs asked.

"No."

"No," he repeated, nodding at the floor.

"What are the visiting hours here at night, Detective Suggs?"

"Early evening. Why?"

"Could you ask Dr. Dommer to have them let me in if I come by after then?"

"Yeah but . . . I mean, you already talked to her."

"She needs some company. If I have the time, maybe . . ." I shrugged and Suggs did too.

It wasn't that he didn't like me or was unconcerned about his job. He just didn't have much sympathy for the woman and her situation. She was a witness or a suspect but nothing more than that.

15

The only one home when I got there was Frenchie the dog. He barked from the moment I walked in the door. It was a high-pitched, yapping sort of a bark that told me who my mother was and who my father was and how badly my butt stank. Accepting the abuse, I read the newspaper while sitting on the love seat in the no-man's-land between the kitchen and the living room.

The police had opened fire on a Muslim mosque on Fifty-sixth and South Broadway. They rushed the building and found nineteen men sprawled on the blood-stained floor. No one was shot, the article said, but they were lacerated by flying glass.

The reason given for the attack was that a shot was fired from an upper floor of the building. But the real reason was in the adjacent article saying that twelve of fifteen thousand

National Guardsmen had been pulled out of Los Angeles overnight. The police were afraid of losing their authority, so they responded with deadly force.

Nola's death took on a new importance as I read the reports. I didn't want the police killing our dark-skinned citizens any more than the deputy commissioner wanted to rekindle the riots. Gerald Jordan and I probably wouldn't agree about what time the sun rose in the morning but we were together on wanting to find Little Scarlet's killer.

Gemini 5 had lifted off by then and the Marines claimed to have killed 550 Vietcong guerrillas in a coordinated attack. Martin Luther King had been in Watts talking about the aftermath of the riots with Negro leaders, and astrophysicists were worried that an asteroid named Icarus would collide with Earth in three years' time.

To some people that space rock would have come as a blessing from God. Something sent down to Earth to shake off the invisible chains and manacles holding down five people for every one that's walking around free.

The school bus brought Feather home a few minutes shy of four and Bonnie came home only moments later. Those kids were less hers than mine but she loved them as much as two blood mothers. The fact that she was a few minutes late made her very unhappy. But Feather didn't notice because she had me there. And she was a daddy's girl from the word go.

Feather read to me from her textbook. It was a story about an old walrus who had to swim five thousand miles from somewhere in South America to Antarctica. Along the way the walrus saw all kinds of amazing things in the water and on the shore. He saw whales as big as islands and sea birds of every size and shape.

Feather started reading her lessons out loud because that's what I had done with her brother when he dropped out of school. She loved Jesus more than anyone else in the world and patterned herself after him even though she was a much better student.

After the reading we talked and after that we watched TV as a family. I had my hand on Bonnie's thigh and my mind a little further up than that but our night of passion was not to be.

The phone rang at 8:30, half an hour after Feather had gone to bed and in the middle of the dishes. I thought it would be Juice telling us that he was staying with friends at the shore but it wasn't.

"Easy," Bonnie said after answering the line. "It's Raymond."

Taking the phone I said, "Hey, Mouse."

"Hey, Easy. You callin' for a discount?"

"What's that supposed to mean?"

"I figure you musta heard that I'm in business and you callin' in for some cut-rate prices."

"What kinda business?"

"Sellin'," he said impatiently.

"Sellin' what?"

"You name it, Ease. I got everything from steaks to Smirnoff, from stuffed chairs to diamond rings."

It made perfect sense that Mouse would have been a part of the black market that had to grow up out of the riots. He had already been in the business of moving merchandise stolen by people he knew who worked at various warehouses. A looting event like the riots would have presented itself as a golden opportunity. And Raymond Alexander wasn't one to let an opportunity go to waste.

"I don't want to buy anything, Ray."

"Then why you callin'?"

"I need some help, man."

"Help?"

"I'm lookin' into this thing and I might need somebody to stand at my back."

"Easy, I'm doin' business here, brother. I can't be runnin' around like it was a party. I got to be at work."

I smiled to myself. If Raymond were going out to rob a bank, he'd have EttaMae make him a sandwich for lunch on the run.

"That's okay, man. You all right?"

"I got money comin' outta my pockets, they so full."

"Okay. I'll call you later."

"Hold up, Ease."

"What?"

"You in trouble?"

"Naw. Don't worry. It's just somethin' I'm lookin' into."

"What is it?"

I told him about Nola Payne and her aunt, about the white man and the car thief named Loverboy.

"Okay," he said. "You know I got to go make a pickup anyway. You wait at your place and me an' Hauser be over in forty-five."

"Where you comin' from?"

"Santa Monica. That's where I'm set up."

I TRIED TO apologize to Bonnie but she kissed it away.

"I know you have to go, baby," she told me. "I'm proud of you."

"I like to spend time with you when you're home, honey," I said. "I just have to go out and —"

93

"Be our hero," she whispered.

We were standing on the front porch, between the spaces where I once grew roses to celebrate our love. Later I cut the roses down when I thought Bonnie loved another man. I did it to show her how angry I was but somehow the emptiness came to mean more to us than the flowers had.

A big Andy's Supermarket truck was rumbling up the street. I was surprised to see such a big truck on a side street. I was amazed to see it stop in front of my house.

"Easy!" Mouse yelled from the passenger's window about two stories high. "Come on up, man."

Bonnie and I laughed and embraced each other. She kissed me again and I ran toward the semi.

I remember thinking, as Mouse reached down to help me, that it was as if I were living in one of Feather's fairy-tale books. Only this was an adult fairy tale. So instead of a flying carpet I had a six-axle produce delivery truck and instead of an evil ogre I had a well-to-do white man who shot virtuous young black women after raping and strangling them.

16

Easy Rawlins, meet Randolph Hauser," Mouse said as I took my place next to the passenger's window. When I pulled the door shut I could see Bonnie going back into the house. Watching our door close brought a tightening around my heart — the symptom of a premonition that was indecipherable and unsettling.

"How you doin'?" the big, redheaded white man said to me.

He stuck out a hand bulging with the muscle of a working man. I shook it and was immediately convinced of his strength.

"Good," I said. "You on a delivery run."

"Deliverin' the goods," he said and then he let out a big laugh.

Randolph Hauser was the opposite of Mouse in almost every way. He was white, nearly fat with muscle, and he had blunt features compared to Ray's chiseled and fine ones.

"What's that mean?" I asked simply.

The white man slipped the truck into gear and took off with a roar.

"Don't your boy know the score, Raymond?" Hauser asked.

"He can count higher than you can think, white boy," Mouse replied. "Easy walk up to a haystack and pick up a gold pin quicker than you could find a straw."

"What are you doin' with this truck, Ray?" I asked.

"I do my pickups around this time, Easy. It's late but not too late. And with Hauser here drivin', the cops let us be."

"Not too late for what?" I asked.

It always took a while to get a bead on what Mouse was doing. He was naturally crafty, keeping in practice even when talking to people he trusted.

"I already told you. The pickup."

"What are we picking up?"

"Don't never know till we get there." He gave me a broad smile. "That's the wonder of this here job. Ain't that right, white boy?"

"Yesiree, son," Hauser said. "This is the best job I had since drivin' shotgun on a regular route we used to bring in from Baja."

He shifted gears again and we rumbled east on Olympic.

The streets were pretty quiet and so was I.

We were just turning onto Western when Hauser asked, "So what about the stuff they take over to your place?"

"What about it?" Mouse said in a less than friendly tone.

"We said that we were going to split the profits —"

"On what we move outta your place, brother. Out of there. Whatever I keep for me is mine."

I could see that Hauser wasn't happy about loot he was missing out on. But I knew, and he did too, that despite his size

Mouse was unafraid of any man. If Hauser wanted to argue he'd better be serious because Mouse was always ready to arrange a meeting with Death.

Hauser drove us all the way down Western past El Segundo, to a lonely spot between the Western Avenue public golf course and the Gardenia Airport. We backed up to a dark warehouse down there. While we were climbing out of the cab the door to the loading dock came open.

I realized that Hauser was even bigger than I thought. He was at least six four and right around three hundred pounds. His red hair was thick and wavy and his shoulders were so big that they seemed like some other creature rising up behind him. He wore jeans and a light blue work shirt over a dark blue T-shirt.

Looking at him I wondered about the origin of Nola Payne's red hair color. Maybe Hauser's ancestors owned Nola's. Maybe they ran together, hiding from the English.

Mouse was clad in white coveralls with a white T-shirt that looked to be silk. There was a sapphire hat pin stuck to his lapel and he carried a canvas money bag like the ones tellers use in banks.

Mouse led us up a ramp and to a table at the center of the room. There were groups of black men on either side, about thirty men in all. Each group of two or three men stood amid their looted goods. One group had television sets, while another had pushed in five or six washing machines. Some had cans of food. One solitary man had a small green duffel bag slung over his shoulder.

Mouse sat at the table and met with the men one group at a time. He'd make an offer and then they would argue. A couple of the groups left with their goods. When a deal was struck,

Mouse took the payment from his money bag. The men worked loading the merchandise onto the truck under Hauser's watchful eye.

There were boxes of transistor radios, trays of watches, seven racks of suits, and about a dozen fur coats. The truck had a forty-foot trailer but it was full to capacity by the time the deals were through.

The last man to see Raymond was the one with the duffel bag. He was tall and dark-skinned with small eyes and what I can only call a sensual mouth. Raymond took this man to the side to keep their talk secret. Both of them came away smiling and Mouse was toting the bag.

"You see, Easy," he said to me. "This here is work."

"I guess so," I said.

When the truck was loaded nearly to capacity we climbed back in the cab and Hauser drove off. He went south to Rosecrans Avenue and then turned right toward the sea.

"I thought you said that this would be a big haul?" Hauser complained.

"You got TVs, dishwashers, air-conditioners, and enough clothes to dress the whole National Guard," Mouse said, "and you think you ain't got a big haul? Shit."

"What you got in that duffel bag?" Hauser wanted to know.

"None'a your business what I got. What I got is mine. We already made that deal."

"You know I ain't a punk, Ray."

"Then don't ack like one. I got my pick'a what the people come to us is sellin'. If it wasn't for me you wouldn't have nuthin' at all."

"How does this work, Raymond?" I asked.

I didn't really care to know but I thought I could cut down the ire between the partners if I could shift the subject a bit.

"Well, you know, Ease," he said, "people I know be takin' stuff hand over fist down in the riots and when they got a whole houseful they need to lay it off fast. You know sellin' washin' machines one at a time got jailbird written all over it. So I got this warehouse from Jewelle and told whoever it was doin' business to come here at night . . ."

"Jewelle know what you're doing in her place?" I asked. I still felt protective of the young woman even though she was my superior in every form of business.

"I didn't tell her and she didn't ask," Mouse said. "But you know I buy at twenty-fi'e percent'a what Hauser here can get and then we split the profit fifty-fifty."

"But he keeps all the cream for himself," the driver interjected.

"And why the fuck shouldn't I?" Mouse said. "You wouldn't even have a dime if it wasn't for me."

"You're just a go-between," Hauser said in an elevated tone. "You should only be getting ten percent."

"I got your ten percent right here in my pocket."

I was worried that the partners would start fighting right there in the cab. I wasn't concerned about the outcome. I knew that Mouse would kill Hauser no matter how big he was. But we might die when the rig ran off the road. And even if we didn't I'd be implicated in moving stolen goods and a murder.

I was trying to think of some words that would ease the mood when a red light began flashing in the outside mirror. The siren started just after that.

"Shit!" Hauser and Raymond said together.

Raymond pulled out his large .41 caliber pistol.

"Put it away, Ray," I said.

"I ain't lettin' them take me to jail, Easy."

"Put it away, man," I said again.

"I'm not goin' to jail, man."

But he put the pistol behind the seat and we all climbed out on the passenger's side. I strode up to the cops before the others and put my hands in the air. The cops coming at us numbered four. They were all white men. They all had their pistols drawn.

In my left hand I held the letter given to me by Gerald Jordan.

"Before you make a mistake, officers," I said. "Please read this letter."

I hadn't been pistol-whipped for quite some time.

The advance policeman struck me for no reason I could see. He didn't know me. I hadn't committed a crime as far as he knew. My hands were aloft and the only thing I held was a flimsy note. But he hit me so hard that *he* grunted.

I didn't go down, though. And instead of striking back I held out the note.

"You better read this," I said.

"Hold it, Billings," another cop said.

Billings swung at me anyway but I bent my knees and lowered my arm so that the gun swung over my head. I tasted blood on the side of my mouth but all I was worried about was Raymond murdering those four cops.

The one who had told Billings to stop stood in front of me.

"What's that you got there?" the cop asked.

"A letter about me and my friends," I said, "from your boss."

I didn't expect it to work. But the officer read my letter while the rest of the cops braced Hauser and Raymond.

"Where's the key to the back?" Billings was asking Hauser.

"Lost it," the big redhead said.

By then my cop had read the letter.

"This doesn't have anything to do with you in a truck in the middle of the night," he told me.

"Call up and find out," I said.

He was brown-eyed and I would have said brawny if it wasn't for Hauser. Sonny Liston would have looked scrawny in the presence of Raymond's disgruntled partner.

I was trussed up in handcuffs and pressed against the side of the forty-foot trailer — next to my friends.

"Where's the key?" a cop was yelling into Raymond's ear.

"It ain't mines to keep," Raymond said. "And stop spittin' on me."

"Uncuff them," the officer who took my official hall pass said.

"What?" Billings asked belligerently.

"Which word didn't you understand?"

I could see the two cops got along about as well as Mouse and Hauser. But that meant nothing to me. My chains were released and three of the cops stood back. The leader, the one who read my note, came up to me then.

"Can I be of any assistance, Mr. Rawlins?" he asked.

It was worth the whole night just to see the look of wide-eyed shock enter Mouse's face. In all the years I'd known him, since we were in our teens, I had never surprised my friend. He was a force of nature, the spawn of some nether god. There was nothing a mortal like me could do that would take him off guard.

But I did that night.

"As a matter of fact, yes, Officer," I said. "Could you let your friends know that Mr. Alexander here and his friend Mr. Hauser will be doing work with me for the next few nights? I really wouldn't want them to be bothered anymore."

"You got it," he said. He didn't even sound angry. Gerald Jordan was not only the enemy of my people but, in some ways, more powerful than all of us put together.

17

How you do that, Easy?" Mouse asked when we were back on the road.

"Do what?" I asked innocently.

"You know what. Get them cops to treat you like you was the mayor or somethin'."

"You don't expect me to let up on all my secrets, do you, Ray?"

"Come on, man, what did that letter say?"

"It said, 'Listen up, Mr. Policeman, that's Easy Rawlins you talkin' to.'"

"I never saw anything like that in my life," Randolph Hauser said. "That cop called you mister and he didn't even try to look in our truck."

I didn't respond to the compliment. I was just happy that Hauser's estimation of Mouse and his value had risen.

THIRTY MINUTES LATER we reached another warehouse on Hart, not half a block from the ocean. Six or seven white men rushed out on the dock and started unloading. I had found out along the way that Hauser really didn't have the key. He carried a set of open padlocks to secure the van, so if the police did stop him they couldn't get into the truck without metal-cutting tools.

We went to the glass-walled warehouse to smoke and drink coffee while Hauser's men worked.

"That was a good trick, Rawlins," Hauser was saying. "How'd you do it?"

"Charm school," I replied.

The giant looked hard at me for a moment and then he cracked a smile.

"You're all right, son," he said. "I guess Ray is better than I gave him credit for."

"If you borrowed on me," Mouse added, "you'd be a rich man."

We all laughed and smoked for a while and then I wandered out toward the front of the warehouse so that Mouse and the big man could conclude their business.

As a rule I avoided Raymond's illegal business. I knew he was a crook, but what could I do? He was like blood to me. And that night the rules as I had always known them had been suspended. Police opening fire on a house of worship, covering up information about a murder, and employing a black man to get them out of a jam. Our bigoted mayor was set to meet with Martin Luther King. I hadn't even broken the law, telling those policemen that Raymond was working with me. So it didn't disturb me standing in the thieves' den. That was simply another step toward the other side of our liberation.

MOUSE JOINED ME outside the warehouse a few minutes past midnight. He still had that small duffel bag. He was smiling so I knew the money had worked out fine. Mouse only ever had two things on his mind: money and women. Revenge ran a distant third but still you wouldn't want to be on his bad side.

"Ready to go, Easy?"

"Go where?"

"To shake Nate Shelby outta his tree."

His white teeth and gray eyes flashed in the night and a laugh came unbidden from deep in my chest.

THE MENLO JUNKYARD was dark, and so was every other house and business on the street. All except one. That was a house that had a double garage at the end of its driveway.

"You gotta dime, Ease?"

"For what?"

"I got to make a call."

I gave my friend the ten-cent piece and he walked down to the corner where a working phone booth stood. I remember thinking that that had to be the only phone booth in Watts that had not been smashed by rampaging rioters.

Ray talked for a good five minutes. Every now and then I could hear his voice rise in a threatening tone.

"Here's your dime," he said, handing me the coin.

"I thought you needed it for the call."

"I did. But the coin box is broke out so you get your money right back. I been callin' people all over the country from the phones down here."

He took a cigarette from his white coveralls pocket, lit up, and then leaned against the junkyard fence.

"What are we waitin' for?" I asked when he lit a second smoke.

"Magic."

"Come on, Ray. Who did you call?"

"What you had in that note you showed the cops?"

Mouse's revenge ran a slow third but it always crossed the finish line.

I laughed and said, "Okay, Ray. I'll wait for your magic trick."

And so we stood there at 1:15, smoking cigarettes and watching the single lit window on the block. No one was out; not the army or the police force or people in the neighborhood. When we had stood around for about five minutes or so one of the doors to the garage came open and a car drove out. A red Galaxie 500. It came across the street and parked in front of us. The door opened and a big black man with a weathered, angry face got out.

He walked up to Raymond and said, "This what you wanted?"

Mouse turned to me and asked, "This the car you lookin' for, Easy?"

"Is it the one stolen from a white man bein' beat on the second day of the riots?"

Mouse looked at the ugly man.

"Yeah," the man said.

"Then that's the car."

"You got the papers, Nate?" Raymond asked Loverboy.

"Glove compartment."

106

"Did you see what happened that night?" I asked then.

"Who you, mothahfuckah?" Nate replied.

"All you need to do is answer him," Raymond said. "You see him standin' here with me, don't you?"

"Crazy motherfuckin' white man drivin' around lookin' out the window with people burnin' and breakin' and throwin' rocks," Nate said. "They grabbed and beat him good. Tore his clothes all up. He ran away screamin' like a baby. Shit."

"You see where he went to?" I asked.

"Naw, man. I just wanted the car. You lucky I still got it. We so backed up right now that we couldn't chop it till Monday."

Mouse flashed his eyes at me and I shrugged.

"Thanks, Nate," Mouse said in dismissal.

"What about my money?" the car thief asked.

"You *do* want trouble, don't you, son?" Mouse said.

While Loverboy was screwing up the courage to die I opened the car door and took whatever papers there were in the glove compartment. I made a quick search under the front and back seats but found nothing.

I took the keys from the ignition and opened the trunk. That was empty too.

"You can keep the car, man," I said. "All I need is this here."

I returned the keys to Loverboy. He took them from me and then turned to Mouse.

"Is that all?"

"Okay," my friend, the self-appointed sovereign of Watts, said.

We all stood there for a moment, wondering what the exact etiquette was in a situation like that. Was somebody supposed to say thank you or even good-bye?

Nate made a quick move for the car.

When he drove off, Mouse asked me, "Even, Easy?"

"Maybe right now but I believe I'll be in your debt before it's all through."

RAYMOND DROVE ME home. We had a good time on the way, chatting about people we knew. It wasn't until he stopped at the curb in front of my house that I remembered my message.

"I ran into Benita Flag at Cox Bar," I said.

"You did?"

"Yeah. Didn't Ginny tell you?"

"Ginny don't talk to me about women too much."

"Benita was worried about you."

"I bet she was."

It was almost three and I wasn't Benita's lawyer, so I opened my door.

"What you do about your girlfriends, Ease?"

"Say what?"

"Your girlfriends," he repeated. "When they get all cow-eyed and hungry for you."

Juanda popped into my mind but I pushed her away.

"I don't have any girlfriends, Ray. It's just me and Bonnie, that's all."

"You don't get you no pussy on the side?"

"Not lately."

"I cain't live without it. I gots to have me a little taste every now and then. But you know some'a these girls don't hear it when you tell 'em you married and shit. I mean they say okay but then they wanna know how you could love 'em like that and then not move in."

I didn't even smile. This was a true moral conflict for my friend. His understanding of anyone outside of himself was severely limited. He didn't know why Benita didn't understand him, so he cut her off. And the mere fact that she would mention him to me set him on a dark path.

"I'll talk to her, Ray," I said.

"You will?"

"Oh yeah. I'll explain your predicament. She'll understand."

"You know, you all right, Easy," he said. "You all right."

He left me standing in the warm night air appreciating the silence. There I was, a middle-aged city employee. The only thing I should have had on my mind was my bed and my children, my mortgage, and the woman I loved. All of that was waiting for me in the house.

But instead of heeding that domestic call I went to my car, turned over the engine, and drove off.

18

There was a chain drawn to block the driveway to the Miller Neurological Sanatorium. I had to park my car on the street and walk to the door. I was looking for the night bell when a flashlight shone on the side of my head.

"Hold it," a voice said.

It was a man's voice, a white man, probably over sixty, who was not born in the South. There was confidence in the tone but not the threatening kind of self-assurance that comes with holding a gun. This voice expressed the expectation of being obeyed because that was his place in life.

I turned toward the dazzling light and said, "Yes?"

"Clinic's closed."

"My name's Easy Rawlins. I'm on a special visitors list."

"Prove it."

"Prove what? That I'm on the list or that I'm Easy Rawlins?"

The question flummoxed the late-night security guard. He sputtered and then used a key on the door to reception.

"Go on," he told me.

I went in and he came after, flipping the light switch as he did.

I was halfway to the swinging door when he said "Hold it" again.

I swiveled on my heel, seeing the man for the first time, at least with my eyes. He was short and white-haired, in his sixties and unarmed except for that large flashlight. I chided myself for believing in my own deductions. Seeing that I was right about that guard might lull me into thinking that I could see in the dark. And all that meant was that one day I'd make a mistake, fall into a pit, and die.

"What?" I asked the security guard.

"I need to see some identification."

I took out my wallet and produced my driver's license. He scrutinized the document as if looking for counterfeits.

"What's your business here?" he asked.

I snatched my license from his hands and turned away. As I went through the swinging door he cried, "Hey you," but I kept on going.

There was no evidence that he was treating me like that because of my race. He was just a guard taking his job a little too seriously. But I had been asked those questions too many times in my life to shrug off the anger they raised in my heart. If I found myself in a situation where I could ignore a white man in authority I would, even though I might have been wrong.

As I quick-marched down the hall I could hear the guard's slower steps behind me. He wasn't about to let me get away with disregarding his authority.

I got to H-12 and opened the door without knocking. Geneva Landry was sitting up in her bed and a young black woman sat in the chair. A lamp glowed on a table in the corner, giving the white hospital room the feeling of home.

"Tommy, what's going on?" a woman's voice asked from down the hall behind me.

"An intruder, Nurse Brown," the security guard said from the opposite end.

"Are you Tina Monroe?" I asked the young black woman sitting in the chair.

"Yes I am. And who are you?"

"I'm Easy Rawlins. I think Marianne Plump gave you my number."

At that moment a huge white woman in a nurse's uniform entered the room.

"If you are not off of these premises in one minute I will call the police." There was a ragged timbre to her voice.

The little speech seemed rehearsed. I supposed that she'd sat around for many nights wondering what she could say to convince a trespasser to leave.

"Hello, Mr. Rawlins," Geneva Landry said. She had bags under her eyes and her words were a little slurred.

"This is Mr. Rawlins, Nurse Brown," Tina Monroe was saying. "He has permission from Dr. Dommer to visit Miss Landry at any time."

"Why is Miss Landry awake?" was Brown's answer. "Haven't you given her her medicine?"

"Yes. But she was nervous so I'm sitting here with her for a while — until she relaxes a little more."

"Give her another dose," Brown said in an almost threatening tone.

"The charts don't allow for that, Nurse Brown," the serious black nurse replied.

"Excuse me," I said then.

"What?" Nurse Brown said.

"I'm here on official police business. I have to speak to Miss Landry and Miss Monroe. So if you don't mind, we need some privacy."

The guard and the nurse didn't want to obey but even they knew that it was a new world.

"Come on, Tommy," Nurse Brown said. "Let's go check Dr. Dommer's instructions."

They turned away slowly, looking for a way back in even as they exited.

"What are you doin' here at this time'a night, Mr. Rawlins?" Geneva asked me. "Have you found that man?"

I perched myself at the foot of the high bed.

"I found out how I could find him," I said. "But I can't do anything about it until morning so I thought I'd drop by and make sure that you were fine. I just thought I'd look in and see you sleepin'. You know you do need your rest."

"They give me pills that put me about halfway 'sleep. Then I start thinkin' about Nola and I wake up. But Tina comes in and talks to me."

"Everything's going to be all right, Miss Landry," the nurse said.

She was filled with the beauty of youth. Her light brown skin and luscious hair, her child's hands and woman's figure. Her lips were in the shape of a chubby heart and her eyes were always looking somewhere else to keep you from seeing the hunger they held. And even though everything about her was geared to making babies and a home she sat there night after night with Geneva Landry, listening to her grief and loss.

"You're a godsend," Geneva said and her eyes fluttered, filling with tears.

"In a day or two it will all be settled," I said. "And I'll make sure that Nola gets a nice service."

"You will?" she asked.

"Yes ma'am."

"Mr. Rawlins?" Tina Monroe asked.

"Yes?"

"Are you going to stay here for a while?"

"Until mornin' I guess."

Tina stood up. "I have to make my rounds and I won't feel so bad doing it if you stay here with Miss Landry."

"No problem."

I watched the young black woman in white move through the doorway.

"She's beautiful," Geneva Landry said.

"She sure is," I added. And I meant it even though it wasn't really true. Tina was handsome, she was well built, but not beautiful.

"It's nice that she can come and sit with you," I added.

"Oh yes. You know I think I might go crazy in here if it wasn't for her. I start thinkin' about Nola and my mind feels like there's razor blades in it."

"Don't think about it," I said. "Let it go."

Geneva had lost weight in the few hours since I had seen her. Her face was drawn and her eyes drifted in her head even when she was talking to me.

"I cain't help it, Mr. Rawlins. I should have told Nola to get away from that white man. I know what men like that can do to a woman or a girl."

"Men like what?" I asked.

"White," she said as if I were a fool. "White men. They rotten. I mean they smile and say nice things in company but when they get you alone it's another story . . . another story altogether."

She started to cry and I took her hands in mine.

"You don't want to cry, Miss Landry," I said. "Nola's in heaven, you know. She's in a better place. And the man who harmed her will pay the price. I promise you that."

"Will he lose an eye like the one he took from my beautiful Scarlet?"

"More," I said. "More."

The promise of retribution seemed to calm Geneva. She kissed my forearm and then laid a cheek against it. I pulled one hand free and stroked her cheek. She sighed and shuddered and then drifted off into a deep sleep.

I sat there for over an hour stroking her face now and then. Whenever I touched her she started and then smiled.

Light filled the small window near her bed. The birds began their morning songs and Tina returned. When she saw me sitting so close to the sleeping woman she smiled.

"She's a darling," Tina said.

She leaned over the bed and kissed the older woman's brow. At the time I thought that was the most beautiful thing I'd ever seen. The feeling Tina had for her charge made my heart run hot.

When we went out into the hall she told me, "My shift's over in fifteen minutes."

I looked at my watch. It was five forty-five.

"Can we go get some coffee after?"

"Okay."

19

Nip's Coffee Shop on Olympic opened at six. We got there fifteen minutes later but there were already a dozen or more customers eating scrambled eggs and dough-nuts, drinking reconstituted orange juice and coffee that tasted mostly like the urn it came from.

We sat in a window booth across from each other.

Tina didn't have a beautiful face. It would have been plain if it weren't for that inner light young people have. As it was she probably had her pick of the young men down in the riot area. I tried not to think about it and so I started talking.

"Marianne said that you two see each other in the morning," I said.

"Uh-huh," Tina replied. "She usually comes in at about eight-fifteen and then we talk until she has to be on the job at nine."

"But you get off at six."

"I use the coffee room to study for my RN tests after work," she said. "And when Marianne come in we talk about it. She's real sweet. Don't know nuthin' but at least she willin' to find out."

"What can I get for ya?" a man asked.

It was the chef. He was skinny everywhere but his stomach, which was half the size of a volleyball. He wore white pants with a checkered T-shirt and a pale blue apron. If he shaved that morning it didn't take. His chin was still gray. His eyebrows were so long that they resembled horns. There was even hair growing out of the man's ears.

He'd come from behind the stove to take our orders. The waitress, a small strawberry-blond thing, was behind the counter, staring at us with a terrified expression on her face.

"I could use a couple'a scrambled eggs and ham with orange juice and some dark toast," I said, smiling for the man. "And coffee for the both of us."

"Juice and an English muffin," Tina added.

He jotted down our order and strode back to the kitchen. On the way he threw the receipt pad at the waitress.

She took up two coffee cups and brought them to our table. She was so shaky that the saucers under our cups were filled with coffee.

I watched the waitress going back to the counter. Once she looked over her shoulder. When our eyes met she bumped into a customer sitting on his stool.

"Watch it there, Margie," the jovial man said to the waitress. "My wife might have spies in the kitchen."

Margie, I thought.

"She's a good woman," Tina said.

"Miss Landry?"

"Yes."

"She seems nice," I said, "but I guess she's had a real hard time."

"You don't know the half of it," Tina said. "Miss Landry been through the wringer three times and now the Lord got her goin' back again."

"You mean Nola's death."

"Yes I do. Her niece gettin' killed like that is gonna take years off that poor woman's life. She's getting weaker every day."

"What did happen to her?" I asked.

"Nola?"

"No. What happened to Geneva? She told me that there were things that happened to her that she never told Nola, that if she had told her maybe she'd still be alive. What do you think she meant by that?"

"I . . ."

"Here you go," a woman said.

It was Margie again. She was trembling, barely able to put our order down on the table. She wouldn't look either one of us in the eye. And as soon as the plates and glasses were down she scurried away.

I took a big mouthful of scrambled egg. It was delicious. Cooked in butter and just an instant past runny. That skinny chef knew what he was doing.

"What do you have to do with all this, Mr. Rawlins?" Tina asked me.

"I got a little office down on Central and Eighty-six," I said. "It's just a room with a toilet down the hall. On one side of me there's a guy sells dollar life insurance to people doin' day work. Across the hall is Terry Draughtman. He's the pool table expert for all of Watts and thereabouts. If you got trouble with your pitch or your bumpers you come to Terry and he'll fix you right up.

"My office door says 'Easy Rawlins — Research and Delivery.' And that's what I do. You can find me any Tuesday or Thursday evening and most of the day on Saturday. If you have a problem and you want some advice, I do that."

"What about the office on the other side of you?" Tina asked.

"It used to be a bookkeeper, but he had a heart attack and died. After that nobody has stayed in there more than a month or two."

For some reason that made Tina smile.

"So who are you helping right now?" she asked.

"You," I said.

"Me?"

"You live down in SouthCentral L.A., don't you?"

"Yeah?"

"Now what do you think is gonna happen down there when people find out that a pious colored woman was killed by a white man? When they find out that he raped her and strangled her and then shot her in the eye?"

"Oh."

"I'm lookin' for that white man and I'd like to know what happened."

"But Miss Landry already told you," Tina said.

"She didn't see her niece get killed. She never even saw him. And Nola didn't have a pistol or any other gun in her house."

"What does that have to do with anything?"

"If Nola didn't have a gun, then what did this white man shoot her with?"

"His own gun," she said.

"And if he brought a gun with him, then why didn't he open fire on the mob that beat him?"

That argument made her forehead furrow and her head cock to the side.

"So you think Miss Landry's makin' it all up?" she asked.

"No," I said. "I think that she's just filling in some of the spaces with her own experiences."

"And that's why you wanna know about what Miss Landry said about what she shoulda told Nola?"

I nodded and took another big forkful of egg.

"Why didn't you ask her yourself when we were in her room?"

"It's like you say," I said. "She looked weak, fragile. I figured maybe you'd know."

"Maybe so but . . . I mean she's talkin' to me because it's a confidence and she thinks I'll keep her secret."

"Did she ask you not to tell?" I asked.

"No. But I'm sure she wouldn't like it."

"If what she told you didn't have to do with who else might have killed Nola then I won't tell anybody," I said. "I just want to know how to understand why she thinks that white man killed Nola."

"It's 'cause of what happened to her that she's so upset," Tina said. "But that don't mean that white man didn't kill her."

"What happened to her?"

"She, I mean her father used to work for this white man outside of Lafayette —"

"Louisiana?"

"Uh-huh. Anyway, they grew pecans down there and Miss Landry's father would spend the whole day out on the plantation takin' care of the trees. And when the white man knew that her father would be gone a long time he'd go up and find little Ginny and do things to her. Things that most women wouldn't let their husbands do."

"How old was she?"

"It started when she was twelve," Tina said. "He did that to her three or four times a week. And when she'd cry and beg him not to, he'd tell her that if her father ever found out, they'd have to kill him because he would go crazy and try and kill a white man if they didn't."

"So she never told anyone?"

"No. And that's why she's so upset. She feels that if she had told Nola, then Nola woulda known that you couldn't trust a white man. That all white men wanted to do was rape and defile black women."

Tina felt the pain of her charge.

I took her hand and she grabbed on to me. What had happened to Geneva Landry could happen to any black woman. She had to take mountains of abuse while protecting her blood. She could never speak about the atrocities done to her while at the same time she dressed the wounds of her loved ones. Of course they both hated the white man who took refuge in a black woman's home.

But even with all that I had to wonder — where did that pistol come from?

AT THE CASH register I had to wave to get the cook's attention.

"How much we owe?" I asked him.

"Margie," he shouted to the waitress. "The man wants his check."

The blond waif shook her head and ran through a door at the back of the restaurant.

"Go on," the cook said to me. "I guess it's on the house today."

20

I dropped Tina off at her bus stop on Pico and then drove toward the address for Peter Rhone on Castle Heights a few blocks south of Cattaraugus. I had all of Mr. Rhone's information on his registration forms taken from the Galaxie 500.

I got lost for a while driving around the Palms area looking for a way to Rhone's house. On the way I thought about Margie. I knew Nips Coffee Shop from the time I bought my house down on Genesee. I had seen the small waitress there for the past three years. She never remembered me, though. I gave my order and she filled it with neither a smile nor a frown on her face. But today she was afraid to be in my company. She still didn't recognize me and so, as I drove around the white neighborhood, I began to see that my history with white people was much more complex than I had ever thought it was. On the one hand Margie had ignored my existence, and on the other I scared her to death. And even while she feared me she still didn't know me. And what about that cook? How did his impatience with her fears fit in?

I didn't come up with an answer. But after forty-five minutes of driving in circles I found Peter Rhone's home.

It was coral pink and box shaped. The roof was flat and the drainpipes were painted a light rust color. The front door was turquoise, and white dahlias decorated the fence around his lawn. There was a lemon-yellow Chevy in the driveway and only one banister for the three wooden steps that led to the front door.

Four weeks ago this house would have sold for three times the amount that the same home would have gone for in Watts. Now the multiplier was more probably five.

"Hello," she said, answering my knock.

She was a small woman with brown hair piled up into a helmet on the top of her head. She was thirty but wearing braces.

"Peter Rhone," I said.

"He's sick," she told me.

"Yeah," I said. "I know what happened to him. But you have to believe me when I tell you that he really needs to talk to me. Now."

"What's your name?"

"My name is John Lancer. I think I might have some information that he would want to know."

"What is it about, Mr. Lancer?"

"It's private."

"I'm his wife."

"And I'm sure he will want to talk to you about what I have to say. But believe me, ma'am, it is not my place to talk about it first."

She blinked three times and then turned her head.

"Peter. Peter, it's some man named Lancer."

She turned back to me and looked me up and down. I was wearing the same work clothes I had on when I went down to Nola's neighborhood. Realizing this set off a chain reaction of thoughts. First I thought that I needed a bath and a shave as soon as possible. Then I wondered why I hadn't even yawned, when I'd been up and moving for well over twenty-four hours. I also realized that I hadn't spoken to Bonnie since leaving with Mouse. Thinking of Bonnie reminded me of Juanda. Luckily, before I could go too far down that road a man appeared out of the mist of the Rhones' screen door.

There was a deep cut on the left side of his swollen lower lip, a knot over his right eye, and two fingers of his left hand were taped together.

"Yes?" he asked affably in spite of his obvious discomfort.

"Peter Rhone?"

"Yes. And you are?"

"My name is John Lancer."

"Oh. Do I know you?"

"I think you might have met my cousin Nola when you were down on Grape Street a few days ago."

"I think so," he said. "She was the neighbor of the people that took me in."

Mrs. Rhone was paying close attention to our lies.

"Yeah," I said. "That's what she said. Anyway, Mr. Rhone, I have something very important to discuss with you. I'm sorry but it has to be private."

"I told him that you were sick, Peter," his wife said.

"That's okay, Theda," he told her. "You know I owe these

people something. Mr. Lancer, there's a park just a few blocks down from here. We could go sit on a bench there for a while."

I smiled and nodded.

"Peter," Mrs. Rhone said.

"It's okay, honey."

He pulled the screen door open and said, "It's just a few blocks. We can walk."

We walked out of the flowery yard and turned right onto Castle Heights.

Peter Rhone was a tall man and good-looking in a boyish kind of way. He was lean and fair with blond hair and blue eyes — just the kind of man who had no business in Watts when there was a riot going on.

I noticed that he limped slightly when he walked.

"Looks like it's cooling down a bit," he said as we strolled toward the corner.

"Yeah. But the heat's still here," I replied.

"I like a hot day," he said. "It'll be cold enough, long enough later on."

We were at the corner.

"So tell me what happened when you were at Nola's," I said.

"What do you mean?"

"I mean — what happened?"

"Are you her husband?" he asked then. That was the first moment I had an inkling that the situation was much more complex than I had even suspected.

"Nola's dead," I said.

Peter stopped walking. He grabbed me by the forearm.

"What? What happened?" There were already tears in his eyes. "What happened?"

"That's what I wanted to ask you."

Peter glanced back toward his house. I did too.

Theda Rhone was standing on the sidewalk, looking at us.

"Come on," Rhone said. "Let's keep walking."

He turned and started moving at a fast pace.

I kept up with him. Walking is what I did all day long at Sojourner Truth. There was both an upper and a lower campus and space enough for over thirty-five hundred students. Some days I didn't sit at all.

As we walked he kept asking what happened. Finally I told him about Nola and Geneva and her claims.

At the end of the third block we came to a small park. It had four or five trees and two benches. Peter sat and started rocking.

"Who could have done such a thing?" he said. "Who?"

"Everybody I've talked to has got their money on you."

"Me? Why would I? She saved my life."

"Maybe she wanted something you couldn't give," I suggested.

"Like what?"

"Maybe she was going to call your wife."

"Why would she? I was going to leave Theda. I told Nola that."

"Come again?"

"I loved your cousin. Didn't she tell you that?"

"Well," I said. "I have to admit that I misled you, Mr. Rhone. My name is Easy Rawlins and the first time I saw Nola was on a coroner's slab."

"I, I don't understand. What do you have to do with her . . ." His words trailed off because he didn't want to call her dead.

"The police are stepping lightly around this murder —"

"Murder," he repeated the word.

"Yeah. Anyway, the cops called on me because I know people

around the neighborhood and I can ask questions without arousing too much attention. You know public attention to her murder could set off the riots all over again."

"I don't understand, Mr. Rawlins. Who would want to kill Nola?"

There we were again. By now I was more than half convinced that he hadn't killed her. Rhone wasn't trying to hide anything from me. He was frightened but not for himself. Nola was still alive in this man's heart.

"Do you own a gun, Peter?"

"A twenty-five-caliber pistol."

"Where is it?"

"In my house. In the dresser."

It was a beautiful day. Low eighties and fairly clear. There was a robin singing somewhere and the traffic was sparse.

"Why don't you tell me what happened, Peter? Then maybe I can help make some sense out of it all."

21

I don't understand, Mr. Rawlins," Peter Rhone said. "Are you with the police department?"

"No. Not with them. If I was, I would have turned you in the minute I got your name. But they asked me to help them solve Nola's murder before the newspapers got hold of it because they want to keep a lid on Watts."

"So you're a detective?"

"Think of me as a concerned citizen who has the ear of the police and you have a good idea of what I'm doing here."

"I don't know," he said. "Maybe I shouldn't be talking to you."

"Fine," I said. "But when I give the police your address they'll have you in jail and up on charges before you can explain to your wife what you were doing down there in a black woman's arms."

Peter Rhone was staring deeply into my eyes. His face was

quivering and his fingers were more jittery than those of a two-year-old who's just eaten a chocolate bar.

"The news hasn't said anything about Nola . . . There were no reports."

"She was strangled and then she was shot. Beaten too," I said.

It was no proof but it broke the man down emotionally. His head lowered nearly to his knees.

"I wondered why she wasn't home," he said. "I've been calling every chance I get. She didn't come in to work either."

"She's dead," I said again.

"What did you want to know?" he asked.

"Did you kill Nola?"

"No. No."

"Did you have sex with her on Tuesday night?"

His forehead touched his left knee.

"Yes," he said.

"She was willing?"

"Very much. Very much. She was so happy that I was there and, and . . . she kissed me. That's what started it. She kissed me."

"Why did you go to her house in the first place?"

"I had driven down to Grape Street looking for her."

"You already knew her?"

"Yes. Didn't you know? She works in the office where I do on Wilshire. Nola's the daytime switchboard operator at Trevor Enterprises."

"What do you do there?"

"I broker advertising deals. You see, people come to us to find out where they should advertise. We have contacts throughout the southland, so people, especially companies with out-of-town staffs, rely on us for intelligence."

"And how well did you know Nola?" I asked.

"The operator's room is next to my office," he said. "And somehow we started bringing in coffee for each other every other day. Usually it was just a drop-off but sometimes we'd gab a little bit before getting to work. At first, you know, I was just nice to her because the operator is the most important job at Trevor Ent."

"How's that?"

"A lot of times people call in wanting help but they have to rely on Nola to route the call to the right person. She was a smart girl so she knew a good prospect when it came in. And if it was good she'd give it to me if it seemed up my alley. Not a bad dividend for two cups of coffee a week.

"But after a while I started liking her. She was smart. Read all the magazines and papers that came through the office and she knew more about baseball than I did. We were friends."

"So how does that turn into you making love to her with the city burning down around your heads?" I asked.

"When the riots started, Theda went down to La Jolla to visit her uncle and aunt. They're her closest family and they were afraid that a race war was coming. Crazy. I went to work in the morning and Nola didn't come in. I worried about her all day and then finally I called in the afternoon. She was so frightened. I could hear it in her voice. She hadn't come to work because she had to take the bus and she was afraid of snipers. So I told her that I'd come and get her and drop her off with some friends that lived down around Venice."

"So you worked until the end of the day and then drove down into the riot?"

I had always been amazed by the ignorance that white people showed about blacks. Most of the times I was angry at their lack of awareness — this time I was enthralled. Peter

Rhone might have been the only white man in L.A. who wanted to drive down into Watts in order to save a colored woman from the riots.

"And they got you," I said.

"Yeah." Peter nodded his battered head. "Beat me pretty bad. All I could do was run toward Nola's address. And there she was. She threw a blanket over me and took me into her building. They knocked out a tooth and I was bleeding from the head. There I was, trying to save her and she saved me instead.

"We talked for three days. She told me all about her family and her Aunt Geneva. I told her about my wife. She had a boyfriend but she wasn't in love with him."

His mentioning Geneva Landry reminded me of something.

"Why didn't Geneva know your last name?" I asked.

"What?"

"Didn't she talk to her aunt every day?"

"Yeah. Little Scarlet would call her aunt at sunset each day. Geneva would call at other times too — whenever she was scared."

"What did you call her?"

"Little Scarlet. That was her nickname. After we got, uh, close she wanted me to call her that."

I couldn't see how a rapist-murderer could possibly learn his victim's pet name.

"Well, why didn't she tell her that the white man she saved was from her job?" I asked anyway.

"Because I'm married. She didn't want to start any gossip about me."

"And how did you get out of there?"

"Early . . . early on Wednesday morning Nola got her neighbor to take me home. I paid him fifty dollars."

"Did he see you with Nola?"

"No. She just called him and told him to pick me up in front of the house at three."

"And before all that you fell in love?" I didn't mean to let my cynicism show but it was hard to hide.

"It's true."

And why not? A cute white boy was worth a second look, especially if he was willing to brave the riots to save a young damsel in her tenement tower. He might even be worth a third look. And if he told her that he'd leave his wife to marry her it could well have been too good to pass up. I mean, how many times are there in a young woman's life when a man would give all that up for her? Imagine what kind of father a man like that would make.

"Who was the man who drove you?" I asked.

"Piedmont is what he called himself," Rhone said. "I don't even know if that's a first or last name."

"What did he look like?"

"Your height but not so filled out," he said. "Same color as you are and he had very long fingers and arms. And . . . and he had a mole right in the center of his forehead. I remember because every once in a while he'd touch it."

"Did you see anybody else while you were laid up at Nola's?"

"No. Neither one of us left the apartment."

"What about Theda?"

"What about her?"

"Didn't she wonder where you were?"

"I called her at her relatives' and said that I'd got caught in the riots and that a family took me in. I said that they didn't have a phone and that I was using a phone booth to call."

"And she believed that?"

"She was staying with people who believed there was a race war unfolding in the streets."

I thought about Margie, a woman who was so afraid of the riots that she couldn't even bring me my bill.

"I better call the police," Peter said.

"No. No," I said. "The last people in the world you wanna talk to right now are the cops. If one word gets out on the airwaves about Nola they'll hang your butt out to dry."

"Why?"

"You really don't know, do you?" I asked.

"Know what?"

"That you crossed the line when you went down to Nola's."

"What should I do?" he asked. "I mean, I don't want Nola's killer to get away. Maybe I could help."

If he was a liar he was good.

I had no idea of what happened in that neat little apartment. Maybe they went crazy after three days. Maybe they fell in love and then they began to hate each other.

All I had to do was give Rhone's name over to Suggs or, better, to Deputy Commissioner Gerald Jordan, and I was free. I'd have a friend in a high place while the police tried to untangle the knots.

But I didn't trust the police to do their job and I didn't think that Rhone was guilty.

"If you're lyin' to me, man," I said, "I will kill you myself."

"I loved Nola," he said with stiff conviction.

"Then wait twenty-four hours."

"For what?"

"I'm gonna do what the cops asked me to do and look for the man killed Nola. If it's you I'll send the cops to your door. If you run I'll find you. But if it ain't you, well, then we'll see."

133

"Thank you," he said.

"You don't have to thank me, man," I said. "This isn't for you. I just don't want the police to let that woman's death slide by because they're worried about somethin' else."

"That's what I'm thanking you for."

22

"Hello?" a black woman said in a gruff but not unfriendly tone.

"Juanda there?" I asked.

As the words came out of my mouth my heart twitched and my stomach turned. I had convinced myself that I was calling the fine young woman because I needed her help. And as I look back on the situation I realize that I really did need her. But there was more than that to the call. I loved Bonnie and had no intention of changing my situation but still I yearned to be in the presence of the chattering young woman who lied to save me and then led me to freedom.

"Hello?" she said in my ear.

"Juanda?"

"Mr. Rawlins."

"Easy," I said. "Call me Easy."

"I was hopin' you would call," she said. There was no pretense in this woman. She wanted to know me and she let me know it.

"Yeah. Well, I think I might need some more help from you if you wouldn't mind."

"I don't mind. You gonna come pick me up?"

I gulped and said, "Yeah."

She gave me her address on a sigh.

I said that I'd be around in the early afternoon.

My next call was to Bonnie.

"Rawlins residence," she said into the receiver.

"Were you ever thinking that we'd get married?" I asked without preamble.

Her response was silence.

"I didn't mean to drop it on you, baby," I said. "I mean . . . I guess I feel a little crazy out here."

"Are you okay, Easy?"

"No."

"What's wrong?"

"I don't think that white boy killed Nola."

"That really isn't up to you, is it?"

"No. But if I don't look at it closely I can't be sure the police will either."

"Why not? That's their job."

"At best their job is keeping the peace," I said. "And right here the peace will be best served by this white man takin' the heat."

"Oh," she said.

"And if he didn't kill her, then somebody else did. But the cops won't care about that. They never worry about exactly who did what. Catchin' crooks is like herdin' cattle for them. So what if one or two get away? They're bound to be caught somewhere down the line. And if they round up an innocent man, they'll just tell ya that he probably did somethin' else they didn't catch him for."

"But Easy," Bonnie said.

"What?" I lit up a Lucky Strike.

"You don't have the kind of resources that the police do. You can't go out there and find some killer that you know nothing about."

"You're right about that, honey. But . . ."

"What?"

"That's why those people were out there shootin' and burnin' and throwin' rocks. Because they're sick and tired of knowin' that they can't ever get it right. They're tired'a bein' told that they can't win."

"Did they win?" she asked me.

"They mighta been wrong," I said. "But at least they tried."

"Okay."

It was more than her giving in to my hardheaded ways. She knew that I needed her blessing to go out so far from safety.

"I love you," we both said together.

After she hung up I slammed the pay phone handset down so hard that it broke in my hand.

I DROPPED BY my office at Sojourner Truth before going to meet Juanda. I had an extra suit of clothes in a locked closet there. It was a rabbit gray two-piece ensemble with a single-button jacket. I also had a cream-colored shirt and bone shoes. I took the clothes down to the boy's gym, where I showered and shaved, powdered, and dabbed on cologne. There were still a few soldiers and policemen prowling the campus but the aftermath of the riot was winding down.

JUANDA WAS WAITING out in front of her door on Grape Street. She had preened a bit too. She was wearing a white miniskirt and a tight-fitting multicolored striped blouse. She wore no hose or socks and only simple leatherlike sandals. She wore no jewelry and had nothing in her hair.

Juanda's hair was not straightened, which was rare for Negro women in the ghettos of America at that time. Her hair was natural and only slightly trimmed. There was a wildness to it that was almost pubic.

She smiled for me when I hopped out to open her door.

"That's another reason I like older men," she said when we were both seated and on our way.

"What's that?"

"They remember to be gentlemen even after you kissed 'em."

"But you never kissed me," I said.

"Not yet."

I STARTED DRIVING and Juanda began to talk. She told me about her cousin Byford who had recently come to Los Angeles from Texas by hitchhiking. His mother, Juanda's mother's sister, had died suddenly and he was alone in the world.

Juanda's mother, Ula, had been angry at Byford's mother for over twenty years. It seems that when their mother died, Ula suspected her sister Elba of having taken their mother's set of cameos that she'd received from a rich white lady she worked for.

That was why Ula left Galveston, because she couldn't stand living in the same town as her thieving sister.

The sisters were estranged, so all that Byford, who was only thirteen, knew was that his Auntie Ula lived somewhere in L.A. He stuck out his thumb and made it all the way to southern California, getting rides with young white longhairs mainly.

He found his auntie by walking the streets of Watts asking anybody he met, did they know an Ula Rivers.

"Byford is pure country," Juanda was saying. "I mean, he go barefoot everywhere and only drink from jelly jars. Sometimes he even go to the baffroom in the backyard if somebody in the toilet an' he cain't hold it . . ."

I could have listened to her for weeks without getting tired. She was from down home, Louisiana and Texas. She was more than twenty years my junior but we could have been twins raised in the same house, under the same sun.

I knew many young teens like her who attended Sojourner Truth. But they were children and I harbored the mistaken belief that I had left my rude roots behind. I owned apartment buildings and a dozen suits that cost over a hundred dollars each. But a tight dress on a strong country body along with the prattle that I hadn't heard since childhood sent a thrill through my heart.

Juanda's conversation was like home cooking was to me after five years' soldiering in Africa and Europe. I didn't stop eating for a week after I got home.

WE HEADED WEST toward Grand Street downtown. There we came to a small hotel called The Oxford. It had a fine restaurant on the first floor called Pepe's. The maître d' was a chubby, golden-hued Iranian named Albert who liked me because I once proved that he was in San Diego when his wife's mother's house had been robbed. Albert had married a white woman whose parents hated him. He had never experienced racism of that nature before. Being Persian, he disliked many other peoples but never for something as inconsequential as skin color or an accent.

"Mr. Rawlins," he said, giving me a broad grin.

The room was dim because, like most L.A. restaurants, Pepe's had no windows. That's because the sun in the southland was too strong and the heat generated by windows didn't make for comfortable dining.

Most of the fifteen tables were set for two at lunchtime. The chairs had leather padded arms and seats.

The dining room was nearly full. All of the other diners were white.

Albert led us to a secluded corner table that had a banquette made for two. He didn't say anything about Juanda's faux leather or revealing attire. He would have seated us if we were wearing jeans and straw hats.

Once we were comfortable Albert asked, "Is there anything that the lady does not eat?"

"Juanda?" I said, passing the question on to her.

"I don't like squash or fish," she told me.

"Then we won't bring you any," Albert said.

He went away and Juanda hummed a long appreciative note.

"You come here a lot?" she asked.

"Not often," I said. "I did Albert a favor once and he told me that I could always eat here free of charge."

"Don't the people own the restaurant get mad at that?"

"His brother owns the hotel."

"Damn."

"Juanda?"

"Yeah, Easy?" Even the way she said my name exhilarated me.

"Do you know a man named Piedmont?"

"Uh-huh."

"What's he like?"

"He's a man. Big long arms and bug eyes. He used to be a boxer but then he got hurt and by the time he was better he was too lazy to go to the gym anymore."

"Is he a bad man like Loverboy?"

"No. He okay."

"Your salads," Albert said.

He put two plates before us. They were green salads made up of frisée lettuce, cherry tomatoes, cut green beans, and a strong garlic vinaigrette.

Juanda loved it. And I loved her loving it.

"You know how I can get in touch with Piedmont?" I asked as she was eating her third slice of French bread.

"Why?"

"Because I think he might help me find a man I'm looking for."

"Can I at least finish my salad before you start askin' me all kinds'a questions?" she asked playfully.

"Sure," I said.

I watched her concentrate on the lettuce and bread. She ate all of the greens, except for the beans, and then used her bread to mop up the dressing.

Albert must have been watching because as soon as she was through he brought the entrée. It was chicken breasts stuffed with ham and white cheese, accompanied by mashed potatoes under a Cognac sauce.

"Is this to your liking, miss?" he asked Juanda.

"It's great," she said.

This elicited a big smile from the round Persian. His hairline was receding and his eyes were cunning but Albert was a man I knew that I could trust.

When he left, Juanda said, "I don't know if I should tell you about Piedmont."

"Why not?"

"Because then you might not call me no more."

She gazed into my eyes and I froze, realizing that what she said was true.

"I live with a woman," I said.

"Will you kiss me one time?"

"I have two kids," I continued, "three if you count one that left with her mother eleven years ago."

"Just one kiss and you have to promise that you will call me one more time at least."

I wasn't thinking about Nola or Geneva or Bonnie right then. I leaned over to give Juanda a chaste kiss on the lips but when her fingers caressed my neck I lingered and even drifted to plant a gentle peck on her throat.

When I leaned back Juanda was smiling.

"He live on Croesus only a couple'a blocks from the corner where you met me," she said. "I don't know the number but it's this big ugly red house that got a bright orange door."

Albert brought crème brûlée for dessert and Juanda was in heaven.

WHEN WE GOT to the car I unlocked her door and opened it.

"You see?" she said. "You'd open the door for me even after we've had a dozen kids."

ON THE RIDE back to her home Juanda talked about her experience in high school. She had gone to Jordan High and got good grades until halfway through the eleventh grade.

"... then I messed up," she said.

"What happened?"

"I met this boy. His name was Dean and he was fiiiiine. Uh. He'd already dropped out but he'd sneak into the schoolyard and stand outside my homeroom door waitin' for the passin' period. I'd tell him that I had to go to class but he put his hand on my waist and I couldn't say no. They finally expelled me."

"Expelled you? Why?"

"'Cause I wouldn't listen," she said. "'Cause I thought I was a woman and they couldn't treat me like a child no more."

The riots and Nola Payne's death and Juanda's heaving chest were pumping in my veins. I was happy when we got to her block.

I pulled to the curb. She turned to me and touched my forearm.

"You gonna call me again, right?" she asked.

"Yes."

"When?"

"No more than two days."

"You still got my number?"

I recited it from memory. That made Juanda grin. She jumped out and I sped off. In the rearview mirror I could see her waving.

23

I knocked on the bright orange door. Then I knocked again. I don't know how long I stood there. I was in no hurry. I had death and sex and race on the brain. No matter which way I turned in my mind, there was one of those vast problems.

"That's the problem with most'a you black mens, Easy," Jackson Blue had once said to me. "White people think we stupid but it's the other way around. We got so much on our minds all the time that we ain't got no time for little things like exactly what time it is or the rent. Shit. Here he askin' you about long division and you thinkin' 'bout Lisa Langly's long legs, who you gonna have to fight to get next to her, and why this ugly white man think anything he say gonna make a bit'a difference to you when you get out in the street."

I smiled remembering the cowardly genius's glib words. Jackson was the smartest man I had ever known. I thought that maybe I should talk to him about the riots when I was finished with my official work.

The orange door came open. A tall man in a crimson minister's suit was standing there before me.

"Yes?" he asked.

"Are you Piedmont?"

"No. My name is Lister, Reverend Lister. Who are you?"

"My name is Easy Rawlins, Reverend. And I need to have a conversation with a man named Piedmont."

"Brother Piedmont isn't here right now," the minister said with a paper-thin smile on his sculpted lips. "What is your business with him?"

Lister was the color of tanned leather that had been left out in the sun too long. He wasn't light skinned but he was lighter than he had once been. All of his facial features were small but well arranged. His hands were weak and he had big bare feet. His shoulders were small but he carried them with authority so I decided to treat him with the respect he demanded.

"Mr. Piedmont gave a man a ride the other night. That man is in some trouble and Piedmont is the only person who might clear him."

The cherry-frocked minister pondered me for quite a while and then he smiled and nodded.

"Come in, Brother Rawlins," he said. "We can wait for Harley together."

We entered a large room. It must have been almost the whole first floor of the three-story house. The pine floor and walls and ceiling were painted bright red. This chamber was bare except for a twelve-foot gray couch against the far wall with a small raised dais set opposite.

This room, I was sure, was Lister's church. When the congregation was having a service, they would come out with folding chairs for his acolytes.

We walked to the long gray couch and Lister gestured for me to sit. After I was situated he sat a few feet away. As soon as he was comfortable a woman wearing a wraparound purple dress came in. She had a glass in each hand and a yellow cloth wrapped around her head.

She stopped a few feet from Lister and nodded.

"Lemonade?" she said.

"Yes, Vica," Lister said. "Mr. Rawlins?"

"Sure."

The woman, girl really, served the minister first and then handed me a glass. She looked directly at me and smiled. Her earnestness called up a moment's shyness in me, so I looked down. It was then I noticed that she too was barefoot.

"Vica," Lister said.

"Yes, Reverend?"

"When Brother Piedmont comes in will you tell him that there's a Mr. Rawlins here to see him?"

"Yes, Reverend."

She left the room.

"Won't Brother Piedmont be coming through the front door?" I asked.

Instead of answering me Lister asked, "What is his name?"

"Who?"

"The man that needs Harley's help."

"DeFranco," I said easily. "Bobby DeFranco. He's a white boy."

"I see."

"Do the bare feet mean something?" I asked.

"Jesus went barefoot in the world," Lister said. "So did our ancestors under the African sun."

I wondered if Africa was all that barefooted but I didn't want to argue. I wanted to keep the minister talking so as not to have to tell him too many lies.

I took a sip of the lemonade. It was sweet for my taste but fresh-squeezed.

"What about Vica?" I asked.

"What about her?"

"She work for you?"

"She works for our master, as we all do, brother."

There was a minor strain of fanaticism in the minister's tone. But I didn't care. I once heard that extreme times call for extreme measures. Living in Watts was extreme three hundred and sixty-five days a year.

"Twenty-three adults live here among us, Brother Rawlins," Lister said. "The women serve and raise children while the men work to pay for our bread."

"I don't hear any kids."

"The school is in the basement." He smiled and then added, "I thought that you had come to join us."

"Join you what?"

"We've had six converts since the riots," he said. "People looking for hope in a world gone crazy."

"Might not be a bad idea," I speculated. "What do you have to do to join up?"

"Not much. Give yourself over to our master. Dedicate your life and worldly possessions to our family."

"That's all?"

Reverend Lister smiled.

"Do you know him, Harley?" he said, looking at me but talking to someone else.

"No suh."

147

The voice came from a door behind the red minister. A tall brown man with long arms and bulging eyes came out. He wore a gray Nehru jacket and blue jeans. There was a raised mole in the center of his forehead.

As Piedmont approached us the minister rose.

"I will leave you men to your business," he said. "And, Brother Rawlins . . ."

"Yes sir?"

"Your life is the only thing you truly have to give."

He turned and walked away. I watched him, thinking, rather resentfully, that what he had said might prove to be the most important lesson of my life.

"Do I know you, brother?" Piedmont asked as he lowered himself onto the couch.

"Nola Payne," I said. "And Peter Rhone."

Even as I spoke he rose up.

"Let's take it outside," he said.

Piedmont had long legs too. I had to jump up and scurry to make it with him to the door. He went through and I followed but after I crossed the threshold I turned to look once more at the consecrated living room. Vica had come back and was removing the lemonade glass I'd put on the floor in my haste to leave. She had gotten down on one knee, a voluptuous purple sail with a yellow flag dipping into a crimson sea. My breath caught as Piedmont pulled the orange door shut.

I believed at that moment that I would one day be compelled to give up my life and that when the time came I would go gladly.

I shivered at the thought and turned away.

24

On the sidewalk and two houses down Harley Piedmont stopped walking and confronted me.

"What the fuck you want, niggah?"

I remembered that the googly-eyed Piedmont had been a boxer. Boxers as a rule are peaceful men outside the ring but when they feel cornered they can be very dangerous.

"No problem, Brother Piedmont," I said mildly, keeping my hands at my sides. "I just been hired by a woman named Geneva Landry to find out what happened to her niece — Nola."

Piedmont's eyes grew even larger and a bead of sweat ran a jagged line from his forehead down between his eyes, forming into a large drop at the tip of his nose. The droplet hung there precariously like a long ash at the end of a burning cigarette.

Watching him sweat reminded me that it was a hot day. Maybe he was simply overheated. Or maybe he'd come back to Nola's place and raped and murdered her.

"What happened to Nola?" he asked.

"That's what I asked Mr. Rhone," I said. "He told me that she called you to take him home over in Palms. So I wondered if you had talked to the young lady again after letting him off."

"Why would I do that?"

"Maybe to tell her that he got home all right," I suggested. "Maybe because you all are friends. All I know is that Geneva is beside herself and the police don't wanna hear from her."

"Police? What do the god-danged police got to do with this?"

"Are you listenin'?" I asked. "Nola's missin'. That's a police matter."

"Man, who knows where she's gone or why? Maybe she's with her boyfriend. Maybe, maybe . . ." But there were no other explanations he could imagine.

"Yeah," I said, agreeing with his silence.

"So what the fuck is it to you?" Piedmont was feeling cornered again.

"I just need to know did you see her again after you took Rhone home."

"No," he said brusquely.

He took a step away from me.

"Maybe somebody else at the red house knows," I said.

That simple speculation stopped him in his tracks.

"No. I'm the one drove the man. Why the hell you think the congregation knows?"

"I don't know," I said. "After you turned in your fifty dollars to the community jar, maybe they sent somebody over to thank her or something."

I knew damn well that Piedmont hadn't turned in the money he'd gotten for driving Rhone. When he'd joined the congregation he probably didn't have twenty dollars to his name. Now that he was a member in good standing he probably did little jobs now and then, donating that money to the community pot. But something big like the fifty dollars he collected from Pete Rhone went in his pocket as silently as a shark sinking down under a swimmer's dangling feet.

"Why you wanna be messin' wit' me, man?" he said.

"All I want, Mr. Piedmont, is for you to tell me what you know about the night you drove that white man home."

"I pulled up in front of her house," he said. "The white man jumped in, told me where he lived, and I drove off. That's it."

"Did Nola come down to see him off?"

"Yeah. I think so. I mean, he waved at the doorway but she didn't come out."

"Did you see anything else?"

"Naw, man. It was three o'clock in the mornin'. And they still had the curfew. Wasn't nobody out except me and that white boy . . . and a old bum push a shoppin' cart an' live in a vacant lot down the street."

For a moment I saw only white. It was like I had been struck by lightning and everything was bleached out and bright.

"What old bum?" I whispered.

"I'ont know his name. All I know is he live in a cardboard lean-to over off 'a Grape."

"How long?"

"How long what?" he asked.

"How long has he lived there?"

"Couple'a months. I don't know. Bums come and go around here. On'y reason I even knew who he was is 'cause one day he asked me for a dime. I told him to get a job."

"Where off Grape?" I asked.

"Why?"

"Not why," I said. "Where?"

For an instant I think Piedmont was angry at my tone. There was even a shift in his shoulders indicating he was considering throwing something at me. It would have been the biggest mistake in his boxing career. The rage in my blood right then would have broken his jaw and a few ribs. He saw the fury and told me where to find the empty lot.

I WENT TO my car first. There I pulled the tire iron from the trunk and made my way to the lot. It was between what was once a grocery store and the chain-link fence of a single-family home. He'd piled ten or twelve sheets of heavy cardboard against the market wall. I cleared away the makeshift paper roof with two swipes of my iron club. I was ready to swing again but there was no one home. Lucky for me because I would have killed him if it was who I suspected.

There were all the comforts of a camping life in the hovel. A glass bottle half filled with water, a dirty green blanket on a foam mat. He had a fork and three cans of sardines, a chipped china plate, and three *Playboy* magazines. On his one solid wall he'd scrawled a poem in red lipstick:

Dirty girls get mud in their eye

They eat maggots and die

Break brains bad things bad things

They all die down in my pantry.

Under his filthy pillow was a square green tin with the emblem of a crown on the silhouette of a man's head at the center of the lid. Inside the tin there were three .22 caliber shells.

I went down on my knees in the dirt and rested my head against the wall. The anger in my heart was monumental. I thought back some months to a young woman named Jackie Jay and her Middle Eastern boyfriend, Musa Tanous. Jackie had been beaten to death and the cops thought that the killer was Musa. But I came to believe that a hobo named Harold had done it. I'd found Jackie's doll collection in Harold's lean-to and I'd seen some of her clothes in his stolen shopping cart.

The police didn't believe me and I never saw Harold again. But I was convinced that he killed Jackie because he thought that Musa was a white man and he wanted revenge on the black woman who dared to become a white man's lover.

"Hey you, Easy Rawlins!" someone shouted.

I didn't respond. I didn't know who it was calling me but I couldn't take my mind off of Harold and Jackie and now Nola on a silver bed in a white room hidden by the same police department that refused to believe my story.

"Hey!" the voice shouted again.

Hearing the threat in his tone my body rose without my willing it to do so. I turned to see that I was faced with four men, the foremost of whom was Newell.

"You sucker punched me yesterday," the broad-shouldered man said.

I lifted my iron in reply.

Two of the men who were with him took involuntary steps backward.

"Whu-oh," the third one said.

"You think I'm ascared'a that crowbar?" he asked me.

I kicked him in the groin and then swung the iron at his cohorts, hitting one of them in the shoulder.

"Get the fuck outta here or I'ma kill you motherfuckahs!" I shouted at the men.

They ran and I didn't blame them. Easy Rawlins was a crazy man right then. Insane.

Newell was in the dirt moaning when I knelt down next to him.

"Do you want me to start hittin' you with this thing?" I asked him.

He shook his head.

"Are you scared of this crowbar now?" I asked.

He nodded so I knew he could distinguish between the words I said.

"What was the name of the bum lived in here?"

"Harold," he said in a pained whisper.

I left him there for someone else to save. Saving wasn't my business right then. I was ready to go out and kill a man named Harold.

25

I entered the Seventy-seventh Street police station not fifteen minutes after leaving Newell. I'd gotten out of the car
with the tire iron in my hand but when a woman passing by
jerked her head and skipped away from me I realized that I
should put my weapon down.

Walking back to the car, I felt every step like I was walking
through water. I was wasting time. What I needed to do was
find Harold and kill him. I opened the trunk and threw the tire
iron in and then I sprinted for the police station.

I ran up to the front door breathing hard and sweating.
Anyone looking at me would have thought that I was a man in
trouble. I'm sure that's what the desk sergeant thought.

"Yes?" he asked, scrutinizing me from head to toe.

"Detective Suggs, please," I said.

"And who are you?"

The only feature I remember about that white man was that he had red hair. Red hair like Nola Payne had. Little Scarlet murdered by Harold the tramp. If thoughts could kill, people would have fallen dead for a mile all around me.

"Easy Rawlins," I said. "Easy Rawlins."

"And what's your problem, Mr. Rawlins?"

"Murder," I said. "He asked me about a murder and I found out something he wants to know."

I could see the cop trying to block me with some unspoken logic in his mind. The man looks crazy, he seemed to be thinking, but then again Suggs was only visiting the Seventy-seventh. I probably did know him.

There were quite a few policemen in the station. I suppose they were on overtime, making sure the people in the neighborhood didn't burn them down.

"Have a seat," Red said.

I went over near the bench across from his desk but stayed on my feet.

"I said sit down," the desk sergeant commanded.

"Don't wanna sit," I said.

"You heard the man," a voice to my right said.

It was from a tall uniformed cop standing nearby. He had gray hair, a young face, and a hand on his baton. I didn't say anything to him, just stood there and stared.

"Do you want me to sit you down?" the gray-haired, boy-faced man asked.

"Fuck you."

"Corless," a voice I recognized said. "Stand down."

"But, Lieutenant —"

"Stand down," Detective Suggs said again.

He came in between me and the angry uniform.

"Fuck you," I said again.

The gray head lunged at me but he was met by a surprisingly quick left hook thrown by the sloppy detective. Corless went down quickly and though he tried to jump back up he couldn't find his legs.

Suggs took me by the arm and led me down a hall behind the sergeant's desk and to an office that was a storage room not three days before. A dozen reams of paper were piled on the table he used for a desk and a three-foot pile of first-aid kits was stacked against the wall. There was a rack of shotguns on the floor and a gaping file cabinet filled with parking tickets and other traffic citations that kept the door from fully opening.

Suggs slammed the door shut.

"What's wrong with you, Rawlins?" he said. "You off your rocker?"

"I know who killed Nola Payne."

"Who?"

"A guy named Harold."

"Harold what?"

"Don't know his last name. But he killed her. I'm sure of that."

"How do you know?"

I told Suggs about Musa Tanous and Jackie Jay, about how I met Harold once and then saw his lean-to filled with her belongings. I told him about the crazy notes he left near both crime scenes.

"Nola and the white man she was with either became lovers or Harold thought that they had. Either way, he killed her for having that white man in her place."

I decided to leave Peter Rhone, Harley Piedmont, and Juanda

out of my story. I knew who the killer was but if I threw any more names at the cops, they'd go off on some other track. And I wasn't about to let that happen.

"How do you know that Harold was in the neighborhood?" Suggs asked. He was a good cop.

"I walked around," I said. "Just lookin' to get the lay of the land and I saw his teepee. It was made the same way as the last one I saw."

"Have a seat, Mr. Rawlins," Suggs offered.

He lifted a box full of files from a folding metal chair and slapped the seat a couple of times to move the dust around. Then he climbed over some other boxes to get to the chair behind the ancient maple desk.

I sat too.

Suggs's fawn-colored eyes seemed to be asking me for something. He took a deep breath and let out a sigh.

"I'm not leavin' here until you do somethin' about Harold," I said. "Last time I told the cops — right here in this station — they said I was crazy to think that a bum could be that good at killin'."

"I believe you," Suggs said.

I didn't know what he meant by that. I mean, he could have been saying that he believed that the cops in the station would say such a thing. But that didn't mean he bought my story about Harold.

Suggs laid his hand on a green folder filled with maybe two hundred sheets of paper.

"While I've been here waiting for you to come up with something," he said, "I've been taking up my time looking at the files of the open homicide cases of women in the neighborhood. At first I only went back one year but now I'm up to seven . . ."

It had only been a couple of days. That kind of work would have meant he was on the job almost around the clock.

". . . and I found something disturbing," he continued, opening the file. On the front page he had typed a long list of names down the left side with a shorter list to the right. "Thirty-seven unsolved homicides of women under forty. Most of them were in relationships with violent men. But six were not and four more were involved with men who had no history of violence. Your Jackie Jay was one of those."

He turned the page to a handwritten sheet.

"Each of the ten was strangled, a few of them were beaten, and one was stabbed after she was dead. None were raped. I don't believe that Nola Payne was raped either. Two of the women were married to white men."

He looked up at me and I felt that a door opened somewhere. It was as if I had been held prisoner for so long that I'd forgotten there ever was a door to freedom. And now that it was open I didn't know exactly what to do.

"You found that just by lookin' through the files?" I asked.

Suggs nodded.

"You mean somebody around here could have sat down in this messy room and read the files and come up with this list?"

"Yeah." Suggs's admission carried a heavy weight with it. "I mean, I'm pretty good at this kind of work. That's why they have me on the case but somebody should have picked it up before this."

"And what about women killed that you found killers for?" I asked. "What about some innocent men up in jail for women that Harold killed?"

Melvin hadn't thought of that. He turned his eyes toward a tan filing cabinet in the corner.

"One thing at a time," he said. "Tell me what you know about this Harold right now."

I told him all I knew. It wasn't much. He was on the short side and medium brown. I remembered that his hairline was beginning to recede and his beard hairs were at least half gray. When I'd met him he looked about fifty to me, but on thinking about it later, I thought that street life had aged him prematurely. He had big hands that seemed a little bloated. He had spent at least a few nights in the drunk tank and he drove a shopping cart. His mother was still alive and lived in L.A., a fact he let drop in the one three-minute conversation I had with him. He had never looked me directly in the eye.

Suggs took notes while I talked and when I was finished he snapped his little notepad shut.

"Not much," he said.

"I know. I've spent months driving around South L.A. looking for him. But it's a big city. I thought maybe he migrated away. But if his mother is here, I hoped that he either came back to see her or that he never left."

"I'll put out the word on this Harold," Suggs said. "But you should be out there lookin' for him too. Did you find out anything about the white man that stayed with Nola?"

"No."

"Well," he said, "that's probably for the best anyway. Jordan's office won't care about our theories on some black Jack the Ripper out around here. No sir they sure wouldn't. Find the white man and truss him up like a Thanksgiving turkey — that's Jordan's speed."

26

Suggs accompanied me out of the precinct. Half the policemen in the station came out to watch our passage. If I'd gone alone I would have been drawn into a fight I could have never won. Suggs knew that and walked me all the way to my car. There he extended his hand to me again. I shook it. It had been a long time since I felt that a white policeman saw eye to eye with me. The least I could do was take his hand in friendship.

I had the urge to get out in the streets and search for Harold but I knew better. Los Angeles is a big place. Anyone can hide there. There are docks and train yards and so many back alleys that it would take you two months to search them all once.

No, I wouldn't get far by driving around, so I went home to see my beautiful patchwork family.

The little yellow dog, Frenchie, met me at the door. He snarled and barked his disapproval at my presence.

"I'm home," I called, thinking that Bonnie and Feather would be in the kitchen sharing girl talk and making dinner.

"Hey, Easy," a somewhat masculine voice said.

Jackson Blue rose up out of the love seat.

Jackson was very dark, slender, and short. I'd known him since my early years in Houston. We were what you would call friends but he certainly was not someone I could trust.

Jackson's own mother couldn't trust him. He was a liar by nature and a thief from the first day he could close his hands around some other baby's rattle. But on the plus side he smiled easily, knew all of the important gossip within a twenty-mile radius, and had an IQ probably on a par with some of the greatest geniuses of history.

One of Jackson's most endearing qualities was his cowardice combined with a willingness to get involved with some of the worst criminals you could imagine. He was always looking over his shoulder or cowering in some dark corner. He laughed easily and I was sure that he stayed so slim so that he'd have the edge when he might have to outrun some irate partner in crime.

"Jackson," I said.

Now that he was standing I could see that he was wearing a tailored two-piece gray flannel suit with a white shirt, a dark maroon tie, and glasses with thick black rims. I tried to think of why he would be wearing such a getup. But no matter what came to mind there was no justification for it.

"You like?" he asked with a grin, holding up his cuffs and giving a wink.

"Halloween?" I asked, gesturing at the suit.

"You a regular Redd Foxx. No. This is a business suit. I'm a businessman."

"Hi, honey," Bonnie said, coming out of the kitchen.

"Daddy!" Feather yelled, careening between Bonnie and Jackson and slamming into my legs.

Feather hugged my right thigh, Bonnie kissed my cheek, and Jackson got into it by giving me a handshake. It was one of the few moments at that time that stands out for me as peaceful and whole. There I was, a man surrounded by friendship and love.

"Uncle Jackson says that there's people in the South Pacific got two heads," Feather said.

"Maybe if they buy a head of lettuce at the store," I told her.

Feather giggled and then laughed until she fell to the floor.

Bonnie picked her up and I kissed her.

"What you doin' here, Jackson?" I asked.

"Anybody ever need help, they come to Easy Rawlins," he said.

Maybe I should have turned him away. I already had two or three full-time jobs to accomplish in the next week or so. Jackson wasn't deserving of special consideration because he was so undependable. But no one I ever knew had a mind like his. And I was going to need some special thinking if I was going to go out after Harold the woman killer.

"What's up, Jackson?"

Bonnie whirled Feather around and whisked her back into the kitchen.

Jackson sat in the love seat and I pulled up a two-rung step stool that Bonnie had bought so that she could get up on the high shelves.

"It's Jewelle," he said. He adjusted his glasses as he spoke.

"Since when you been wearin' glasses, Blue?"

"You like 'em? I just got 'em last week. Bought 'em up in Beverly Hills — on Rodeo Drive."

"Near-sighted?" I asked.

Jackson grinned. "No, brother. My eyesight's twenty-ten. You a small man like me, need an edge with all these violent peoples runnin' up and down the street."

He handed me the glasses and I tried them on. It was like looking through the windshield of my car — no change at all. I handed them back.

"I don't get it. Glasses make you look like an egghead. What's the angle?"

Jackson smiled again.

"You know I been studyin' the binary language of machines," he said.

Computers had been Jackson's passion for some time. He had been holed up in a small apartment managed by his lover, Jewelle MacDonald, for well over a year reading about how those thinking machines worked.

I said all of this by nodding.

"Well," he said, "a while ago I decided to see if I could get me a job at a bank or some insurance company workin' on their computers. I know the IBM languages called BAL and COBOL and FORTRAN. I know all the loops and peripheries and the JCL too."

I had no idea what he was talking about but it still gave me an inner glee to know that a ghetto-bred black man like Jackson could know all the rich white businessmen's secrets.

"So what's that got to do with your glasses?" I asked.

"I been goin' out on job interviews for the last five weeks," he said. "At first I was wearin' my light blue suit but I could see that that wasn't the way a businessman's supposed to be dressed. I got me some Brooks Brothers then but still I couldn't get a job. Finally I realized that I had to do somethin' about bein' black."

We both chuckled. If anyone was a black man it was Jackson. His skin, his accent, the way he laughed at a joke.

"It came to me," he went on, "that even though I'm little the white people were still scared'a me. So I had to make it so I didn't seem scary."

"Damn," I said in deep appreciation for his uncharacteristically subtle solution. "So you put on those glasses with the ugly frames so the people at the bank would think that you're a Poindexter."

"Tried 'em out this afternoon," he said. "And three people said I'm as good as hired."

"Damn, Jackson. Damn. You're good."

It was rare that I complimented Blue. He grinned to show his appreciation.

"That's the favor I need," he said.

"I thought it was Jewelle needed help?"

"She does — in a way."

"Uh-huh. What's the scam, Jackson?"

"No scam, man. I swear."

"No? Then let's hear it."

"You know about that big shoppin' center they puttin' up over near Slauson?" he asked.

"The one on Figueroa?"

"That's the one."

"What about it?"

"The name on the papers is the Bigelow Corporation," he said. "But you know almost every dime comes from JJ. She bankrolled the project thinkin' we was gonna be rich."

It made sense that the young Jewelle and Jackson had gotten together. He was a technical and philosophical whiz, while she had a knack with real estate and finance that put me to shame. And Jewelle didn't mind caring for a man older than her by decades. She had been with my real estate agent, Mofass. He was quite a few years past sixty when he died. And Jewelle wasn't put off by a man who lived a rough life either. Mofass had died in a murder-suicide protecting Jewelle from her homicidal auntie.

". . . so," Jackson was saying, "I need to work until JJ get on her feet. You know she gonna have to sell almost everything she own to keep the wolf from the door. That house up in the canyon and every apartment buildin' she got. She says she's gonna come live with me down in Santa Monica."

"You like that?"

"She been payin' my bills for a long time, Easy. Don't matter what I like."

It takes a woman to make a man. That's what my cousin Rames used to say. I never knew what he really meant until that moment.

"So what is it you need from me, Jackson?"

"You remember that answerin' machine I hooked up for that numbers thing?"

"You mean when those white gangsters were tryin' to kill you?" I asked. "You mean the reason you livin' in Santa Monica today? So they don't find you and shoot you in the back'a your head?"

"Yeah," he said, giving me the evil eye. "I wanna put that machine on your office phone."

"Why?"

"I gave your number for a reference. I said that your number was for the office of Tyler Office Machines. I said that I fixed your cash registers and time clocks."

And there it was again. Jackson couldn't fly straight down if you threw him off a cliff. He could have gotten a job as a filing clerk or a secretary and worked his way up to the computer room. But that wasn't how he operated. Get in quick, burn down everything, and then run like hell — that was Jackson's way.

"Sure," I said. "I'd be happy to."

I even smiled.

Jackson didn't like it. He was ready to give me some long sob story about how we both owed so much to Jewelle and how he was finally trying to settle down and use his mind. He wasn't used to me saying yes without an argument.

"What's up, Easy?" he asked cautiously.

"Let's wait till after dinner," I said. "Then we can go down and put in your machine and maybe you could do a little something for me."

27

Bonnie and Feather had made short ribs roasted in a spicy Jamaican sauce. They also served rice with some red beans mixed in and collard greens cooked with kale, onions, and salt pork. There were corn muffins to soak up the juices and for dessert we had Feather's favorite: strawberry Jell-O made with a cup of melted ice cream folded in.

Like most naturally thin men Jackson had a good appetite. He took thirds on everything and would have kept on eating if I hadn't pulled him out of his chair.

I kissed my weepy daughter good-bye and asked Bonnie to tell Jesus if he called that I expected to see him by the next day.

"OKAY, EASY, WHAT kinda trouble you in?" Jackson said when we were less than a block from my house.

I could have tortured him but with Harold on the streets I didn't have the leisure to act coy. I told him the whole story starting from the time I helped Musa Tanous prove that he hadn't killed the beautiful teenager Jackie Jay.

"And the cops didn't believe you up until this new woman got killed?" was Jackson's response.

"It's only one cop believe me now," I said. "It's just the three of us if you wanna help."

"Me? What can I do, Easy?"

"Talk to me, Jackson. Talk to me. You one'a the only men I know can talk about the streets with me. I mean Mouse knows the street but he only knows one way."

"That sounds like what you would want with a man like this here Harold," Jackson said. "Mouse would do what's right in a situation like that."

"I got to find the man first."

Jackson nodded and sat back in his seat. Then he scratched his left ear with a baby finger and I knew he was applying his mind to my problem.

I was so upset about Harold and the riots and the sweet sugar talk of Juanda that there wasn't much room in my head for logical thought. I wanted to use Jackson as a kind of a jump start.

We got to my office and installed his answering gizmo. It was a big box that he wired directly to the jack. If the phone rang, it picked up after the third ring and gave out a prerecorded message.

Jackson wrote a little speech for me to give and I did it without any Texas or Louisiana in my voice. After that Jackson put his feet up on the edge of a small trash can and grabbed the back of his neck with both hands.

"What you think about these riots, Easy?" he asked, beating me to the punch.

"I don't know."

"Me neither. Me neither. I just cain't see how people gonna get out in the street and waste that much energy when all you gonna get is some scratched-up shit don't even match the carpet on yo' floors."

"It was more than that, man," I said. "It's hot and they been sittin' on our necks forever."

"I don't see nobody sittin' on our necks, Easy." Jackson looked around, indicating that it was just him and me in the room.

"No? Did they ever send a letter to your mama's farm askin' you to go to college and say that they'd be happy to pay for your courses?"

"'Course not."

"Did your teachers tell you that you were the smartest kid in school and you need to go to college?"

"Are you crazy, Easy?"

"They don't do it out at Sojourner Truth but maybe two times in a year. And you know that's wrong."

"And me throwin' rocks gonna change that?"

"Maybe not for you."

"Definitely not," Jackson said. "Especially if I get arrested or killed."

I could still smell the smoke from the streets in my office.

"I need to find this man Harold," I said. "You got any ideas?"

"I'm not gonna get my hands dirty, Easy. I'ma take this here job as a computer man and I ain't never gonna be in these streets again."

"Okay," I said. "You just point me in the right direction and pull the trigger. That's all you got to do."

I could feel my language turning toward my southern roots. Jackson brought out the country in me.

"There's a flop house over on Manchester near Avalon. You know it?"

"Gray bungalow," I said, "with boarded-up windows."

"That's the place. White guy run it. Man named Bill. I think he was a preacher or a priest or sumpin' but he got the call and put that place in. He wanna help people when they down. You know I been there a few times myself. Before I got it together and started —"

"Livin' off of Jewelle," I said, cutting off whatever story he'd invented to make it seem like he was making it on his own.

"Why you wanna fuck wit' me, Easy? Fuck wit' me and then ask me for my advice."

"Excuse me," I said. "Go on."

"Bill's a good guy. He likes Negroes and he knows about that foot on the neck thing you talkin' 'bout. I mean, he's part of the problem but he mean well."

"What's that supposed to mean —'part of the problem'?"

"It's like when the doctor I used to have would give me a penicillin injection and every two weeks later I'd come down sick again," he said. "Finally after about a year I went to the medical library at UCLA and looked up about those anti-biotics. I realized that he never gave me enough. That way he had me comin' back for more. You know that doctor wasn't no better than a pusher. The only difference with Bill is that he don't have enough medicine to pass around. One bowl of soup and a sandwich and a cot — that's all he can give ya. And you know, Easy, when you only give enough medicine to keep the disease down, it gets stronger down there and come back with a vengeance."

"So you think Father Bill there would know about Harold?" I asked.

"Yes sir. I sure do. Every brother been down on his luck been to Brother Bill's mission at one time or other. Everybody."

"So what should I do?"

Jackson smiled and hunched his shoulders.

"I ain't gonna get my hands dirty, Easy," he said. "But that don't mean you have to come out clean."

ON THE RIDE back to my house we talked about the internally rhyming irony of the phrases "space shots" and "race riots." Using that as his argument Jackson postulated that there was some sort of mathematical and poetic necessity that brings about a balance in scientific, economic, and social extremes.

"You can't have a rich man if you don't have a poor one, Easy," he said. "You can't have a clean floor unless you got somewhere to put the dirt."

"What you gonna do if you get that job, Jackson?"

"Work."

"I mean really."

"I'm a changed man, Easy," the man who most resembled a black coyote said. "No more shit, brother. I'ma make a nest for Jewelle and feather it with hard-earned cash."

I rubbed my bristly chin and wondered. Maybe the world had changed in the fires of the riots. Maybe I had to let go of the order of things that I had always known.

It made me feel unsure and hopeful like a man weak from hunger who stumbles upon an empty store filled with delicacies. How much could I eat before they came to take me away?

28

Jackson left me on the sidewalk in front of my house. He climbed into a yellow pickup truck. I was sure that there was some story around him driving that truck but I didn't ask. It was very late and he wanted to get home and tell Jewelle about his new job.

BONNIE WAS NAKED on top of the covers. She moved her head and gasped when I came into the room but I could tell that she was still asleep.

"Mama?" she cried.

I whispered, "It's okay."

"Papa?"

"Go to sleep."

I sat down on the bed next to her and put my palm against her forehead.

I sat there looking at her body. Bonnie had a curvaceous but lean body with a great mound of pubic hair and powerful thighs that had been made strong by walking thousands of miles through her Guyanese childhood.

"I love them," she said.

"Who?"

"Both of them."

She could have been talking about the children or her parents, who she thought had come into the room. But my suspicious imagination jumped to another conclusion.

"Easy and Joguye?"

"I want to go fishin'," she complained.

"Who?" I asked again.

"We can ride the big fish and go down to the seas and under the coral."

"Who?"

"What?" she asked, still asleep. "What did you say?" she asked, and I knew she was awake.

"I didn't mean to wake you up," I said.

"What did you ask me, Easy?" She sat up without covering herself.

"You were talking in your sleep."

"What did I say?"

"Something about fishing and coral at the bottom of the sea."

Bonnie smiled.

"About my home," she said. "Papa used to take me fishing but he stopped when I started to become a woman."

"Why wouldn't he take you then?"

"Because he didn't want to make me into a boy, that's what he said."

I wanted to ask her if Joguye Cham had taken her fishing when they spent their holiday on Madagascar. But my courage fled when she was awake.

I stood up and took two steps toward the door.

"Are you coming to bed?" she asked.

"Not yet."

"What time is it?"

"Late. You get back to sleep."

I went out into the little living room. A few moments later Bonnie followed wearing her robe. I knew that Jesus must have been home because she only put on that garment to hide from his eager teenage eyes.

"You want some tea?" she asked me.

"Yeah."

WE SAT AT the small table in the living room drinking tea, using the lemons from our own tree for spice.

I told her about Harold and Suggs and the women who were murdered but no one knew that there was a connection between them.

She asked me to come to bed but I told her to go on, that I wasn't tired.

"But you have to sleep," she said.

"All I have to do is die and pay taxes," I replied.

After that we talked about all kinds of things. About how Jesus seemed to be becoming a man without all of the teenage rock and roll nonsense that was going on in every other house on the block. We talked about liquored plantains and fruit-cakes and how she used to swim naked in the ocean.

"I would swim out so far that I could hardly see the shore," she said. "I'd do that in the summer when it was hot and only very far out did the water turn cool."

"Swimmin' instead'a riotin'," I said.

"I suppose we were freer then," she agreed. "I mean inside of us. We were colonized but still our home belonged to us."

"I wish I could have seen you way out there," I said. "I wish I was a fisherman and you got hung up in my net. That's a fish story right there."

Bonnie kissed me and then turned so that she could lean against my chest.

I held her, thinking about the southern oceans surrounding her as I did with my arms.

29

At sunup Bonnie and I went down to a breakfast stand facing the beach in Santa Monica. The sands were empty at six-fifteen. We talked about nothing for a while and then we turned up our cuffs and walked along the shore.

Bonnie was the first woman ever to make me feel guilty about being a man. I felt bad about my heart racing whenever I saw Juanda. Here I had a wonderful woman who knew the world from a whole different perspective. She read Latin and had traveled extensively in Eastern Africa and elsewhere. She was beautiful and trusting and she never questioned my crazy little office or the work I did in the divide between the police and black L.A.

She never demanded that I marry her, even though I knew that was what she wanted.

I decided not to call Juanda when we were walking along the sand.

I dropped Bonnie off at the house at ten-forty-five.

BY ELEVEN Dr. Dommer was telling me that Geneva had fallen into a coma.

"What happened?" I asked.

The weak man's eyebrows twitched like big furry caterpillars being jolted with electricity. He shook his head and frowned.

"I don't know. Maybe there was an underlying condition that was exacerbated by her shock," he said. "We've taken blood and put her on an antibiotic IV. That's all we can do for a while."

He placed a hand on my shoulder for a moment and then walked off.

It came to me that Tina Monroe and I were Miss Landry's closest friends and we didn't really know her. Geneva Landry was just part of different jobs that each of us was doing.

I thought about going down to her room but I realized that there wasn't time for that luxury.

It was my job to find Harold.

BILL'S SHELTER. The words were spray-painted in orange over the door to the gray building.

I was in my work clothes again. I had shoes on my feet that should have been thrown out and no socks at all. My beard hairs were coming in. More of them than I would have liked were showing up white. My eyes were bloodshot and the skin beneath my eyes hung down like budding turkey wattles. Lack of sleep and grooming made me perfect for Jackson Blue's plan.

The door opened into a large room with a high ceiling. There was a table with enough space to seat a double dozen to the left and a desk faced by four couches set out like so many rows on the right.

There was an industrial-size rotating fan on a pole roaring from one corner. But it didn't do much to relieve the heat.

There were chairs everywhere and men too — black men of every hue and age and state of disrepair. A group of four men were playing a very loud game of dominoes to the left of the desk while groups of two and three were talking here and there. One man was having a lively conversation with himself next to a boarded-up window. I counted fifteen in the room including me and the small snaky man sitting behind the walnut desk.

It smelled like fifteen men who were down on their luck. There were body odors of every type and other smells meant to mask or clean up after them.

The room was lit by eight or nine lamps and one set of neon lights hanging by ropes from the ceiling. This was because all of the windows were boarded over. Between the smells and despair, the darkness, and the shouting I felt myself being pressed as if the room were trying to eject me.

I gagged and winced at the melee before me. My disguise was finished by the time I reached the desk.

"Yeah, bub?" the little man sitting behind the desk asked.

"Somebody said I could stay here," I said, not looking him in the eye.

"Who said?"

He was a small man with ocher skin, a Mississippi accent, and mainly Caucasian features — one of the thousands of racial blends brought into existence by the melting pot of the South.

"Man named Blue," I answered.

"Blue what?"

"Jackson Blue."

The man cocked his head way over to the left and squinted.

"Where'd you see him?"

"On Central. I used to know him down in Texas and he was dressed good so I axed 'im to help me out."

"Did he?"

"He 'idn't gimme nuthin' but he told me 'bout here."

"Where's he livin'?" the snaky man asked.

At the same time I became aware of someone standing behind me. I turned around quickly and shouted, "Get on out away from me, muthahfuckah! Step back!"

There were two men who had approached me. One was fat and powerful, while the other was of a normal build. The heavy one wore a trench coat even though it was probably eighty-five degrees in that room. His friend was clad in a white T-shirt and jeans that were two sizes too large. Both men took a big step backward.

All discussion and play in the room stopped. That's just what I wanted. I needed the men in that room to see me and make up their minds that I was just what I looked like: a crazy man down on his luck and ready to protect his boundaries.

"Hey!" the snaky man shouted. "You two know to keep away from the desk when I'm talkin' to a prep."

He was addressing the men I scared away.

"And you," he said to me. "What's your name?"

"Willy," I said. "Willy Mofass."

As I have gotten older I find that I use the names of dead friends to mask my secret passages. I do this partly because it is easy for me to remember their names and partly to keep them alive — at least in my mind.

"Well, Willy," the man said. "You can have soup and bread for dinner and a place to stay for two bits."

"I don't have a nickel much less a quarter," I said. "Blue said that this place was free."

"Ain't nuthin' free, Brother Willy. No sir. You got to pay. But we could let you slide for a day or two. But you got to pay the kitty if you gonna stay here more'n that."

"Where the fuck I'ma get twenty-fi'e cent a day. If I had that right now, I get me a bottle'a wine and climb in a cardboard box down near Metro High."

I knew the layout of Los Angeles. I knew where the hobos went to sleep unmolested.

"Billy will help you get a job," the little man said. "Remember though. No wine on the premises. No drugs or liquor or women neither. This here's a Christian men's shelter. It's clean."

As he said this a light brown roach darted across the desk. That bug was quick but the gatekeeper was quicker. He slammed that roach so hard that the only things left to identify it were two legs and a quivering wing.

30

I camped out at the far end of the sofa furthest away from the desk. The snaky man, Lewis was his name, was a little too interested in the whereabouts of Jackson for me. So I sat there and read the papers.

Gemini 5 was ready to take off. The Russians offered hope for a peace treaty in Vietnam. But mainly the news was about the riots and race relations across the nation.

The news was all the more fuel for Gerald Jordan's fears. A Catholic priest and a seminary student had been gunned down by local lawmen in Hayneville, Alabama. It seems that they had been trying to integrate a country store. Lyndon Baines Johnson declared that the rioters in the streets of L.A. were no better than Klan riders. Two more people died, so the official death toll in the riots had risen to thirty-five. In a statement Martin Luther King made before leaving L.A. he said that he couldn't find the kind of creative and sensitive leadership among our elected officials to solve the problems that caused the riots.

Even Martin Luther King had given up on a nonviolent solution.

"Hey, man," someone said.

I looked up to see a tall young man with bright eyes and a nice smile except for one broken and brown tooth.

"Hey," I replied.

He sat on my couch, about three hand spans distant, looked me up and down and asked, "Where you from?"

"Galveston." It was true pretty much. I had come from a lot of places. Baton Rouge, New Iberia, New Orleans, Houston, Galveston, and many other towns. I had been to Africa, Italy, France, and Germany during the war. And someone had shot at me at least once in every location.

"You know a man name of Tiny?" the young man asked me.

"I know a whole slew'a Tinys: A man, another man, a woman, and one don't know what he is."

The young man smiled again.

"You read?" he asked.

I nodded and folded the newspaper across my lap.

"I wanna read," he said.

"Why?"

"What you mean 'why'? You read, don't you, niggah?" Just that fast the pleasant young man was ready to fight.

"All I did was ask you why, man," I said. "You know, people always got a reason t'do somethin' and I collect reasons."

"Collect 'em?"

"Yeah. Somebody tell me they go to church I ask 'em why. I wanna know if they go there because they love the Lord or because they afraid'a hell. Somebody tell me that they like America I ask 'em why. You know, I once knew a woman loved a man so hard that she'd do anything for him. But he beat her just about every Saturday night. When I asked her why she said, "'Cause he give me flowers every Sunday — just about.'"

By the time I was through with my explanation the young man's anger was gone.

"You crazy, niggah," he said.

"You know a old boy name of Harold?" I asked then. "Short guy, kinda wide. His hands is kinda fat like."

The young man shook his head. "Naw. You got two dollars?"

"I got half a pack of Lucky Strikes. You want one?"

We smoked for a while and two other men came up to us. They looked like brothers with their coal-colored skin and bloodshot eyes. They both had long hair that was matted and infused with dust.

"Mickey," one of the men said to me.

"Terry," the other said.

We shook hands and I supplied them with cigarettes. We all smoked and talked about the streets. I lied. They lied. We all laughed. And slowly I began to get used to the heat and electric light, the smells and despair.

AT ABOUT SIX, three black men — one old, one young, and one in between — all dressed in clean white pants and white T-shirts, came out with bent-up pewter bowls that they placed around the large table. They also put out steel-ware cutlery and blue and green plastic tumblers. The residents had just started to rise and move toward the table when a door behind Lewis's desk opened and a big white man came out.

He was very fat. So much so that his eyes were almost shut from the flesh pressing from all sides. After taking in his girth I realized that the man was also tall. Taller than I am and I'm six one, at least I was when I got drafted. They tell me that you shrink with the years of worry we go through.

That fat man didn't look like he ever worried about anything.

"Hey, Bill!" Lewis shouted.

Ten or twelve of the residents echoed the snake's greeting.

Bill smiled. He wore a green jacket and black trousers. His shoes reminded me of catcher's gloves and he carried a cane whose tip never touched the ground.

His hands were enormous with fingers that might have been babies' limbs. His dense brown hair only covered the sides of his head and his crown rose from the thicket like a battlement or a moon.

I was fascinated by this massive Caucasian the way some white children in Germany were amazed by me and my black skin.

Maybe he felt my gaze. He turned his head toward me and strode toward my couch. I rose to meet him — half out of respect and half from fear.

"Bill," he said introducing himself.

"Willy," I said, but I was so impressed I almost said Easy.

"Short for William?" he asked.

"Yes sir."

"Me too. We have the same name, you and me."

I thought that there wasn't anyone in the world who could do for a name what he could. He could have been Emperor Bill, Conqueror Bill, Bill the Magnificent.

Even though he turned out to be important to my investigation, Bill's effect on me had to do with something else. He had all of the charisma of Mouse in a package that was appropriate for such grandeur. A giant who dominated all that he saw, was aware of everything in his world. I was sure that Lewis's greeting was normal fare in Bill's life. He would command respect without asking for or even desiring it. I had only been in his presence for a minute or two and I'd already forgotten that he was a white man.

"Down on your luck, Willy?" he asked.

"I don't know," I said. "I guess there's a lotta others got it worse. I'd like a place to sleep, though."

"Done," he said. "Come, sit with me."

I followed the big man to a seat at the table and sat on his left side. Lewis took the chair to his right and then the rest of the men took their seats. The men in white brought out a large tureen and went from man to man, ladling out a stew of potatoes with beef, lamb, and chicken. They also put down cheese sandwiches as they went.

The food was good. Very good. I ate heartily, realizing that I hadn't eaten much or slept at all since Detective Suggs had drafted me into service for the LAPD.

"Where you from, Willy?" Bill asked.

"Galveston," I remembered. "From down around the docks."

"Never been there," he said. "What do you think of this place?"

"L.A.?"

"No. The shelter."

"We sure could use it," I said. "You know, it was better bein' poor down south. At least there you could go back to the country and find a barn to sleep in, catch some fish, sumpin'. Here they would just as soon see you starve."

"Amen," Bill said, and it didn't seem forced. "How long have you been in town?"

"I been in and around L.A. for years," I said. "It's just that I can't seem to catch hold of enough money to make a go of it. But I ain't give up yet."

Bill turned his attention to his other guests after that. He talked to everybody, even the man who talked only to himself.

That man was named Roderick, and when Bill asked him how he was, Roderick said, "Somebody wants to know how you doin', Rod." And then he answered, "I'm doin' pretty good, they keep them doctors off and don't let 'em put them needles in my eyes."

That made me think about Geneva and Geneva reminded me of Nola Payne. Before you know it Harold was on my mind.

The dinner went on for about forty-five minutes or so. I didn't want to be too obvious about Harold because someone there might warn him off. So I just ate and marveled at Bill the Shelter King.

31

I was walking through a full meat locker, wearing only a T-shirt and cotton pants. It was freezing in there. The carcasses were black women hanging from hooks. I recognized all of them but couldn't put a name to anyone. Women I had known from Texas to California as lovers and co-workers, neighbors and friends. They were naked and hard, beyond hope for any heaven or afterlife. They were hung in rows that went on forever and it came to me that I might be in hell. There wasn't much light but I could see. And as long as I kept on walking, I thought, I wouldn't freeze.

Then I came across Nola Payne. Her reddish hair was plastered down over her eyes. I stopped even though I knew I ran the risk of freezing. I almost brushed the hair from her face but then I understood that if I touched any one of the dead women He would know I was there.

I turned around and saw Bonnie and Juanda side by side on hooks. They were both cramped and uncomfortable looking as if they had been frozen in quarters too small for them to spread out in. I felt crystalline tears form in my eyes and I reached out . . .

The moment I touched Bonnie a heavy hand fell on my shoulder. It spun me around and there was Bill, King of the Underworld.

"Don't mess with my dinner, Easy," he proclaimed.

I shouted and sprang up out of the cot where I had fallen asleep. My heart felt as if it had grown two sizes too large for my chest. And the despair I felt was beyond anything I had ever imagined except when I was a child and my mother died while I slept.

The room smelled of sixteen men down on their luck. There were snores and farts and sighs and darkness. I knew where I was but for a moment I couldn't remember how I got there.

Slowly it came to me.

After dinner I talked with Lewis for a while. He asked me about Jackson Blue from every angle he could think of. How long had I known him? What kind of gig was he into? Where was he going? And even how was he dressed?

I realized that the men that had been after Jackson must have put out a bounty on the Coal Coyote's hide.

I tried to mask it well enough. I said that I saw him now and again in Compton, that he was involved with a counterfeiter that printed down in L.A. but distributed his product in Frisco and Vegas. But that was all hearsay, I added. I also said that Jackson was wearing the outlandish styles of Carnaby Street, elevator shoes and bell-bottoms, ruffled shirts and a feather in his hat.

After that I retreated to the dormitory cot, where I pretended to sleep for a few minutes.

When I awoke it was very late.

I rose up from my cot and moved through the maze of sleeping men toward a strip of light that betrayed the door.

"Do you see that man, Rod?"

"Uh-huh, yeah I do."

"I wonder where he's goin'?"

"It ain't none'a your business, mister. Keep your eyes to yourself."

I smiled at Roderick's conversation with himself. He wasn't crazy, just obvious and out loud. I would have had the same thoughts if I had seen someone walk by my bunk in that dark and hopeless room.

THE DOOR BEHIND Lewis's desk was unlocked and the light switch was on the left. The filing cabinet stood against yet another boarded-up window. It was locked but that didn't matter. I had lifted a steel spoon from the dinner table and the bolt gave with very little pressure.

I started with the 1964 file of residents' names. There were one hundred eighty-three sign-in sheets, filled in on both sides, one side for each evening. I scanned the far left side for the letter "H." I found quite a few Henrys and fewer entries with the name Hank. Harvey made a better showing than I would have figured. Howard was the most common name and there was one each for Hudie, Hildebrandt, and Hy. There were six Harolds. Brown, Smith, Smith, Lakely, Ostenberg, and Bryant.

I was writing down the last name when I felt the breeze on the back of my neck. Instantly the temperature dropped down to what it was in the freezer of my nightmare. I knew before I spun around that it would be Bill and not Lewis facing me.

He was wearing an impossibly large white terry cloth robe and somehow he seemed to have gotten even taller and broader.

"Hey, Bill," I said with hardly a waver.

"What are you doing there, Willy?"

"Lookin' up names."

"What for?"

"There's a man I need to find and I was hoping that he spent a night or two here with you."

It was the calmness Bill showed that frightened me. It carried all of the certainty of a powerful predator eyeing a snack.

"I don't keep any money in here, Willy," he said.

I handed him the list that I had scrawled. I had only written the last names.

He glanced at the list and said, "You've been lying to me, haven't you, Willy?"

I didn't respond because I didn't know which lie he was referring to.

"This handwriting," he said. "It's not done by some man who can't quite catch hold. I've told Lewis to look at the way the men sign in. He doesn't understand but I bet you do."

"He murdered two women," I said.

"Who did?"

"The man I'm looking for."

"And you think he stayed here?"

"I'm sure of it," I said. "He was just the kind of man who would need a place like this from time to time. If it was raining too hard for too long or maybe if he was too sick to hustle up a meal."

I had a small pistol in my pocket, that and the letter from Gerald Jordan. I didn't want to shoot anybody but if Bill got mad I knew that my only defense would be homicide.

He crushed the list in his hand.

"Get out of here, Willy," he said. "I don't know who you are or what it is you're really after but my guys here have the right to their own private lives. I won't help you."

He was standing in front of the door.

Realizing that I wouldn't move until he did he took a step to the side. I went by him quickly and, just as swiftly, he followed me until I reached the front door of the shelter.

I went through and turned to him.

"I'm sorry, Bill," I said. "I know that you're doing a good thing down here and I didn't mean to cause you trouble."

I think he smiled briefly before closing the door. That made me wonder if he knew that I'd submitted the names on that list to memory, making his gesture more perfunctory than it seemed.

I thought about that all the way through the early-morning streets, so dark and empty. Somewhere out there Harold was hiding. But soon I'd find him. I didn't think that he'd survive our second meeting.

32

Los Angeles is a desert city. Plants don't grow except for the sufferance of irrigation. The soil is hard and yellow and the sun shines more than three hundred days a year. It doesn't rain much and there's no snow at all. People come here to escape the necessity of seasons. They talk about the weather like it was their personal pot of gold.

They come here for the daylight and the warmth of the sun, flocking to the beaches and planning barbecues. Los Angeles is a town of baseball and football, croquet and golf. The city is oriented toward the heat of the sun. And when the night comes, people curl up in their beds and dream about the morning and all the promise of light.

L.A. is not a town for night owls. You come for the acreage and the vistas but in order to pay for that, most people work so hard that night is only a place to rest.

Those people who finally understand that perfect weather only means that you could work even harder often become disillusioned. After that they either move back to where they came from or they drop out and live in the shadows.

Those folks need a nightlife. And where there's a need there's always an offering.

Stud's All Night Holiday was one such offering. It was a bungalow built to be a school. But there was a property dispute and lawsuit and finally the city backed off. I don't know how Ronette Lee got hold of the lease but every night she ran a bar/coffeehouse/restaurant from sundown till sunup out of that would-be school.

It was off the road but the cops knew she was there. They knew but didn't bother her because she filled the needs of all the people who needed respite — and also she was a good tipper.

THE CLASSROOM HAD a dozen round tables and a bar. A door behind the bar led to another classroom, where Ronette's daughter, Maxine, cooked and stewed.

The women didn't get along. That's because Ronette hated men and Maxine couldn't get enough of us. And that was only the beginning of their discord. Maxine didn't like the taste of salt, so Ronette criticized her cooking. Ronette wanted to move back to St. Louis but Maxine hated the cold. I had never heard either one of them say a kind word to the other but I rarely saw them apart.

At four a.m. there were maybe a dozen souls at Stud's. When I entered I waved at Ronette and made the gesture for coffee. For someone else the signal might have meant beer. But Ronette knew I had given up alcohol.

Benita Flag was sitting at a small table alone and miserable. Her shoulders sagged and her hair was a mess. When she looked up I could see that her makeup had been running with her tears.

Sadness is a kind of beacon for me. That's why I frequented the late-night spot.

"Hey, Benny," I said, moving a chair to her table.

"Did you see him?"

"Yeah."

"Is he okay?" she asked. Her voice was rising toward hysteria. I realized that she really was worried about his well-being.

"Oh yeah," I said. "Mouse is fine. You know any kind of social upheaval makes for business opportunities. And Raymond is definitely what you call an opportunist."

I smiled and she at least tried to.

"You know what I'm sayin', don't you?" I asked.

"What?"

"Mouse is like a thundershower at the end of a hot day. If lightning don't strike you the rain will cool you down. It brings you back to life."

Benita smiled and took a very deep breath.

"Yeah," she said. "That's Raymond."

"But a storm like that just passes by, Benny. And when it's gone it's gone. I mean even if it hits you again it won't stay around."

Benita was staring into my face. Her intensity brought back the beauty I knew.

"But I love him, Easy. He come into my life and I never even knew you could feel like that for anybody else. When he walk out to go to the store I ache till he's back again. When he say my name in conversation I feel somethin' so strong I get dizzy."

What could I say to that? She was in love — or something. And whatever that was, it would be wrong to take it away.

"You got any relatives outta town?" I asked.

"A cousin in San Diego."

"Maybe after a while you should go visit her. Maybe the sea will do you some good."

Ronette came up to the table then.

"Easy," she said, setting down my coffee, and to Benny, "Girl, you need to go to the bathroom and fix your face."

Ronette was solidly built and the color of tarnished bronze. She had straightened hair that swirled at the top of her head like a squat tornado that had been turned upside down.

"I'm lookin' for a Harold," I said to Ronette.

"Funny, it look like you lookin' for a Helen."

Benita was touching her face to see if she should follow Ronette's suggestion.

"His last name," I said, ignoring her joke, "could be Lakely or Ostenberg or Bryant." I decided to leave out Brown and Smith. I concentrated on the less common names, hoping my man would be one of them.

"Excuse me," Benita said.

She got up and went toward the bathroom.

"Sounds like white men," Ronette said.

"It ain't a woman and it ain't a white man," I replied. "Have you heard their names?"

"No, Easy. I don't know no Harolds at all. Not no black ones."

"You know we all have white men's names," I said.

"Say what?"

"Our names. None of them come from Africa."

"That's why you always frownin', Easy," she said.

"What's that?"

"Studyin' somethin' till it don't even look like what it is no more. That's what makes you so sad."

I couldn't deny it. She was right.

Ronette saw my silence as a victory. She snorted and smiled and strode off to her bar. I watched her. She had a good figure for a woman in her mid-forties. She liked being watched by men, and women too. She just didn't want their opinions.

When Benita got back to the table she looked like another woman. There was a store-bought sexiness about her, from the false eyelashes to the fire-engine-red nails.

She sat down and started in as if she had never heard of Raymond or had a broken heart. She asked me about my job at Sojourner Truth and my kids. I found out all about her grandfather who was descended from chiefs of the Seminole tribe out of Florida. She talked until the sky began to lighten.

When I said that I had to leave she asked for a ride.

When we got to her door on San Pedro she asked me inside. I could tell that she was fragile and for some reason I felt responsible for Raymond's romantic misdemeanor.

Once inside she made me another coffee. She wanted a kiss for her troubles but I suggested that she might want to bathe first.

I ran the tub for her, making it especially warm.

She came in wearing a pink robe. Before I could leave the bathroom she let the garment drop to the floor. I saw why Mouse once wanted her and then I closed the door.

BENITA HAD A very small place. It was just two rooms and a hot plate. And the rooms were small. The telephone sat on a small triangular table that had three legs. Underneath it sat a phone book.

The Smiths alone took up seven pages. The Browns only had a page and a column.

Lakely and Ostenberg had five listings apiece and Bryant was little more than a third of a column of names.

I studied the book, jotting down numbers until the sun was bright. Then I peeked into the bathroom.

Benita was sound asleep in the tub, snoring and dreaming of real love.

33

I left Benita's before she woke up. That way she could feel kindly toward me without having to face her drunken failure at seducing her lover's best friend.

I needed to talk to Detective Suggs but in the light of morning and with a few hours' sleep from Bill's Shelter, I knew that I shouldn't go waltzing into the Seventy-seventh after the argument of the day before. So I went to a phone booth on Hooper and called like any other ordinary citizen.

"Seventy-seventh Precinct Police Station," the male operator said.

"Detective Suggs."

"Who is this?"

"Ezekiel Rawlins."

"And what is the call pertaining to?"

"He called me," I said to avoid further bad blood with the department. "So I wouldn't know."

The operator hesitated but then he connected the pin in the switchboard.

The phone only rang once.

"Suggs."

"I need to speak with you, Detective."

"You got something?"

"Enough to talk about."

"Bring it in," he said.

"No. Let's meet. At my office. I'll be there by nine." I hung up after that. I couldn't help it. The letter in my pocket gave me true power for the first time ever in my life. I didn't have to answer to Suggs but I wanted even more. I wanted him to answer to me.

I STOPPED BY Steinman's Shoe Repair before going up to my office. The doorway was boarded over and a sign that read CLOSED DUE TO DAMAGES had been nailed from the center plank. I made up my mind to call Theodore soon, to find out what he needed. It came to me then that my side job of trading favors had become more geographic than it was racial. I felt responsible for Theodore because he lived in my adopted neighborhood, not because of the color of his skin.

My office was a comfort to see. The plain table desk and bookshelves were filled with hardbacks I'd purchased from Paris Minton's Florence Avenue Bookshop. He'd introduced me to the depth as well as the breadth of American Negro literature. I had always known that we had a literature but Paris showed me dozens of novels and nonfiction books that I had never known existed.

I started reading a copy of *Banjo* by Claude McKay that I'd bought from Paris a few weeks before. It was a beautiful edition, orange with black silhouettes of jazz musicians and women and swimmers on the wharf in Marseilles. It was a rare find at that time: a book about people of many colors getting together on foreign shores. The dialect McKay wrote in was a little too country for my sensibilities but I recognized the words and their inflections. On the title page, just below the title, there was a little phrase, *A Story Without a Plot*. I think that's what I liked best about the book. After all, isn't that the way most of the people I knew lived? We went from day to day with no real direction or endpoint. We just lived through the day, praying for another. Even in the best of times that was the best you could hope for.

The knock on the door was soft, almost feminine, but I knew it was Suggs.

"Come on in."

He wore a black suit. You know it has to be bad when you can see the wrinkles in black cloth. His white shirt seemed askew even with the red tie, and today he wore a hat. A green one with a yellow feather in the band.

"You didn't have to get dressed up for me," I said.

He was carrying a white paper bag in one hand and a brief-case in the other. He walked up to my visitor's chair and sat down heavily. I could see in his exhausted posture that he had missed as much sleep as I had.

"Coffee and some doughnuts," he said, placing the bag on the desk.

Another seminal moment in my life that I associated with

the riots: a cop, a city official, bringing me coffee and cake. If I had gone down to the neighborhood barbershop and told the men there that tale, they would have laughed me into the street.

I took the coffee and a cherry-filled doughnut. And then I rolled out an edited version of my visit to Bill's Shelter.

"How can you be sure that our Harold was one of the ones who stayed at this joint?" the cop asked.

"I can't be," I said. "But it's someplace to start. Bill's is the kinda place let a man like Harold be crazy but not have to answer for it. They don't try and sell you anything or change you. It's just a bed and a meal — a perfect place for our man. I figured that you could put some muscle into the Smiths and Joneses and I'll concentrate on the others."

Suggs stared at me with those watercolor eyes of his. He had mastered the textbook cop expression — the look that didn't give away a thing.

"There could be as many as twenty-one," he said at last.

"Twenty-one what?"

"Women."

I was back in the frozen slaughterhouse, surrounded by dead women cut down in the prime of their lives; black women who shared their love with a white man and then paid the ultimate price for betraying Harold's stiff sense of morality.

I clenched my jaw hard enough to crack a tooth.

Suggs opened his briefcase and handed me a sheaf of single-page reports.

Each page contained two photographs of a young black woman — one in life and the other in death.

"The bodies were almost all left on their backs," Suggs was

saying. "A couple weren't quite dead when he left them. That accounts for the few odd positions."

"You think it was all him?" I asked.

"Maybe not every one," Suggs said. "But there are also probably some that I missed. It's a shame. The homicide detectives should have picked it up. I'm really very sorry about this, Mr. Rawlins."

An apology. A week before, it would have meant something to me. But right then I couldn't even meet his eye. I was afraid that if I saw his sorrow, it might dredge up the rage and impotence I felt. So instead, I kept my eyes down and my mouth shut.

After a few minutes I heard the chair scrape the floor and his footsteps trailed away. Finally my door closed and I was alone with the dead women.

Suggs had done a good job. He'd read the files and typed up an abbreviated report, which he stapled to the back of each one.

Phyllis Hart was thirty-three when she died, choked to death in her auntie's backyard on the fourteenth of July.

Many of them had known white men. Maybe all of them had. Suggs had called family members to get some of the details. He even asked about a man living in the street named Harold. There were three people who had seen a hobo hanging around.

Solvé Jackson was killed in her own bed. Her boyfriend, Terry McGee, was arrested for the crime. He had an alibi and witnesses to his whereabouts but still the jury found him guilty.

I sat there reading about dead women until I knew everything Sugg's report had to say.

After a while I noticed that the tape on Jackson's recording device had moved. I flipped the switch to "rewind" and then to "play."

"Hello," a man's voice said. "This is Conrad Hale of the Cross County Fidelity Bank. Your company's name was given as a reference for a Mr. Jackson Blue. Could you please return this call as soon as possible? We are considering hiring Mr. Blue in a responsible position and were wondering about his work history with your firm. I'm calling on Saturday, so you may not get this until Monday morning. But if you get this message earlier I'll give you my home phone too. We are anxious to get going with Mr. Blue. We'd like to put him to work as soon as possible."

There was a similar call from Leighton Car Insurance but they didn't leave a home phone.

I realized that I had been of two minds about giving Blue a fake recommendation. It hadn't felt right. I needed his help, so I said I would do it, but I still didn't like it. With that stack of dead black women on my desk now, I felt differently. Nobody cared about them. I had told the police about what I suspected about Jackie Jay's death. I'm sure there had been other complaints with so many women dead. But the denizens of Watts were under the law with no say. We were no different than pieces on a game board.

I dialed the banker's number. He answered on the first ring.

"Conrad Hale."

"Mr. Hale," I said, "this is Eugene Nelson, manager of Tyler Office Machines. I hope it isn't a problem calling you on a Sunday."

"Not at all, Mr. Nelson. I have to hire ten men in the assembler lab here at the bank and your Mr. Blue is only the third person we've interviewed who passed the IBM exam."

My voice was devoid of any accent. My words were a plain wrapper over a five-pound lie. Jackson was a mechanical whiz kid, I told Hale. He understood any machine and its inner workings. He worked overtime. He handled sensitive information. He was the most trustworthy employee I'd ever had.

On Monday, if necessary, I would extend my lies to Leighton Car Insurance.

I was happy to have Jackson on the inside of the world that ignored the women on my desk. I would have put Mouse in the White House if I could have.

34

There came another knock on the door.

I wondered if Suggs had found another twenty-one dead women. Maybe there were children too and old people and ministers. Maybe there was a whole factory of death working twenty-four hours a day under the city. Black people being thrown down onto rolling spikes that chopped them into pieces and then dropped the pieces into vats of acid. Maybe they were selling our blood and using our teeth and bones for ivory.

"Mr. Rawlins," Juanda said, peeking into the office from the half-open door. "Can I come in?"

I stood up as she entered, closing the door behind her.

She was wearing a pink dress that only came down to the middle of her thigh.

I walked toward her and she to me. I put my arms around her and held her as tight as I did my mother when I was six and she was still alive. We may have kissed — I really don't remember.

"You're crying," she said.

I didn't even know that.

Somehow I was sitting on my desk. Juanda was standing next to me, holding me like the young mother she dreamt of becoming. My tears stopped. But the rage was still singing inside me.

"How did you know where I was?" I asked her.

"Phone book," she said simply. "I needed to see you."

"Somebody after you?"

"Naw," she said. "I'm after you."

I took a deep breath. My heart was pounding and I had an erection that I was sure she could see through my pants. My mind was tuning in and out like a radio receiver ranging over all of the things I was feeling and the things I had to do.

I wanted sex with that gorgeous young woman. Right there on the table with no foreplay or pretense. I wanted to be as blunt as she was, grunting out the anger in my body.

But that brought my fine tuner back to Harold. That was Harold running my mind, making me just like him.

"I love my girlfriend, Juanda," I said.

"That's okay. I don't mind."

I pulled her arms from around my neck, standing up as I did so. I ran my hands down to her elbows and walked her toward the chair where Detective Suggs last sat.

"I'm just not that young anymore, baby," I said. "If I was in the bed with you, then I'd have to give up something."

"I ain't askin' for that."

"But I would," I said. "You know I would. That's why you're here. You can read me like a first-grade primer."

She cracked a grin and pushed her shoulder in my direction.

"That's why I like you," she said. "'Cause you so smart. I bet you read all those books on that shelf over there."

"Yeah," I said. "Just about."

I moved back to my chair. She crossed her legs and my heart thrummed. I needed a woman so much right then that I would have probably gotten excited over her picking her nose.

"You know a guy used to live in a cardboard shelter in a vacant lot over there on Grape?" I asked her.

"Oh yeah," she said. "Harold."

"He killed Nola Payne and a whole lotta other women."

"What?"

"Killed her. Dead. He's been killin' black women for years. Any time one of them gets in with a man looks white to Harold, he kills 'em."

"No."

"Yes."

Juanda had learned from a long line of tough black women to show a hard face even when she was laughing. But the crime I suggested wiped all that away. She uncrossed her legs and sat forward.

"For real?"

"Can you tell me anything about him?" I replied.

"No. Not me. All he ever said was good mornin' to me. He really killed Nola?"

"Yeah."

"How do you know? Nobody done said she dead."

"Listen, Juanda. This is a serious thing here. Harold is a dangerous man. I don't want you talkin' about it because if he knows you and if he thinks you know about him he will kill you without thinking twice. You hear me?"

"Uh-huh. Yeah."

"He's a killer and I'm gonna take him down."

"Nola's dead?"

"Yeah. Her aunt Geneva found her and called the cops. They thought that it was a white guy did it, so they brought me in to help because they couldn't work too well so soon after the riots. But it wasn't that white man. It was Harold. He's been killin' black women around here for years."

"He has? Why didn't somebody stop him?"

"Because nobody cares about black women bein' killed," I said harshly. "Nobody cares about you, girl. A man could cut your throat and throw you in the river and if a cop see you floatin' by he wouldn't even drag you in because he might get his shoes wet."

I experienced a vicious satisfaction hurting Juanda like that. It was wrong but I was angry.

"Can you drive me home, Mr. Rawlins?"

"Sure I can," I said. "I'm going to give you my number here too. If you get scared or find out something you call me. I got an answering machine now and I'll be sure to get the message."

I walked her down to my car and then drove her home.

On the way she didn't chatter about her relatives and the events of her life. She pulled close to me and put her head on my shoulder.

I don't think I ever wanted to be with a woman more in all my life. I wanted to lick the tears from her face.

35

I came back to my office after dropping Juanda off at her auntie's house. We were halfway to Grape Street when she decided that she didn't want to be around where Harold had just been living. We kissed when she got out but that was just reassurance. She was scared.

I knew that by warning Juanda I ran the risk of people starting to talk about Harold and running him into hiding but I had no other choice. Juanda was a woman and there was a woman killer in her neighborhood. No secret was worth her life.

TANYA BRYANT, Bill Bryant, Joseph, Martin, JaneAnne, Penelope, and Felicia all lived in colored neighborhoods. I called their numbers asking for Harold. Not one of them knew a Harold with their last name. At least none of them admitted to it. There were two H. Bryant listings. Harvey and Helena.

Only Tom Lakely of the phone book Lakelys lived in a Negro community. But he didn't answer his phone.

There were no Ostenbergs anywhere near SouthCentral L.A.

I knew that Harold didn't have a phone, but he did have a relative. I tried to think about Harold. We only spoke for a few minutes the day I was snooping around Jackie Jay's neighborhood. He talked about having the flu, about the police arresting him. About Jackie. He said that he didn't know her at first but then he said . . . he said that his mother's name started with a "J." What was her name?

I was forty-five that year and my memory, though still pretty strong, had begun to drop certain details. Names of relatives and friends from long ago slowly floated away. Numbers and sequences blended together. I remembered the smelly Harold telling me that Jackie's name started with a "J" just like his mother's. But the name was . . . the name was . . .

I finally decided that it didn't matter. I had the first letter. That would have to be enough.

I pulled out my phone book, and starting with the Brown listings, I called every "J" in our neighborhood. Janes and Joes answered most often. There was a Jeanette, a Julia, a Jules, and a Jay. One woman answered and I asked her if she had a son named Harold.

"No, mister," she said. "Are you sure he said Jocelyn Brown was his mama?"

Jocelyn!

"Yes ma'am," I said. "Thank you, ma'am."

I spent the rest of the afternoon going through the Smiths. I called until the tip of my pointer finger was sore from dialing.

I made a few notes about people who sounded cagey, but no one seemed to be a good prospect.

Once when I hung up, the phone rang.

"Hello?"

"Hi, baby," Bonnie said. "Are you still looking for that man?"

"Uh-huh."

"I've been trying to call you for hours but the phone line was always busy."

"I think I might know the killer's last name," I said. "I've been calling all day trying to get a line on my guy Harold."

"Do you need some help?"

I was born as poor as it gets in America. No running water, no heat, and only internal organ meat to eat once or twice a week if we were lucky. I never owned a new article of clothing until I was sixteen and already on my own for seven years. In my mind I still had that home to return to but I was no longer poor. Bonnie's offer and Juanda's embrace were gifts many a rich man could never claim. I was saved by the love of black women. Harold wouldn't live to see 1966.

"Well," I said, "I've only been calling in the Negro neighborhoods. I figure that his mother would be around here. But maybe they're in the valley or down around Santa Monica. Maybe you could call those numbers."

"Sure," she said happily.

"You can't give your name or anything else," I said. "You can't sound like there's any problem at all."

"Okay."

I gave her the last names and Jocelyn. She took a deep breath and told me that she loved me.

I hung up the phone, wondering how long my perfect life could last.

The phone rang again.

"They call, Easy?" he asked even before I could say hello.

"Yeah, Jackson, they sure did. And I hope you plan to do right by these people and Jewelle."

"What they say, man?"

"I only talked to the banker," I said. "He gave me his home number. He said that they wanted to hire you for a responsible position. I told him that you were trustworthy and good. I hope you don't make me a liar."

"Easy, he don't even know who you is, brother. It's not like you put your name on the line."

"It's just like that, man. It's just like that."

"Well, don't you worry, brother. I know them machines better'n the men who made 'em and I haven't even seen one yet."

Of all his failings, one thing Jackson didn't suffer from was false pride. If he said that he was good at something, he was most probably the best. And if he said he was the best, then all the masters had better run and hide.

"I got somethin' for ya, Ease," he said.

"What's that?"

"Boy name'a Harold. He cranky and mean and been livin' in the street since he lost his job in nineteen fifty-six."

"Where?"

"He been stayin' at a mission over on Imperial Highway. They serve two meals a day there and let people stay as long as they don't cause no trouble."

"Did you get Harold's last name?"

"Brown," Jackson said. "Harold Brown."

I held my breath. My luck was incredible. All I had to do was sit at my desk and whatever I wanted — sex or love or information — just poured in over my phone and through the door.

"I don't get it, Jackson. Where'd you find all'a this?"

"Axed around, man. Axed around. You know, Easy, you takin' care'a me. I sure in hell better make sure that you doin' fine."

"Who did you ask?"

"I got to keep my secrets now, Ease."

"This is no time to play with me, Jackson."

"There's a sister work for the Congress of Negro Baptist Churches used to like me some," he said. "I called and asked her if she knew how I could get a line on a man that's homeless. I told her that his son just died. You know when you tell a woman about the death of a man's son she's all upset. Anyway, she give me a list of missions and I just called until I found the man meet your needs."

"They just told you who he was?"

"I reeled out a story, Easy. You not the only one can do that. I told 'em that a man from their place, a big boy named Harold, had found my wallet and give it back to me wit' all the money in it. I said that I wanted to reward him. You know wit' a success story like that they was ready to let me spend a night with one'a their sisters."

I could almost hear his grin.

"You a good man, Jackson," I said. "You're a dog but you're a good man."

36

If the Watts Community Men's Shelter was on public school grounds it would have been called a gymnasium. It was a large empty space like an airplane hangar with pitted pine floors. The walls were thirty feet high and the only windows lined the ceiling. On one side there were rows of canvas cots and on the other, rows of tables with benches along them. There must have been five dozen men in the room. The smell of mayonnaise and body odor was overwhelming.

"Can I help you?" a young man asked.

He was black but his hair was straight, not straightened. His words were clear and well articulated but there was a whisper of Spanish somewhere.

"I'm lookin' for Harold Brown," I said.

The young man, who was slender and well groomed, hesitated. I knew then that I was going to have trouble finding my quarry.

"This isn't a hotel, sir," he said. "People come here for food and shelter. There's no entertaining here."

"It's very important that I see Harold Brown," I said. "Extremely important."

"A lacerated foot or a chest infection," he said. "Those are the things important around here. A good night's sleep is what we strive for."

I looked out over the crowd of brown and black men. Some of them were probably made homeless by the riots but the majority were permanent inhabitants of the streets of L.A., San Diego, San Francisco, and every other stop along the rails. Their clothes, no matter the original color, mostly tended toward gray and their shoulders stooped under the almost metaphorical weight of poverty.

"So you not gonna help me?" I asked the prissy gatekeeper.

"If you needed a place to stay I would," he said.

But it was too late for that.

I took two steps past his desk.

"Sir," he said, rising to his feet.

I ignored him, walking further toward the gang of lost souls.

"Bernard, Teddy," the young man said.

To my left I saw two brawny black men straighten up. They wore makeshift uniforms of yellow T-shirts and black slacks.

They were large and young but still I contemplated going up against them. Maybe if they were closer I would have thrown myself into it. But they were ten paces away. By the time they'd taken six steps my common sense kicked in.

"All right," I said to one. "I'm goin'."

I walked out of the front door onto Imperial Highway. I was mad at myself. If somebody told Harold I was looking for him he'd run and I might never find him again.

There was a phone booth across the street. I decided to call Suggs and wait at the entrance hoping that there wasn't a back exit that Harold would decide to use. For a moment I thought about calling Raymond, to get him to guard the back door. But I knew better than to get the cops and Mouse working on the same job. If he decided to kill Harold he might take a few policemen along with him.

"Hey, mister," someone said. "Mister."

He was a small man. Smaller than Jackson Blue and lighter skinned than Mouse. He was young and hunched over. He wore stained blue coveralls and yellow rubber flip-flops on bare feet that a man of sixty could have called his own.

"What?"

"You lookin' for Harold Brown?"

"Uh-huh. You know him?"

"Yes sir. I sure do."

"I need to talk to Harold. Could you get me to him?" I asked. I wanted Harold on my own. I wanted to mess him up before giving him to the cops. I wanted to kick him when he was down.

"I could tell him that I had some wine and that he should meet me in the alley over on that side of the mission," the little man suggested.

He pointed and I took out a five-dollar bill. I folded the note and then tore it in half along the crease.

"Here's half'a what it's worth to me," I said. "Bring Harold over there and I'll give you the rest."

The creepy little man took the scrap of money and scuttled away, his heels slapping against yellow rubber. As he slipped into the front door of the mission I moved toward the entrance of the alley on the left side of the building.

I lit up a cigarette and stared at the city from that particular point of view.

Los Angeles ghettos were different from any other poor black neighborhood I had ever seen. The avenues and boulevards were wide and well paved. Even the poorest streets had houses with lawns and running water to keep the grass green. There were palm trees on almost every block and the residential sidewalks were lined with private cars. Every house had electricity to see by and natural gas to cook with. There were televisions, radios, washing machines, and dryers in houses up and down the street.

Poverty took on a new class in L.A. Anyone looking in from the outside might think that this was a vibrant economic community. But the people there were still penned in, excluded, underrepresented in everything from Congress to the movie screens, from country clubs to colleges.

But there was something else different. The riots were beginning to wear off. Life was becoming what was to become normal after all of the stores had been burned down. People were going to work. The police and National Guard were less present.

The black revolutionary scattershot aimed at overthrowing the oppression of white America was over, or at least it seemed to be. People were talking and laughing on street corners. White businessmen, at least a few, were returning to their stores.

"Hey you!" someone called.

I turned and saw the scrawny man who had promised to bring Harold. He was far down in the alley next to a big green Dumpster.

I walked toward him, unafraid. I was sure that he'd have cooked up some lie about how he tried to find Harold but could not. He knew that the good Mr. Brown would be back later, though, and if I'd just give him the other half of that five-spot he'd be happy to arrange a meeting.

I had been in the street longer than I'd lived in any house. I knew how it worked. There was a natural order to the way things happened. I didn't mind playing along.

But as I approached my informant he was casting glances to his left into a recess between buildings. My pace slowed slightly. The crafty little man might have seen me as a mark, someone who could be mugged. The smart thing to do would have been to turn around. But I was too angry for that. Bums didn't roll citizens, I told myself. They begged maybe or cajoled but they didn't mug everyday people.

When I was three steps from the little man someone walked out from the crevice. It was a big man. Not as big as Bill but large enough to put me into a lighter-weight class.

"You lookin' for me, mothahfuckah?" the big black man asked.

What could I say?

He stepped forward reaching for me.

I stepped backward. Not quite fast enough.

His fingertips felt like steel rods scraping against my chest. I gave up running and leaned forward putting all of my weight into a blow to his jaw.

I'm a big man and strong too. The man I hit felt it. He even backed up half a step. He shook his head. I was hoping that was the beginning of a downward slump but then he grabbed me again. I went aloft, something I hadn't experienced in many a year. The next thing I knew I was flying back down into the crevice that the angry man had come from. I might have flown all the way to the foothills if it weren't for the brick wall in my path.

Most of the pain was in my lungs but there was plenty left over for my neck, head, and spine. I hit the ground and slumped to the side, which was a good thing because it caused the big man's foot to miss my head by at least an inch.

I got to my feet. How I did it I will never know. I stood up straight just in time to get a backhand that lifted me higher still. I hit the wall again and instinctively ducked. The instinct was right. He missed my head but got in a body blow. I fell to my knees and put my hands out in front of me. When he tried to kick me, like I knew he would, I grabbed his ankle and stood straight up, pressing my hands high and pushing out so that King Kong would take a spill.

The little man who had brought me there was jumping up and down, yapping about something. I couldn't make out what he was saying. The pain was so strong in my body that no other sensation could get a toehold.

The big man was on his back, then risen up on one elbow, then staggering to his feet. All this time I was panting in short hacking breaths against the wall, wanting to run but unable to call forth the strength.

"Kill him, Harold," the little man shouted.

I was happy that I could make out his words. But that wasn't my Harold. It was just a big ugly Harold who was made out of pig iron and cast in a bathtub.

Harold swung his fist and hit me in the shoulder. I sprang forth as if leaping from a diving board. My hands were at my sides and the top of my head aimed for the big man's nose.

I felt the collision in my sinuses, fell to the side, and hit the ground. When I looked up I saw Harold looming above me. There was blood gushing from his nose and a mean look on his face. I scrambled to my knees and crawled. I knew I couldn't escape him but I had to try. I had to find the right Harold and do to him what this Harold had done to me.

I made it about five feet and then turned to see the progress he'd made.

The big man looked at me and wavered. Finally he fell flat on his back, knocking up a plume of dust. The little man was still shouting. I couldn't understand him again.

I got to my feet and staggered away. I made it to my car and slumped down on the hood. The metal was hot from the unrelenting sunlight. No one came to save me from frying out there. After a while I began to sweat profusely. Somehow that gave me the strength to get to my feet, unlock the door, and turn over the engine.

I drove away from there wondering if I was driving on the right side of the road and if the wrong Harold had done enough damage to take my life.

37

I don't know how my driving was doing but there were a few blaring horns along the way. I had probably gone a mile or so when I realized I had no idea where I was headed. The wrong Harold had put the hurt to me, as the young people used to say around that time. I was reeling in my seat, driving my car like it was a boat.

I had to laugh, even through all that pain. So many young men go out on the street looking to get into a fight. They talk about how they beat some fool who cursed or insulted them. But all they needed was one fight with a man like the wrong Harold and all of their heroic notions of street fighting would go out the window. I didn't beat that big ugly man. All I did was keep him from stomping me to death. I saved my life but I'd have pains and bruises to remind me of my folly for more than a month. No. There was nothing glorious about getting tossed around like a rag doll and hit so hard that you could taste it.

I didn't know what to do. I couldn't use a phone or go ask questions. There was a big knot over my right eye, and my lower lip was swollen too. I drove to Compton, to Tucker Street. That was a dead end with a stand of avocado trees where the road should have continued. I pulled off the road and parked between two dark-leaf trees. I opened the door and she was standing there. Tall and black-skinned, handsome with glints of beauty left over from a glorious youth, Mama Jo was like an African myth come to life in the New World, where no one could believe in her unless they felt her magic.

"I wondered when you was gonna get here," she said in a deep voice that was not wholly masculine or feminine.

"It's a wonder I made it at all," I said.

I opened the door and reached out to her. She pulled me by the arms until I was standing. Then she supported me, helping me to navigate through the trees until we got to her cabin.

Mama Jo always lived in hidden places. She raised armadillos and ate delicacies like alligator and shark meat. She made medicines and potions for poor superstitious black people and if you wanted she would read your fortune.

I never wanted her to tell me my future but she said she wouldn't even if I asked her.

"You not the kind'a man should know what lies ahead," she'd tell me. "It won't make a difference and you got too much to do to be slowed up thinkin' about it."

She half carried me into her one-room home and laid me out on a mattress on the floor. By that time Jo was over sixty. But she still had the spark that made me make love to her when

I wasn't yet out of my teens. Sometimes I still wonder about what might have been if I had stayed out there with her as she asked me to do.

I watched her sitting at her long oak table mixing powders in a wooden bowl.

"Jo," I said.

"Rest, baby," she said, shushing me.

It was a hot day but Jo's place was cool, covered as it was by the shade of a dozen trees. And it was also partially submerged in the soil. The floor was at least six feet below ground level.

It was dark in there too. Candles and lanterns lit the cavern-like space. A shelf over her table contained various animal skulls. One of these was a human, her first lover and the father of her son, both named Domaque.

Jo was a woman of great power and knowledge: a witch by anyone's definition at any time in the history of mankind.

She took a dirty green bottle and poured a greenish liquid from it into the wooden bowl. She lifted my head for me to drink and I did. Whatever it was she was giving me I knew that it would be good. I knew it because she had saved my life once and on another occasion she literally brought Mouse back from the dead.

Things got a little hazy after I drank the brew, which managed to be both slimy and chalky. I remember her putting poultices on my head and mouth. I thought I saw a great black feathered bird spreading his wings on a branch behind her.

"Easy Rawlins!" I heard her deformed son announce as was his wont whenever he saw me.

I was looking at the roof and slowly it disappeared. Above me were ten thousand stars on a backdrop of black. The air in my nostrils was crisp and cold and I was the only person in the wide world, safe at last from the pain of hatred and the pain of love.

The events of the past two weeks — the riots, the death of Nola Payne, the pursuit of Harold the woman killer, and the memories that Juanda kindled in me all came together and spun me out like a bird clipped by a stone. I was spinning through the sky, seeing pieces of everything — out of control.

Then I crashed. For a moment the aching from my fight was excruciating, then I felt nothing, and then I knew nothing.

"YOU CAN GET up now, baby," Jo said.

"Hi, Easy," her hunchbacked son cried.

"Hey, Dom. How you doin'?"

"Hey, Ease," Mouse said. I couldn't see him from where I lay but it was him.

A large black bird cried and flared its wings.

"You got a crow as a pet?" I asked Jo as I sat up on the floor mat.

"Raven," she said. "This here's a raven. Talks an' everything. He keeps me company."

"Who did this to you, Easy?" Mouse asked.

He was standing to the side. Just looking at him made me smile.

Mouse was wearing a greenish gray two-piece suit with a black shirt and a tie made up of every shade of yellow that you could imagine. His shoes were fashioned from alligator skin.

"Poor Howard make you those shoes?"

"Oh yeah. You know Howard got his cousins bringin' up gator hide from bayou country. He sellin' 'em for four hunnert dollars a pair."

Howard was a dark-skinned Cajun acquaintance of ours from Louisiana. He lived in the wilds around L.A. because he was a fugitive from Louisiana justice. He had killed a white man, so running was the only choice he had.

"You gonna answer my question?" Mouse asked.

"It was just a misunderstandin', Ray. Nuthin' to get upset about."

"How you feelin', darlin'?" Jo asked me.

She'd always had a soft spot for me. I could still hear it in her tone.

"Good," I said. "Great. I don't hardly hurt at all." I was a country boy again, even in the way I spoke.

She handed me a mirror and I saw that all of the swelling on my face had gone. Her teas and poultices rivaled the medicines most doctors prescribed.

"You got to take it easy, baby," she said. "You know a man's body don't bounce back too fast after he pass forty."

"You wanna go fishin', Easy?" Domaque shouted.

I turned to Jo's powerful and lopsided son. He was big and mis-shapen in almost every part of his body. Something was wrong with his nasal passages, so his mouth hung open showing crooked teeth and red gums. His arms and legs were all different lengths and his mind, though extremely intelligent, held on to all of the innocence of childhood. The first time you saw Dom he'd scare you silly but if you knew him you would feel that you'd met one of the finest human beings on this earth.

"No, Dom. I got to do some huntin' first. But you know, my boy Jesus has built him a sailboat."

"Really?"

"Oh yeah. It floats and goes where he tells it to. I bet he'd take us out for some fishin'."

The glee on that child-man's face gave me one of my first feelings of true happiness since the riots began.

"I got to go," I said.

I rose to my feet. I was fully dressed except that Jo had taken off my socks and shoes.

While I tied my laces she said, "Here, drink this, Easy." She proffered a cloudy quartz bottle.

"What is it?"

"It's what you need, baby. You gonna take that body back into the street, you better have a little get-up-n-go."

I drank the liquid down in one swallow. There wasn't any alcohol in it but it certainly had a kick.

"After six hours get yourself into bed, honey," she said.

"Don't forget about Jesus," Dom said.

"I'll ride with ya, Easy," Mouse informed me. "When Jo called about you, LaMarque drove me over. He needed the car to impress some girl."

As we walked out from between Jo's trees her elixir hit me. I felt like I could go out and run a ten-mile race.

38

You talked to Benita?" Raymond asked me after I'd driven
about six blocks.

I don't know what it was that Jo had given me but I could
feel the blood pumping in my veins. I was wide awake and ready
for anything — even the implied threat in Raymond's tone.

"Yeah," I said confidently. "Yes I did."

"What for?"

"I was just goin' around lookin' for my boy — Harold. I run
into her at Stud's."

"What she say?"

"That she loves you, that she misses you, that you broke her
heart."

"Then what?"

I pulled the car to the curb, came to a halt, and yanked on
the parking brake.

"I took her home," I said. "Then I read the phone book while she fell asleep in the bathtub. After that I left. You wanna make somethin' outta that?"

Ray's gray eyes seemed to flash as he looked at me.

He was a small man. That's where most men who went up against him made their biggest mistake. They thought that a small man had to cave in to a bigger one. They didn't know that Mouse was strong as a man twice his size. But that's not what made him dangerous. Mouse was fast and he was a killer. He killed without a second thought or a moment's remorse. He was a soldier who had been at war his entire life.

"What's wrong with you, Easy? You crazy or sumpin'?"

"You wouldn't understand, Ray. What's been goin' on the last few days don't mean nuthin' but business to you. But this shit has fucked me up. I'm lookin' for this killer and the streets I'm walkin' down today ain't what they were last week. I'm your friend, Ray. But you know that girl has let herself go all the way down to the ground over you. She could die."

"Die? What she gonna die from, man? It's not poison."

I was breathing hard. I knew that my friend could see it. I hoped he knew that I wasn't a threat to him.

"Black women, Ray. You know how they are. Tough as you ever wanna be. Go up against a whole gang to protect her man. Ready to walk away if you do her wrong the next day. But you know about her heart. You know when you talk that sweet shit, she gonna believe every word even if she knows it ain't true. And when you leave her alone it eats at her like acid.

"I went home with her because she needed someone to look after her. I ain't interested in your girl. I just don't want her to feel like she's all alone."

While I spoke Ray didn't say a word. He just stared with those killer eyes. For all I knew he was waiting for me to finish so he could say I had my last words.

But instead of killing me he scratched his nose.

"You know they's hardly anybody talk to me like that, Ease. I once killed a man fightin' over a woman and you know that woman was his wife. But you right. Just 'cause I tell 'er about Etta don't mean I don't snake up in there an' confuse her mind. Yeah."

He turned around and faced forward. We sat there for a while and then I turned over the engine.

I let Raymond off at his house. He got out of the car and walked away without another word.

I drove off thinking that I would never take another one of Mama Jo's potions without asking her how it was going to affect me.

IT WAS NIGHTTIME and I hadn't spoken to Bonnie in quite a while. I was running low on gas too. So I pulled into an A-Plus gas station on Normandie and waited for the attendant. It was a white guy in a tan jumpsuit with "A+" printed over his breast pocket. He was back on the job and the end of the riots wasn't three days old.

"What can I get you, mister?" he said.

"Two dollars," I said.

"Right away."

He attached the nozzle to my car and the pump started ringing. I got out and stretched my legs. I took a deep breath that went all the way to my toes. There was a phone booth at the corner of the lot. I took a few steps toward it, when three squad cars ran up on the curb and surrounded me.

Those three cars contained a dozen policemen.

One of them yelled, "Put your hands where I can see them!" He had a shotgun pointed at me.

All the cops had guns out. Six of them took positions around the perimeter of the station and the rest pounced on me.

In a normal state of mind I would have held out my hands in surrender. But with Mama Jo's drug in me my whole body, from my fingers to my anklebones, went rigid. It took all of those young white men to subdue me. I didn't say a word and I didn't fight. I just stood there thinking that those men were no more than rodents trying to intimidate me with their squeals.

Once they got me down they had a problem because there wasn't any room in their cars for a prisoner. None of them wanted to be on foot and in uniform in the black neighborhood after nightfall. They had learned to respect the anger that glared at them from the darkness.

It was the station attendant who suggested they use my car.

It took three of them, one driving and the other two holding me in the backseat, to drive me to city hall.

And when we got there it took five men to heft my dead weight into a large, well-appointed room.

They dropped me on the floor but I didn't feel it. I had become the soul of resistance. I could stay like that for years, I believed. No one would ever defeat me again. They'd have to kill me.

"Get up, Mr. Rawlins," Gerald Jordan said.

I took what felt like my first breath since my arrest and stood up. At the door behind me were the five cops that had carried me. Detective Suggs was there. So were two high-ranking police-men in fancy dress.

Somebody took the handcuffs from my wrists.

Suggs looked a little subdued. But that was okay by me. I had the fortitude of ten men inside of me.

"What the fuck you grab me off the street like that for, man?" I said to the deputy chief.

A hand grabbed me from behind but I flung it off.

Jordan raised his hand to tell the rank and file to stand back.

"I've been talking to Detective Suggs," Jordan said.

He looked every bit as slick and evil as he had the first time we met. The only thing different about him was that the red mark under his eye seemed larger. I decided that this meant I had done something to upset him.

I liked that.

"Yeah," I said. "So what?"

"He tells me that you're looking for a mendicant named Harold. He said that you don't even know his last name but that you believe this Harold killed Nola Payne."

I didn't say anything. Why should I?

"Is this true?" Jordan asked.

"What the fuck do you want, man?" I replied.

"Don't push your luck, son," one of the fancy black uni-forms said.

That had an effect on me. I was born understanding those very words, delivered in that very tone. I and everybody I'd known had survived by gleaning the white man's final threat.

His words shook me but Jo's potion poured over them like salt on a garden slug.

"Listen, man," I said to the uniform, "I'm here because you

called on me. I got a job to do and I will do it. But I'm not gonna smile at you or kiss your mothahfuckin' hand. I'm not gonna let you tell me what it is I should be doin' neither. So if that's why I'm here, either throw me in a cell or let me be."

Suggs, who had been looking at his feet, glanced upward at his bosses. I could tell that he was awed by my outburst and that they were stymied by my resolve.

"This is not going to help your case, Rawlins," Jordan said.

"There's only one thing I want, Jerry. I want to find the man who killed Nola Payne. I want him either on death row or dead. If you're with me on that, then we don't have a problem. If you not — that's okay too."

"There is no Harold," Jordan said. "I've spoken to every captain in the south L.A. precincts. These killings that you and Detective Suggs are talking about have other, better explanations."

"Sir," Suggs said.

"You be quiet," the other fancy uniform said.

"No sir," Suggs replied, "I can't do that. The people you've been talking to are just trying to cover their own oversights. The cases I brought to you were all done by the same man. I'm sure of that. Mr. Rawlins has a credible suspect . . ."

"You don't know that," Jordan said.

"Yes I do, sir. There's a murderer running loose and if we find him we will be doing what you asked us to do."

"If," Jordan said.

"We ain't gonna find shit stinkin' in here with you," I added.

"You don't want me as an enemy, Mr. Rawlins," Jordan said.

"I don't have any choice about that, Jerry. You know it and I do too. Right here at this minute you and me on the same side even if you don't know it. I'm gonna do what you want me to do but we still gonna be enemies. There ain't no question about that. Never was. Never will be."

Jordan turned to Suggs then.

"You have forty-eight hours," he said. "Either you have a killer in a cell by then or I will have your ass. Both of you."

39

It was close to midnight and I was on the street downtown standing side by side with the white man named Melvin Suggs. He was a cop by trade and I was a criminal by color. But there we were.

"You are one crazy bastard," Suggs said to me.

"Yeah. You right about that."

"What are we going to do now?"

"You got any leads?" I asked him.

"A few. Nothing I can act on tonight."

"Call me at my office by noon tomorrow," I said. "Then we can share notes and maybe get somewhere."

I GOT TO my office a little before one.

There were two messages on my answering machine. The first one was from Bonnie.

"Hi, Easy," she said in that island-soaked, deep-toned voice. "I think I have something. I called a J. Ostenberg in Pasadena. A man named Simon Poundstone answered. He said that his wife, Jocelyn, was named Ostenberg before they were married. She kept her maiden name. He also said that he thought that once she had had a maid who had a son named Harold. I called back later to speak to her but she said that the maid's son was named Harrison not Harold and that she hadn't heard from either one of them for years. But there was something about the way she sounded that I didn't like. I think that she was hiding something.

"Feather misses you, honey," she added. "I think she wants you to come home."

The next message was from Juanda.

"Hi. It's me. I was just sittin' here thinkin' about you and how much I wanted to see you. At first I was gonna call and tell you I saw that man Harold somewhere just to get you ovah heah. But then I thought you'd get mad. Call me, okay? I really wanna see you."

I disengaged Jackson's answering machine and then turned out the light on my desk. I stood up with every intention of getting into my car and driving home to my little family.

I took one step without a hitch. The next step was a little wobbly but still I kept my balance. Number three had me bending a little too far down. The fourth stride brought me to my knees.

I had only enough presence of mind to realize that it was Mama Jo's elixir wearing off. I tried to rise but instead I fell. I was on the floor and then I was floating. As I neared the roof everything went black.

Then a bell started ringing. It was all over the place; loud then soft, long and then in short bursts. It sounded like water fountains and rain forests and waterfalls. But it was a bell. A loud bell. And then it stopped.

I opened my eyes to bright sunlight coming in through the window. I was laid out exactly as I had fallen. The room was hot and my whole body was sweating. I had no headache or even a bad taste in my mouth. Mama Jo could bottle that medicine and make a mint among the down and out.

The phone began to ring again. It sounded odd. There was a pulsing nature to the jingling bell. I got right up and went to the phone. I picked up the handset, said hello, and then fell into my chair. I realized that I couldn't have gotten up again to save my mother's life.

"Rawlins, you okay?" Detective Melvin Suggs asked me.

"What time is it?" I asked.

"It's after one."

"In the afternoon?"

"What's wrong with you?" the cop asked me.

"Are you at the precinct?" I replied.

"Nearby."

"Come and get me. I wanna take a ride out to the valley."

"What for?" he asked, but I was already hanging up the phone.

I sat back in my chair as weak as water. It was a miracle that I didn't spill out under the desk. Sounds came to me from the street crazily. A baby's cry was loud and piercing but a car horn blaring was almost too low to hear. There were birds chattering clearly enough that they seemed to be speaking English, or maybe Spanish. Cars were moving but their mechanical sounds receded into a single rushing sound, like an engorged river flowing a few hundred feet away.

I looked at my hand in awe. It moved and flowed, responded to my every whim like magic. I took a deep breath and felt thankful for the few moments of life I had under a sun that made me sweat and grin.

I was an infant amazed by the miracles surrounding me. I couldn't move but that didn't seem to matter. Whatever I needed would come at the proper time.

I had been meandering in my mind like that for some time when a knock came on the door. I tried to say "Come in," but there wasn't enough air in my lungs.

The door opened and Detective Suggs entered.

I was actually glad to see him. I don't know how many white men I'd seen walk through doors but I doubted if I had ever been as happy as I was when a friend visited. I liked Suggs. Was that Mama Jo's doing? Had my mind somehow been altered to leave behind all of my history, clear my eyes, a man cut loose from his own private anchor of hate?

"What's wrong with you, Rawlins?" the cop asked.

As he approached me, strength flowed into my legs and then arms. I stood up from a long hibernation, hungry for movement, thinking only about my prey.

"I'm fine. Perfectly fine."

"You sounded drunk on the phone."

"I was up late," I explained. "Slept here in my chair. You woke me up."

"So why did you want to go to the valley?"

I GOT J. OSTENBERG'S address out of the phone book. And then I turned on Jackson's answering machine just in case someone called while I was out. On the drive over I explained what

Bonnie had told me, only I said it was an assistant of mine that made the call.

"SO WHEN WERE you going to tell me about Peter Rhone?" Suggs asked on the ride over the mountain.

"Peter who?"

"Don't fool with me, Rawlins. I found him myself. All I had to do was locate the chop shops in the neighborhood. You put a little pressure on a man in an interrogation room and he'll turn in his own mother."

"So he told you about me?"

"No. He gave me the car and the dealer gave me Rhone. He told me about you."

"You arrest him?"

"No. He didn't kill Nola. He might have set fire to his life but he didn't kill that girl."

"Woman," I said.

"Say what?"

"Woman. Nola Payne was a woman just like you and me are men."

Suggs was driving. He turned to me and gave me a quizzical look.

"I don't like bein' called boy," I said. "I don't like our Negro women to be called girls. That's easy enough, right?" It was something I had always wanted to say but hadn't. Between the riots and Mama Jo I was a real mess.

"Oh yeah," Suggs said.

What did he care? He didn't know what made me mad. All he wanted to do was make sure his job was done well.

———

JOCELYN OSTENBERG LIVED in a nice house on Hesby Street off of Muerretta Avenue. It was a two-story Tudor with a broad green lawn and a crooked oak to the side.

I followed Suggs to the front door. He pressed the button but I heard no bell. He knocked.

A few moments later a woman's voice said, "Who is it?"

"Police," Suggs uttered.

"Oh. Wait a minute."

I heard a loud crack of a lock opening, a chain pulled, another bolt thrown back, and then the doorknob turned. I looked around and saw that all of the windows had bars on them.

The white woman who answered was tiny. She wore a drab blue sweater and a long coal-gray skirt. She also wore a fancy black straw hat and gloves. It was midday and she didn't look as if she were about to go out but she had on enough makeup to star in an opera. Her ears would have worked on a fat man five times her size.

"Yes?" she asked Suggs, darting a worried glance at me and then looking away.

Suggs held out his identification. She saw the badge and then nodded.

"My husband is at work," she said.

"We came to ask you a few questions," Suggs said.

"Who is that man with you?" she asked in a confidential tone as if I were across the street, out of earshot.

"He's a material witness, ma'am. We wanted to ask you about a man named Harold. He might be using the same last name as yours."

There was a long silence. Jocelyn Ostenberg was maybe sixty, maybe more. It was hard to tell under all that pancake flour. She had gotten to the age where lies didn't flow easily. She looked at me, at the floor, at the bent oak. Finally she said, "I don't know any Harold."

"No?"

"No sir. I once had a maid named Honey. She had a son named Harrison. Somebody called earlier. They wanted to know about a Harold. Was that someone from your office?"

"No ma'am. What was Honey's last name?"

"Divine," she said but I didn't believe it. "Honey Divine. She died a few years ago, I heard."

"May we come in, ma'am?" Suggs asked then.

"I don't have men in my home when my husband is out, Officer. I'm sorry." She waited for us to bow out.

"Well, okay," Suggs said, about to honor her request.

"How long have you lived in this house, ma'am?" I blurted out before he could complete his sentence.

"Thirty-five years."

I smiled and nodded.

"Well thank you, ma'am," Suggs said.

She nodded and closed the door, making a racket with all of the locks she had to engage.

"That's a dead end," the cop said to me on the stroll back to his car.

"You gonna bust Rhone?" I asked him.

"In thirty-six hours unless we come up with something solid."

"You know he didn't do it."

"I'm comfortable letting the courts decide that."

40

Suggs opened the driver's side door but I just stood there on the patch of grass at the curb.

"You getting in?" he asked me.

"No." I chewed on the word, drawing it out.

"You gonna walk over that hill?"

"They got buses out around here, Detective. I wanna stretch my legs, think a bit."

"You're not about to find a Negro hobo around here, Rawlins. But you might find trouble."

"Why's that?"

"Don't you see where you are?"

"Los Angeles," I said. "That's the city I live in, the city where I work and pay taxes."

Suggs shook his head, dropped into the driver's seat, and took off. I liked him more all the time.

I STARTED AT the far end of the opposite side of the block. Nobody was home at the first house. The lady at the second home looked out between the blinds of a side window at me but never came to the door. There were another few homes where the people were not at home or didn't answer. Finally one door came open. The man standing there was thick around the middle but slender in the shoulders and neck. He wore white pants and a green shirt and so resembled a leek or some other bulb plant.

"What do you want?" he asked, none too friendly.

"I'm looking for my wife's second cousin Harold," I said easily.

"None'a your people livin' around here," he said.

He had green eyes and a pale face.

"He used to use an address around here," I explained, "and my wife was worried about him —"

"Didn't you hear me?" the study in green and white asked.

"So you don't know a black Harold?" I replied.

"I told you —," he said.

I didn't hear the rest because I turned away from him. While I walked down the concrete path toward the sidewalk he shouted at my back.

"You better get out of here, mister. We don't want you or your relatives causing problems here. You aren't welcome here."

On my way to the house next door, I counted the three times he used the word "here." I quickened my pace because it was a toss-up whether his next move would be to get his gun or call the police.

The next three places turned me away too. And then I came to a pink house edged in red toward the other end of the block.

A tallish and older white woman in a banana-colored housecoat came to the door. She looked at me with no apparent fear. Maybe she had no radio or TV and no paperboy either. Maybe no one told her that Los Angeles had just been through a small-scale civil war or maybe she didn't care.

"Yes?"

"Hello, ma'am," I said. "I'm looking for a man, a Negro named Harold. I think he used to live on this block."

"That boy from the Ostenberg home," she said.

"You mean Jocelyn Ostenberg across the street?" I asked.

"Yes sir. That's the one. And it was a shame too."

Out of the corner of my eye I could see a police cruiser turn onto the far end of the block.

"May I come in, ma'am?" I asked.

"Oh yes. Please do," she said.

She moved away from the door and I took a long step into her home, hoping that the cops hadn't seen me.

The house smelled of cat piss and air freshener but that didn't bother me. If the police didn't come to the door within two minutes I was home free. I still had Jordan's letter in my pocket but after my arrest at the gas station I didn't know if it still held any official power.

"Come sit down," the woman said. "My name is Dottie, Dottie Mathers. What's yours?"

"Ezekiel, Miss Mathers," I said. "Ezekiel Rawlins."

The woman turned to me with awe on her face.

"Named after the Bible," I added so that she wouldn't mis-take me for an agent of the Lord.

The room she ushered me into had flowers everywhere. In vases and stitched into the fabric on the couch and stuffed chairs. There was a floral pattern on the wallpaper and little

244

knickknacks on the shelves, coffee table, and windowsills that had various flower motifs. Moving between the images of flowers were cats. White, black, calico, and blond cats rubbing and mewling and looking at me with sultry half-interest.

"Have a seat, young man," Dottie told me.

There was a cat on the seat she offered me. He didn't move until I was almost on top of him.

I counted seven felines and I was sure there were twice that number in and around her house. But none of that bothered me. The cops had not come to the door. I was safely hidden among the flowers and cats in the company of a white woman who didn't seem to care about anything else.

"Tea?" she asked.

"No ma'am. All I wanted to know was about Harold."

"What a shame," she said. "You know he used to come here to my door when he couldn't take it anymore. That was a long time ago. More than twenty-five years. I'm one of the only people left who remembers it and that's why Jocelyn hasn't talked to me in all that time."

"So Harold and his mother used to live at Jocelyn's home?" I asked.

"That's exactly right," Dottie said. "I think her name was Honey."

"You wouldn't happen to remember her last name?"

"Oh yes, I do," Dottie said in a pixilated sort of way. "Honey May. I'll never forget that, because she had two first names. I always thought that was peculiar."

"Honey May," I said, committing the name to memory.

"That's right. She seemed like a nice girl but I think she must have had a problem with the bottle."

"Why do you say that?" I asked.

"She just left one day. Didn't even take little Harold with her. Left him with Jocelyn."

She had taken a seat in the middle of the flowery red-and-blue-and-green sofa. Dottie had a long face that was meaty around the jowls. Her nose was hefty and her cheeks round. In that face I saw Jocelyn's face. I had been distracted by the large ears but now that I remembered it I could see the features of the Ostenberg woman again.

"Jocelyn kept the boy," Dottie was saying. "I suppose it was very Christian of her but you know, everybody would have been better off if she would have found some nice colored people to take him in."

"Why do you say that, ma'am?"

"Aren't you polite, Ezekiel," she said beaming at me. "It would have been better because Jocelyn was ashamed to have people know that she was raising a colored child. She wouldn't even take him to school. From the time he was five years old she made him walk the nine blocks to Redman Elementary. She never took him to the park or allowed his friends into the house."

"What about her husband?" I asked.

"That man she lives with is her second husband," Dottie said. "He's only been there for sixteen years. Jocelyn's first husband left years before. Harold left Jocelyn's home when he was twelve."

"Twelve years old?"

"Oh yes. I know because he came here to me the day he left. He asked me if he could cut my lawn for fifty cents and I told him yes. After that I never saw him again. Jocelyn told her neighbors that his mother had come to get him. But I knew better. He wanted that fifty cents for a stake to run away from home. And who can blame him? His mother a drunk who aban-

246

doned him and the woman who raised him didn't even hold his hand when they crossed the street."

By then I had forgotten the police.

A cat jumped into my lap and started pressing her nose against my hand. I scratched behind her ears absently. I imagined a lonely black boy living out in a white world where even his mother treated him like dirt.

"You like cats, Mr. Rawlins?" Dottie asked me.

"Better than most people," I replied.

"Hallelujah to that," she said.

41

"Hello?" a man's voice asked.

"May I speak to Miss Ostenberg?" I said into the phone in a booth on Chandler Boulevard.

It was near four in the afternoon and I was waiting for a ride.

"Who is this?" the man asked me.

"Harold," I said, "Ostenberg."

There was a lull and then, "Yes?" a woman's voice said.

"Was Harold's father passing too?" I asked. "Or was Harold just a throwback from your side of the family?"

"Who is this?"

"If you don't want me to have a talk with your husband, you had better tell me how I can get to your son, Jocelyn."

"I'm going to hang up," she warned.

"No you won't," I said. "Because if you do I'll send that policeman to your husband's place of work. He'll be asking about you and your lineage, Jocelyn. How deep will he have to dig to find out who your parents are?"

"I don't know where Harold is," she said, answering two questions with one declaration.

"I need to meet with you, Jocelyn. I need to talk about your son."

"Don't call him that."

"I'll give you an address and you come to me. If you don't I'll huff and puff right in your husband's ear."

"You can't blackmail me, sir," she said from a high saddle.

"I could if I wanted to, ma'am," I replied humbly. "But all I want is Harold. You give me that and I'll let you be."

"And if I meet with you you'll leave me and Simon alone?"

"I don't care about you, Jocelyn. I never heard of you before yesterday and I won't be thinkin' about you tomorrow. But this evening when you come to see me I need you to tell me where I can lay my hands on Harold."

"I told you I don't know where he is."

"Have you had letters from him?"

Silence.

"Do you have any adult pictures of him?" I asked.

Again no answer.

"I need to know anything you got," I said.

"Hey, Easy," Raymond Alexander said. He was rolling to the curb in a golden Continental. A brand-new car.

I held up a hand while telling Jocelyn Ostenberg my office address.

"I want to see you by seven, Jocelyn," I said and then I hung up.

———

"WHAT YOU DOIN' out here, Easy?" Mouse asked me when we were on our way back to SouthCentral L.A.

"Lookin' for Harold."

"You think some Negro bum gonna be out with the white peoples?"

"How are you, Ray?"

I asked because he didn't look good. He was wearing an old pair of dress trousers held up by suspenders and a white T-shirt that was none too clean. He still wore the handmade alligator shoes but had no socks on. Most people would have looked at him and thought he was trying to achieve some kind of rough fashion statement but I knew better. When Mouse's dress got rough, so did he. Something was bothering him and there was an even chance that he'd settle this problem with a gun or knife.

"I can't find Benita," he said.

"No? I've seen her just about everywhere I been."

"I called her and she ain't there," Mouse said. "I asked her friends and they haven't seen her since before you took her home. You know you got me worried about her with all your talk."

There was an accusatory tone to his words, as if it were my fault she was gone.

"She mentioned that she might go see some family down in San Diego," I said. "Why don't you ask her mother if you could get their phone number?"

"Yeah. All right. You know her mother's worried too."

FOR THE ENTIRE ride Mouse was sour and silent. That wouldn't have been pleasant in any companion but with Raymond there was always the added threat of homicide. He was more killer than anything else and so had to be handled gently and with great respect. An angry Mouse was like a grenade with a loose pin, like a hungry lion breathing down your neck.

When we neared my office I asked, "How's business with you and that dude Hauser?"

"Okay, I guess. Mothahfuckah kept houndin' me 'cause I wouldn't let up on my private shit, kept sayin' that he wanted his fair share. I finally had to say that we could either fight or he could get up off'a me. He didn't even wanna pay you."

"Me?"

"Yeah, Easy. You saved our butts, man. Shit, it wasn't just the cops that night. You know them mothahfuckahs had the National Guard too. Even if we woulda killed them cops, they woulda had men with bazookas on us. As it was, we did three more runs and once the police even waved at us. *Waved.*"

With that he reached into a pocket and came out with a thick brown envelope. He handed the packet to me saying, "We made 'leven thousand dollars that night."

The envelope contained a stack of hundred-dollar bills and an emerald ring wrapped in toilet paper.

"Three thousand dollars and a little sumpin' from my private stash."

I held the ring up to the light. The stone was very large, five or six carats at least.

"High-roller pawnshop over on Avalon," Mouse said. "I been thinkin' about them for years. They didn't think anybody could get into their safe but I knew a torch man."

By then we were in front of my office. I couldn't turn down the lucre. Mouse was giving me the money partly because he was my friend and partly because he wanted me to be implicated in his criminal activity. Telling him no would have put us at odds.

I told him to call me if he hadn't found Benita by morning. Then I went up to the only place where I could be the man I wanted to be.

I PUT THE money and the ring into the bottom drawer of my desk.

At home in the garage I had a little box where I kept all the extra monies I had taken in. That was for Feather's college and Jesus' future, whatever that might turn out to be. But Mouse's money was something else. I had to do something with it that would redeem his crimes. I thought about how to achieve that goal but without much success.

After that I went to the window and looked out on the street. There were no National Guards to be seen, but six police cars cruised down my block in the time I stood there.

On my street, the effects of the riots were still in evidence. Small knots of people moved around listlessly from corner to corner. The police would break them up whenever they began to congregate. I saw one man getting arrested for refusing to move on. The riots were kind of like my fight with the wrong Harold. There was no real winner. Fear on one side, defeat on the other.

42

I was reading *Banjo* when she came to the door. The knock was so soft that I couldn't place it at first. It might have been a cat playing with a ball of yarn in the hallway.

But it was Jocelyn Ostenberg. She was still wearing that gray dress and she'd added a brunette wig. There was enough powder on her face to bake bread and her lips looked like they were painted with red nail polish. Rather than trying to be a white woman, she seemed like she was attempting to pass as a member of a lost race of clowns.

"Come in," I said to the garish woman. "Come have a seat."

I returned to my chair after the older woman was seated. She was carrying a big tan bag. I wondered if she had a gun in that purse. It bothered me that the idea wasn't very far-fetched at all.

"What do you want from me, Mr. Rawlins?"

"Your son owes me six hundred dollars," I said. "He stopped me on the street, asking for a handout. I hired him to work on a wall I was building and he ran away with my power tools."

The pinched expression returned to the tiny woman's face.

"You brought the police to my house for a bunch of tools?"

"Good tools," I said. "Power tools. And anyway, it's the principle, not the money."

"How did you find me?"

"On the day he was workin' he talked about his life some. He talked about his mother, Jocelyn, so when he stole my property I looked you up in the book."

It was a weak lie, very weak. But it was all I could manage.

"What do you do here?" she asked me.

"I do research," I said. It was close enough to the truth that I would have probably passed a lie detector test.

"So then why were you building a wall?"

"Tell me where your son is or I will tell your husband that he's married to a Negro woman who has a Negro son running around Watts committing crimes."

"That's extortion," she said. "I could take you to court over that."

"Where's Harold?"

"I don't know. I haven't seen him in years."

"He said that he comes to your house now and then."

"Not for years," she said. There were tears somewhere near.

"When was the last time you saw him?"

"You're not doing this over some old tools."

"I have your number right here, Miss Ostenberg. And I will call your house before you can get there."

"It's not right for you to do this."

"I'm not going to argue with you, lady. Either you give up Harold or you give up your white life."

"Do I look like a black woman to you?" she pleaded.

"You look like Bozo's grandmother," I said. "But I don't care. I would go out in the streets and stage a one-man riot to get to Harold. So either you tell me what I want to know or I'll tell everybody else about you."

I could hardly believe how brutal I was toward that fragile, elderly woman. But I knew that Harold had given rise to all kinds of sorrow and the woman before me had given birth to him. She was responsible and I wouldn't let up.

"Why do you want him so bad?" Jocelyn asked.

"Where is he?" I replied.

"I don't know. You've seen him. He lives in the streets and alleys. He doesn't have a phone or an address. He's a derelict. Only thirty-seven and he's just a bum."

"Tell me about him," I said.

"I told you. He's worthless." Her lips curled into a feral snarl. "He's nothing."

"Is that why he's killing black women who get together with white men?"

For me it was her eyes. They opened wide at the accusation I leveled, wide and brown and down-home. She had the colored curse in her veins. I was sure that she saw it in the mirror every morning before dousing herself with powders and lightening creams, before she put on her wig and gloves and hat.

It wasn't the first time I had met someone like her. And I didn't hate her for hating herself. If everybody in the world despises and hates you, sees your features as ugly and simian, makes jokes about your ways of talking, calls you stupid and beneath contempt; if you have no history, no heroes, and no future where a hero might lead, then you might begin to hate yourself, your face and features, your parents, and even your child. It could all happen and you would never even know it. And then one hot summer's night you just erupt and go burning and shooting and nobody seems to know why.

"What women?" Jocelyn said.

You. The word came into my mind but I didn't say it. Maybe it wasn't even true but I believed it. I believed that Harold Ostenberg had roamed around the streets looking for a place to put his rage. He found women who had betrayed him as his mother had. He killed them and stole their memories.

"The woman across the street said that you made Harold walk to school alone even when he was little," I said.

"Lots of children go to school alone. I was busy keeping the house in order," she said.

"She also told me that Harold ran away when he was just twelve."

"He was a bad seed even then. You know, Mr. Rawlins, that some children are just born bad."

"Who was his father?" I asked.

"I don't see what that has to do with anything," she said. "His father left when Harold was just a baby."

"Was he passing like you?"

"I don't have to put up with this."

"Yes, you do," I said. "Either that or you want me to go to your new white husband with this story."

For a moment I believed that Jocelyn was going to walk out on me. She certainly wanted to. She certainly hated me.

"Carl came from St. Louis," she said, defeated. "We met when we were both working for Third Avenue Bank. He was a loan officer and I was a teller. They thought we were white and we didn't set them straight. But we could tell about each other. It wasn't so wrong. We just wanted to get ahead. We wanted to work together. We bought a house."

"Just a nice white couple from back East."

"You have no right to judge me."

"But black-skinned Harold did," I said. "Somehow you and your light-skinned hubby made a mess in the nursery. Harold would be like a shit stain on your sheets."

"You don't have to be crude," she said.

"I have never once murdered a black woman, Miss Ostenberg. I never once drove a child from my door."

"You don't understand," she said. "Carl left me. He just went to work one day and never came back. I had no friends or family. All I had was Harold and he just couldn't act right."

"You mean he didn't know why he had to pretend to be your maid's child? He didn't know why Honey May was pretending to be his mother?"

"You know her name?" Jocelyn asked.

"I'm looking for Harold," I said. "I intend to find him with or without your help."

"I don't know where he is, Mr. Rawlins. He left me when he was twelve. I haven't seen him since."

"You sure you don't wanna change that story? Once it gets out you won't have a hole to hide in."

She stood up on nearly steady feet and turned her back on me. She walked to the door and out without another word. I'd never felt such hatred in my life but I wasn't quite sure right then of who or what I hated. I wasn't even certain why.

43

There was only one Honey May in the Los Angeles directory. She lived on Crocker between Eighty-seventh Street and Eighty-seventh Place. I could have walked there from my office but I drove because that was the way you got around in L.A. Down the street or across town, you had your car there at the curb waiting to take you where you needed to be.

Honey lived in a blue apartment building, on the second floor.

"Yes?" she said sweetly from behind the closed door.

"It's Easy Rawlins, ma'am," I said. "You don't know me but I've come here to ask you about Harold Ostenberg."

"Oh my," she said. "Oh my."

She opened the door and peered out through the screen.

Honey was a big woman in height and girth and facial features. Her nostrils were cavernous and her eyes were like moons. Only Honey's voice was small. I got the feeling that the one squeaky voice I heard was just a single member of the chorus that must have lived inside that large body.

She held out a big hand in a delicate motion.

"Mr. Rawlings?"

"Rawlins," I said. "My grandfather said that we got the "g" shot off, hightailing it out of Tennessee."

Her grin revealed big teeth. But the smile was quickly replaced by concern. Men had been taking advantage of her by being charming and funny for a whole lifetime — that's what her face was telling me.

"You said somethin' about Harold?" she asked.

"He's in trouble," I said.

"He been that since the day he was born. You wanna come in, Mr. Rawlings?"

I didn't correct her.

Honey's walls were painted violet. She only had four walls to live between because it was just a one-room home. There were framed photographs along the box shelving and prints of paintings tacked on the wall. She had three chairs, one sofa, and a Murphy bed that folded up lengthwise under a window that looked out on a green wall.

"What kind of trouble?" she asked me after I had chosen a seat.

"As bad as you can get," I said. "So bad that nothing worse could possibly be done to him in revenge."

My words hit Honey's face like bombs on a peaceful city.

"It's not his fault," she said. "He cain't help what life made him."

"Do you know where I can find him, Miss May?"

"Are you plannin' to shoot him, Mr. Rawlings?"

That was the likeliest solution to a dispute in the black community at that time. If black men had a problem with each other they rarely went to the police. The law didn't care unless it had to do with white skin or money. Black men settled their own disagreements.

"No ma'am. What Harold's done has to be made public. He's killed women," I said.

"Oh no. No."

"I don't even know how many. But he has to be stopped. Because if he isn't he'll keep on until he dies."

Honey started to cry. I got the feeling that she'd been expecting my visit for many years, that she knew the potential tragedy wrapped up in Harold's hurting heart. But what could she have done with her gentle nature and chocolate skin, her mild demeanor and giant eyes? She was just an exotic witness, an angel, maybe, with no say over the actions of men.

"I'm sorry, Mr. Rawlings. Did he hurt someone close to you?"

"Not really. But since I've been looking for him I've seen things that were just as bad as the war." I paused and then asked, "Do you know where I can find him?"

"I don't know if I should tell you, Mr. Rawlings. You know, I carried that boy in my arms when he couldn't even crawl."

"He's a man now, Miss May. And men have to stand on their own two feet."

"But he's had it so hard," she argued. "You know that no white judge is gonna care about what happened to him."

"Do you have a daughter, Miss May? Or a mother or sister?"

She smiled but it was as if I had reached into her breast and wrenched the grin out against her will.

"Right here." She walked over to a shelf near the window and took down a brass frame containing a Polaroid photograph of a young woman cut from her mold. "Sienna May. She married a man named Helms but we all still call her Sienna May 'cause it sounds right."

I stood up and went over to the window. I took the frame from the big woman's hand and admired it. Then I turned it so that she could see it.

"If Helms was a white man Howard would have choked your girl until her eyes and tongue was poppin' outta her head," I said. "She'd be cold and dead as a Christmas ham in the icebox. And there'd be a dozen other girls layin' right up in there next to her."

Honey grabbed the picture from my hand.

"No!" she said.

"Yes," I replied. "That's just what I said when I realized it almost a year ago. And when I went to the cops and told 'em they said that I must've been mistaken, no vagabond could get around them like that. Now there's another woman dead. And I'm askin' you to help me stop Harold."

"But why should I believe you, Mr. Rawlings?"

"Because you know the man I'm talkin' about. You know where he comes from and what he might do. You see him doin' just what I say and you know why."

Honey May let herself fall onto the sofa. She looked down at her lap and tears fell from her eyes. She shook her head and her shoulders slumped forward.

"It's my fault too," she said. "I knew his mama was colored the minute I laid eyes on her. But I never said so. I didn't argue when she hinted that things would go better for Harold if people thought that I was his mother. But I never lied to Harold. I told him that Miss Ostenberg was his mother and I was just his big mama. I guess I shoulda taken him wit' me when I left. But you know I didn't have the strength."

"Did he come to you after he ran away?" I asked.

"He'd come stay with me and Sienna May now and then. But you know he was so wild. Most the time he was out in the street, livin' in empty lots or shelters."

"Didn't the state come after him?"

"They did but Harold would just run away. They didn't want him all that bad and he always looked older than he was. That's because his face was so hard."

"Do you know where I can find him, Miss May?"

"He comes by here once a year or so," she said to the floor. "Last time was four or five months ago. He said that he liked the north side of Will Rogers Park because there was some good guys like to play dominoes there."

"I won't kill him, Miss May," I said. "I want to but I won't. I'll just make sure the police get him."

She looked up at me with those big eyes.

"I can tell that you're a good man, Mr. Rawlings," she whispered. "But I know Harold too. He wanna be good but he just don't know how."

"Do you have a picture of Harold that I can show to them?"

There was a tiny chest of three drawers next to the Murphy bed. She pulled open the middle drawer and took out a simple dark-wood frame. She handed this to me.

Harold was in his twenties when the picture had been taken, wearing a coat that was too large for him, probably borrowed from the portrait photographer. His eyes weren't as dull and there was some hope in him at that moment. I wondered if he had already started murdering women then.

"Can I have it back when they're through, Mr. Rawlings?" Honey May asked me.

"Just as soon as we're through with it," I said.

We looked at each other, both knowing what my words meant.

44

It was nearly ten at night. No domino players would be out that late. I drove back to my office and called home.

"Hello," Feather said.

"What are you doing up so late, girl?" I asked the daughter of my heart.

"Daddy!" she shouted. "It's you."

"Sure it is, baby girl. Did you think I ran away?"

"I was scared that you were hurt down in the riot places."

"No, baby. I've just been workin' at my office. You know sometimes grown-ups have to work day and night."

"But why can't you come home, Daddy? I miss you."

"I'll be home when you wake up in the morning, baby. I promise."

"You promise?"

"Cross my heart," I said. "Is Bonnie there?"

"Uh-huh. Here."

"Where are you, Easy?" Bonnie asked.

"At the office. What's wrong?"

"A woman named Ginny Wright called at about eight. She said that Benita Flag had been looking around for sleeping pills. She tried to call Raymond but he wasn't home. She said that you might want to know that."

I took a deep breath. The world was feeling too big for me to handle. I wanted to go home and see my family. I wanted to sleep for a week. And when I got up I wanted to go to my job at Sojourner Truth Junior High School, mopping up spilled milk and checking to see that there was no litter in the schoolyard.

"I was gonna come right home, baby," I said. "But I better look into this. Benita is one'a Raymond's friends and she's been under a lotta pressure lately."

"That's okay, Easy," Bonnie cooed. "Jesus is here and he's going to wait until you get back before he goes out on his boat again."

WHEN NOBODY ANSWERED I knocked the door in. If I was wrong about Benita I could always put it back on its hinges. Living poor and black had done many things for me. It had made me a plumber and a carpenter, an electrician and a mason. I could put in windows, take a car engine apart, pave a highway, or run a steam engine. Being poor made more out of many men than any Harvard or army could imagine.

Benita Flag was on her bed with white foam coming from her mouth. She didn't respond to shaking or slaps or cold water in her face.

I could have called an ambulance but poverty had taught me a lesson about that too. I had her at Mercy in less than twelve minutes. They pumped her stomach and shot medicine in her veins. A doctor named Palmer told me that she was so close to death that he didn't know if they had done enough.

"You did the right thing," he told me.

"What good is doin' the right thing if women are dyin' whichever way I look?" I said.

I think the doctor was put off or worried by my words. But he patted my shoulder and showed me to a chair.

What else did I have to do? It was only one in the morning. I had many hours before I would set up watch at the domino tables at Will Rogers Park. Why not sit in a chair at the hospital, waiting to see if yet another woman had died?

THE EMERGENCY ROOM at any hospital in the middle of the night is mainly made up of the consequences of love. Men and women and children with fearful parents. The men and women had gotten into fights over passionate jealousies and the children were there because their parents had nowhere to turn.

I watched a small boy with a purple bruise on his head drifting off to sleep but before he could go there his mother would shake him, saying, "You might have a concussion, honey. You got to stay up."

Two men who had stabbed each other over a woman started fighting in the waiting room and the police had to be called to separate them.

With all that blood and worry I still fell asleep.

I WAS A simple seaman on a great gray battleship going off to war far from America's shores. It was my job to keep the hull bright and shiny and clean. I had thick rope riggings and a platform made from a single plank of oak. All I did day and night was scrub and swab the steel hull from top to bottom, from sunup to sundown. Once I'd cleaned the whole hull it was already dirty at the place where I started. So I'd begin again with no complaint or attempt to shirk my duty.

But after a long while and many, many revolutions of scrubbing I began to wonder why the boat had to be so clean when all it was made for was war. Why shine and glisten on the deep blue sea when it would only come to blood and the deaths of mothers' sons? The sea would still run red, the skies would still resound with cannon. Then the shining hull would be a disgrace and my work would be scorned throughout history.

"Mr. Rawlins?"

It was a nurse.

"Yeah?"

"Miss Flag is awake now," the middle-aged, gray-headed white woman said.

"What time is it?" I asked.

"Sixteen after six."

SHE LOOKED AWFUL in that hospital bed. There were two other beds in the room. Each one had curtains to separate them but they weren't drawn. In one bed was an elderly woman who kept babbling to herself. In the other lay one of the men who had been fighting in the waiting room. His color looked bad. There was a nozzle strapped to his nose, feeding him oxygen, I supposed, and three different intravenous drip sacks putting medicine into his arms. If he had a mother I prayed she didn't see him like that.

"Easy," Benita whispered. "Are you the one saved me?"

"I brought you here," I said. "How you doin', Benny?"

"I feel like a fool," she said. "Please don't tell nobody what happened."

"Are you okay now?"

"Oh yeah. Can you imagine it? Taking them pills, tryin' to kill myself over Raymond?"

"What made you do it?" I asked.

I pulled up a heavy chair with a metal frame.

"Have a seat," the elderly patient said to the air.

"I don't know, Easy. It just hurt so bad that I wanted to go to sleep and never wake up again. It was like I was in a dream, you know? I didn't really think about dyin', just goin' to sleep. And then when I came to and the doctor asked me if I tried to kill myself I said no. And I meant it too. But I can see where everything been leadin' to this. Everybody said that I was takin' this thing with Raymond too hard but I told 'em that they didn't understand. But I guess they did, huh?"

She was drifting a little bit but her words were clear and the burden of love had been lifted from her brow.

"It hurts when somebody you love is gone," I said. "Imagine how your mama would feel if you turned up dead on the floor with foam comin' outta your mouth."

"Yeah." She was looking up at me with wonderment in her eyes. "You saved my life, Easy Rawlins."

"So what you gonna do with it now?"

"I don't know."

"You can come stay at my house a few days if you want," I said. "We don't have an extra room but there's a couch you can sleep on. And my girlfriend will make sure you eat right and have somebody to talk to."

Benita smiled and her face seemed to fill with health.

45

I called Bonnie and told her about the attempted suicide. I asked if we could put Benita up for a while.

"Doesn't she have a mother?" Bonnie asked.

"I promised."

"Okay," Bonnie replied. "But she better understand that I don't want any monkey business under my roof."

I had breakfast at a diner on Success Avenue, soft-boiled eggs over toast. That's what my mother fed me when I was sick. I also had tea with honey and only one cigarette. I ate and read the paper.

The riots were nearly over. There was only one article on the front page that referred to them and that was an argument between Chief Parker and Governor Brown. Brown thought that Parker hurt race relations in L.A., and Parker didn't believe that his police department was guilty of brutality. Other than that, the space shot showed promise and might last eight days, the job prospect in the nation was the best since 1957, and the Vietcong had ambushed some South Vietnamese regulars.

There were no stories about Negro women being murdered by a deranged black man whose mother thought that she was white.

After I was finished I went down to the park benches where men gathered to play dominoes.

The tension from the riots was lifting around the city. People were on their way to work and mothers let their children come to the playground at the park. A few men gathered to play dominoes on the tables. None of them was Harold. I sat down on a slender bench under a tree and watched. I may have fallen asleep a few times because my watch said eleven and it hardly felt like nine-thirty to me. For a while I thought about asking the domino men if they knew Harold but then I decided against it. Someone might warn my quarry and then I would have driven him away.

"SEVENTY-SEVENTH PRECINCT." A woman's voice this time.

"Detective Suggs, please."

"Hold a moment."

The phone rang.

"Detective Suggs."

"I've got a picture of him," I said. "I borrowed it from a woman that wants it back."

"I'll come over to pick it up," he said.

"Don't bother. I'll meet you at the dinette down the street from the station. I'm just callin' to tell you that and that I know where he hangs out a lot."

"Where?"

"Northeast part of Will Rogers Park. Where the men play dominoes."

"Where'd you get that?"

"It doesn't matter, does it, Detective?"

"Ten minutes?" he replied.

"You got it."

I GOT THERE in less than ten minutes but Suggs was already at the counter, drinking coffee from a thick porcelain mug. There was a gutted jelly-filled doughnut on a plate in front of him and two cigarettes in his ashtray.

"Got a light?" I asked him as I sat.

He set fire to my cigarette and I handed him the photograph I got from Honey May.

"So this is Harold the Horror," the cop said. "Just looks like some loser."

"Yeah."

"I'm surprised you brought me this," he said.

"What do you mean?"

"I figured you would go after this clown yourself. I was ready to cover you if he showed up dead after havin' fallen on a bullet or some shit like that."

I laughed then. My head bowed in mirth and I had to hold on so as not to fall off of my stool. It wasn't the joke but the notion that a white cop would let me do my business without interference or condescension tickled me. It was as if I'd died and gone to another man's heaven. This man whose soul I inhabited had been white, and his heaven was filled with ordinary things that were like magic to me.

"No," I said. "I know too much about Harold to kill him like that. People been messin' with him his whole life. Don't get me wrong. I want you to arrest him and I want them to send him to the gas chamber too. But I don't have to do it. No sir. Not me."

I felt the weight of Melvin Suggs's hand on my shoulder. Another friendly gesture.

The police detective stood up and threw a dollar bill on the counter.

"Have some eggs, Rawlins," he said. "You look like shit."

"Thanks. I will."

I had two more soft-boiled eggs and white toast with strawberry jam. You could buy a lot with a buck back then.

I walked back to my building.

Before going upstairs I stopped by Steinman's Shoe Repair. The closed sign was still up but it was tacked on the door that had been wired back into place. I pushed it open and saw Sylvie, Theodore's wife, muse, and best friend. She was a quarter of a head taller than him with the features of a Teutonic goddess. She was slender and I doubted if even her husband knew what her voice sounded like. Mostly she gestured, now and again she whispered, but Sylvie would never raise her voice. I don't know how old she was but she had the kind of beauty that would not fade. Violet eyes and platinum hair, long thin hands and skin akin to the perfect milk that men like Plato dreamed of.

She smiled when she saw me.

"Mr. Rawlins," Theodore said from somewhere behind her.

"Hi, guys," I said. "I saw that the door was open and I just dropped in to make sure things were okay."

Sylvie's smile took on a trace of sadness.

"I'm probably going to close up here, Mr. Rawlins," Theodore said. "It's too much. My insurance agent says that my policy doesn't cover riots and the city refuses to help."

"What about the federal government?" I asked.

He shook his head and Sylvie laid an ethereal hand upon the nape of his neck. The love between them always surprised me. It was like a fairy tale that you one day realized was true.

"You need help moving?" I asked.

It was Theodore's turn to smile.

"You know," I continued, "there's a corner store not far from my house that might be a good place to open a shoe repair shop. It's been vacant a couple'a months. Maybe I could introduce you to the owner."

Sylvie took two steps and kissed me. Her lips formed the words "thank you," and she might have made some sound.

We set up a day for the move and a time to talk with the owner at the empty corner store near my house. It was once a clothes store near Stanley and Pico. It was a space and he was a cobbler and people wore shoes everywhere in the world.

Theodore took the leather saddle from the ruined table and pushed it on me.

"Take this, Mr. Rawlins — Easy," he said.

"I didn't do anything, Theodore," I said. "This is yours."

"But you are helping us," he argued. "You are always trying to help. This is just a, what you call it, a token for our friendship."

I didn't want to take it but Theodore held it out and Sylvie kept smiling. Finally I nodded in defeat and took the ancient riding gear.

I CARRIED MY prize up the southern stairwell to the fourth floor. I walked down the long hall thinking that it was all over.

Suggs would take Harold and somehow prove that he was the killer of Nola Payne. Theodore would move to West L.A. and Jackson Blue would become a computer expert for Cross County Fidelity Bank. I didn't know what to do about Juanda but that was for another day.

I decided to take Benita and Bonnie and the kids for a picnic at Pismo Beach. We could cook and Jesus could take us out fishing one at a time.

I put the key in the lock, thinking that I had done fine. I'd done my job and broke it off before things could go bad. People had died but that wasn't my fault. The city had gone up in flames but maybe that was like a forest fire, cleansing the underbrush, making room for new growth.

When the wood of the doorjamb above my head shattered I thought that it must have been something that fell. But from where? Then the child's cap gun exploding and more shattered wood and a quick pain in my left biceps.

I turned toward the doorway at the far end of the hall, shouting and holding the thick leather saddle in front of my head and chest. I ran as hard as I could toward the door, screaming like a berserker in an ancient war. More shots were fired. One grazed the big knuckle of my left hand. I slammed into the stairwell door, hitting someone who grunted and fell back. The pistol clattered to the floor and I caught a glimpse of the man's shoulder.

As he lunged down the stairs I threw the saddle at him but it missed.

I put a foot down the stairs, not realizing that I had been shot in the calf. The blood dripped down and made a slick on the step. I tumbled for a full flight before coming to a halt and losing consciousness.

46

I must've hit my head pretty hard because even though I thought I was conscious my mind wasn't making the right connections in the ambulance.

"Where did the Germans go?" I asked the medic from my litter.

"What Germans?"

"The ones that killed all those women," I said. "The ones who tried to fool the Allies and killed the women with the white ribbons in their hair."

I remember saying these words. I can still feel the frustration when the attendant said, "You've been hurt but you're going to be okay. Do you know the man who shot you?"

"Must have been the Nazis," I said. I knew that there was something wrong with that statement because of the look on the white kid's face.

"Hand me the hypo, Nick," the attendant said to the man sitting next to the driver.

For a while I was looking out of the window listening to the siren that I took for an air-raid warning. I could almost hear the booming of the Allied cannon.

There was pain in my arm and leg and hand so I didn't feel the morphine while he was injecting it. But soon the blue funk of war gave way to a sunlit yellow world that had never known of battle. The siren became the cry of a huge wild bird and the ambulance was a Greek chariot bringing me home after all those years in hell. I started crying. I asked the attendant if my mother was there.

"What's her phone number?" he asked me.

That was the last thing I remembered for some time.

I AWOKE IN darkness. There was the smell of alcohol and other acrid chemicals in the air. I was between crisp sheets on a bulging mattress in a too-warm room. There were small lights at odd places hovering here and there. The lights illuminated nothing. They merely glistened, like stars in the void.

I had no idea where I was at first. My mind was fuzzy and there were dull aches somewhere on my person. I concentrated very hard and recalled the shots exploding around me. But at first my mind went all the way back to World War II, twenty years earlier, when I was a young man fighting for someone else's freedom.

Then I remembered the splinters from my doorjamb. The shots and Theodore's saddle, which saved my life. It sounded like a cap gun. A .22 caliber, probably a pistol, with low velocity, not enough to rip through hard leather.

I remembered a young German woman, twenty-two if she was a day. Kissing my forehead and learning English, asking me did I have chocolate and sewing needles. I gave her both and then he shot me. No. The girl was a long time ago. I was shot and then I slipped in my own blood . . .

I sat up in the hospital bed, in the warm room. I was alone. My left biceps felt like it was ripping open every time I moved. There was a lamp on the table to my left. I had to twist around and turn it on with my right hand.

Also on the table there was a crayon drawing next to a glass of water. It was a crude green-and-blue picture of a man in a bed with three people standing beside him. My little family had been there. Feather would be in my life for many years. She would love me and I would love her long after all the pain I felt was over.

In the drawer of the table Bonnie had left me a clean change of clothes. I knew it would be there. In the pants pocket was my letter from Gerald Jordan but Bonnie had taken my wallet. She knew that no one would steal a letter but money was another thing.

Who shot me?

It was a man with a pistol who waited for me to come to my office. Somebody who knew me and was afraid of me. A killer who wasn't used to firing a gun. No one who was serious shot at you from that far away with a small-caliber pistol. Then again, nobody with any sense ran at a man shooting at him.

I had three bandages and not too much pain except in my arm.

It had to be Harold. Harold with the same gun he had used to shoot Nola in her dead eye.

After I was dressed I lay back down and closed my eyes.

I fell asleep and dreamt of a German girl sewing up my wounds. She was Sylvie, and Theodore was lurking at the bombed-out doorway with a pistol in his hand.

I jerked upright and bounced on the springy bed to get to my feet. It wasn't bad. Somebody had shot me less than a day ago and I could already get to my feet. I was a soldier, not some citizen or bystander. I had to go out now and find Harold and make sure that he couldn't get at anybody else ever again.

It was very late. More than forty-eight hours had passed since Jordan had laid down his ultimatum. Nobody in the hospital hall was moving. At the nurse's desk a small Asian woman, Japanese I think, was sitting reading a magazine. When I came up to her she jumped from her chair, gasping.

"You shouldn't be out of your bed, sir," she told me.

"Pay phone," I said. "Where?"

"You have to get back to bed."

"Got to make a call. Pay phone."

She scurried to my side and took my arm. I pushed her away and lurched down the hall toward a door marked EXIT. I staggered down the stairs until there were no more and then I pushed open a door.

Across the street from Mercy Hospital was a phone booth. The operator gladly connected the collect call.

"Hello?" she said.

"Will you accept a collect call from Easy?" the operator asked.

"A collect . . . ? Yes, operator. I will."

"Hey, Jewelle," I said. I could hear the thickness in my throat.

"Is that you, Easy?"

"Yeah, baby. How you doin'?"

"Fine. It's four in the mornin'. What's wrong?"

"I been shot."

"What?"

"I'm okay. I mean, not perfect but not bleedin' no more neither."

"Do you need a doctor?"

"Uh-uh. I'm across the street from Mercy Hospital. What I need is a ride. I was wonderin' if Jackson could come get me."

"He's 'sleep," Jewelle said. "And you know he has to be at work tomorrow."

"Already?"

"They need good computer people, Easy. They wanted him today. I'll come get you."

"I didn't mean to get you outta bed, JJ," I said. "It's just —"

"I'll be there, Mr. Rawlins. You just wait."

She hung up and I sat down in the phone booth, feeling the morphine and revenge slithering under my skin.

47

It was a little after five by the time Jewelle parked across the street from the hospital. She had put on a pink dress and dark makeup. I remembered when she was just sixteen, in jeans and in love with my property manager, the grumpy Mofass. Now he was gone and she was a woman.

"I brought you some food and a gun, Easy," she said as I dropped as delicately as I could into the passenger's seat.

I took the paper bag sitting between us and found a .45 pistol, a ham sandwich, and a silver thermos filled with hot black coffee.

"Where to?" Jewelle asked me.

I gave her Jocelyn Ostenberg's address and we took off.

I ate the sandwich even though my stomach didn't want it. The coffee was strong, the way black people made it down

South. The gun was loaded and the safety was off. I'm right-handed, so the wound wouldn't deter me from killing Harold.

"Who shot you, Easy?" the petite Jewelle asked me.

"A man I'm after. A man who kills black women for loving white men. He pulled the trigger but his mother loaded the gun."

"Uh," she grunted disparagingly. "You'd think that people would have enough trouble makin' the rent without all this shootin' and burnin' and killin' everybody."

"Yeah," I said. "But you know there's always somebody with some reason to be mad. I can't hardly throw stones. I mean look at me. Here I am all shot up and bruised and still I'm out here with a gun."

"But you different, Mr. Rawlins," she said. "You the only one I know tryin' to do right by people."

"Jackson said that he's getting' that job to help you out, JJ. That sounds like he's tryin' to do right."

"Yeah. He loves me. I know he does. But you know straight as he tryin' t'be, he still a pretzel in his heart. It tickles me to see him in that suit with those cute glasses don't do nuthin'."

"You love him?"

"Yeah. I love 'im but he ain't you, Mr. Rawlins. No sir. You are the real thing. That's why I got up outta my bed, because it ain't too often that Easy Rawlins calls on somebody for help."

I drifted in my seat for a while then. I was angry at myself for inviting Jocelyn Ostenberg to my office, for giving her a way to come at me. But in that car, with the rising sun making silhouettes of the eastern mountains, beside a woman I'd seen grow up from a child, I felt at ease. I was at home in my own life in spite of everything. Maybe that was the drugs or maybe even shock but I remember feeling safe and comfortable on the drive toward the Ostenberg home.

"Jackson said that you lost everything in the riots," I said after a long time.

"Naw," Jewelle said easily. "It's just tied up my resources. The property's still there and there's sure enough rent to pay the taxes. I got to be creative but the money'll flow back in."

WE PARKED A block away from the Ostenberg house. I didn't want Jocelyn seeing me out there waiting and I didn't need a close-up view to know if Harold came in or if she went out.

It was still very early when we got there, not yet six. Jewelle put her head down on my lap and fell asleep. She'd always felt comfortable with me, as if I had some kind of secret power to keep away danger. There she was with her brilliant business mind thinking that I was the one who could protect her.

I wasn't tired but all the drugs and trauma to my system made me drift in and out of various states of mind. I thought about Juanda and Howard and Jackson and Mouse. I thought about the riots and Gerald Jordan and Melvin Suggs all at the same time. Between all the chemicals and thoughts and wounds I seemed to be able to break up my thoughts and let them blend together.

For most of my life I'd only been able to think about one thing at a time unless I was in danger and had to have eyes in the back of my head. But that morning, when I should have been concentrating on Harold and only Harold, I was putting all the pieces into place all at once.

Jewelle took my hand in her sleep and rolled her head. I looked down on her lovely profile. She was smiling, thinking about Jackson most probably while holding my hand and feeling my warmth.

I realized then that I had almost died in my hallway. I had come within inches and moments of my own death and hadn't stopped even to acknowledge my luck.

I could see Juanda in Jewelle's profile and I knew that we would never be lovers. That made me smile. I could see that Suggs hated Jordan as much as I did and that Harold felt the same pain that drove his mother. Mouse and Harold were in the same place in my mind. And Benita and Nola, and Honey and Geneva were right behind them. Black women at the mercy of black men who couldn't help what they'd become.

My heart was racing trying to keep up with all the overlays in my head. I wanted a cigarette but Jewelle was holding my hand.

A light-colored 'sixty Cadillac drove up to Jocelyn's driveway and pulled in. A man got out and walked up to the door. He fiddled around and then went in. It wasn't Harold. I stayed where I was, wondering what I should do.

A few minutes later the sirens began to howl. At first there was only one and it was pretty far off. It wasn't a fire engine siren; either police or ambulance then. And then there was another, and another. They were coming closer with every moment.

"Get up, baby," I said to Jewelle.

"What is it?" she asked.

"I don't know but you should be awake."

The ambulance wailed up to the front of the Ostenberg home. Two attendants rushed out carrying the gurney. The man from the Cadillac ran out to meet them. Even at the distance I could tell that he was all broken up. His hands kept moving. The ambulance men had to push him aside.

"What is it, Easy?" Jewelle asked.

"I don't know. But you better get out of here. I'll get out and you go home."

"I'm not leavin' you here. You come on with me."

Four police cars came up all at once. Cops rolled out of the cars and into the house. People were coming out of their houses on the next block. The sun was coming up as if even the sky was awakened by the racket.

As the minutes went by, the ambulance attendants didn't reappear. That meant there was either a false alarm or a death.

"It's him!" someone shouted in a maniacal tone. "It's him! It's him!"

I looked out and saw, not fifteen feet from Jewelle's Citroën, the flabby man with the green eyes who had called the police on me the last time I was on Jocelyn's block. He was shouting and jumping in his housecoat and slippers. When our eyes met he shrieked and ran straight for the cops.

"You got a key for the glove compartment?" I asked Jewelle.

"What's wrong with him?" she said, referring to the screaming man.

"Take it off of the key chain and gimme it," I said.

I took the forty-five out of the bag and Jewelle handed me the key. I threw the gun into the glove compartment, locked it, and then swallowed the little brass key just as if I were in some spy movie about to be arrested for attempting to go over the Berlin Wall.

"What's wrong with that man, Easy? Was he talking about us?"

"The cops are going to grab us, JJ. Let's get out of the car and cross our hands in front of us."

Jewelle was a fast study. She got out with me and we waited for the cops that were hurrying out of the Ostenberg house.

Even though we were waiting peacefully we were both grabbed and thrown to the ground. The officers used rough language, calling us niggers and asking questions without waiting for or expecting replies. We were cuffed and yanked to our feet, dragged down the street and thrown through the Ostenberg front doorway.

As we were pulled into the house more policemen arrived. All that pushing and shoving opened the wounds on my leg and arm.

"This one's bleeding," one cop said.

But I wasn't paying attention to their overreactions or the stinging pain I felt. I was looking around the Ostenberg living room.

It was all white.

The carpets and walls, the sofa and even the coffee table were stark white. Even a painting on the wall was a big white house in snow with white children laughing in the window. I wondered if the rest of the house was the same. A policeman grabbed my bandaged arm and a drop of my blood fell onto the thick white rug.

A white man in a brown suit was ushered into the room by two cops. He was an old man and miserable beyond his years. One cop whispered something into his ear and he looked up at me and Jewelle. Then he shook his head and collapsed into their arms. They led him to a white stuffed chair.

He rolled out from the seat and onto the carpet, crying.

I watched him as if he were a distant constellation. I didn't care about Jocelyn's husband any more than some far-off celestial event that occurred before humanity had blighted the earth. He was just a bystander who didn't see the car coming at him. He wasn't important.

48

W hat were you doing in front of the house?" a police sergeant asked me.

We were in the kitchen of the Ostenberg house. I was sitting in a white chair, at a white table, across from a white enamel stove, dripping blood on the white linoleum floor.

Somewhere else in the house the white man was crying.

"I was down the block," I said. "Sitting in the car with my girl."

"How did you get shot?" The sergeant was in his mid-thirties. When he was a teenager he had a bad bout with acne. The scars covered both of his fat cheeks.

"I don't know," I said. "I was going to my office when some-body opened fire."

They had Jewelle in another room but I wasn't worried about her. Jewelle would just say that we were parking, that there was no law against that.

I had given them Jordan's letter but with a black suspect in a crime in a white neighborhood less than a week after the riots, they had to have more than a tardy note from the deputy commissioner.

"What are you doing in this neighborhood?" the scarred sergeant asked.

"Nuthin' special, Officer. Just hangin' around."

"Tell me about this note from Jordan's office."

"That's nothing," I said. "Why don't you tell me what's wrong here. I didn't do anything and haven't seen any crime."

"You open your smart mouth again, nigger," a uniformed officer said, "and I'll break your face for you good."

"Yeah?" I said.

It was as if Mama Jo's elixir was waiting for some insult. The blood in my veins turned hot and I was suddenly ready to fight.

The sergeant didn't know what to do. And I was of no help. I couldn't seem to control my mouth or my actions and I had no proof of what crime had been committed — though I did have my suspicions.

There were four cops with me in the white kitchen. The angry one was meaty and tall. The sides of his neck were red and his eyes were blue. He'd cut himself shaving recently. The scab was near the right corner of his mouth.

I was ready to fight even sitting there with my hands cuffed behind me. It was as if Mama Jo's medicine had opened a door of foolish bravery in my heart and now it came on me whenever I was in jeopardy.

Just then the phone rang. In between the ringing I could hear the white man's cries.

"This is Dietrich," the sergeant said into the phone.

He looked up at me. "Yes."

He gestured at another policeman to undo my handcuffs. "Certainly. Yes sir. I understand."

The manacles were tight on my wrists and they held me in such a way that the ache in my arm worsened. With release I felt a moment of surcease.

"Are you sure?" Sergeant Dietrich said into the phone. "Yes sir. I will. Completely."

He hung up the line and said, "Come with me . . . Mr. Rawlins."

The meaty cop who had threatened me scowled. He wanted to strike out at me but was restrained by the respect that his superior was forced to show. He got close to me though. I'm sure he was hoping that someone would give him permission to drop the hammer on my skull.

Sergeant Dietrich walked me up the stairs to an open door that led into a bedroom with the corpse of Jocelyn Ostenberg lying across it. Her tongue was protruding and her eyes were wide with fright.

He finally got the one he was after, I thought.

There was a small pistol on the floor next to the bed. About half a soda bottle of blood had been spilled down the bed-spread and onto the floor.

"Do you know her?" the sergeant asked.

"Jocelyn Ostenberg," I said. "She's a black woman."

"What?" the meaty cop said.

"Her son is a man named Harold. He killed a woman down in Watts a few days ago."

The police all around me peered closer at the dead face on the bed.

"And what do you have to do with it?" Dietrich asked.

I was staring at the corpse, looking for Harold somewhere in the folds underneath. After he shot me he came back to her,

I thought. Was it her plan to kill him? Did she want to get rid of him for good once he took care of me?

"Was there a trail of blood?" I asked.

"What?"

"Leading from the house? I mean, she shot her attacker, right?"

"You look like you've been shot," the meaty cop who had called me a nigger said.

I ignored him.

"Can you help me out here, Sergeant Dietrich?" I asked.

"Go look around the backyard, Samuels," the sergeant said to my self-proclaimed enemy.

"But, Sergeant —"

"The backyard," Dietrich repeated.

After Samuels was gone Dietrich said, "There was a little blood. Not much. We figured that he used a pillow or something to stanch the bleeding and then made his way out. Mr. Poundstone said that his wife's car was missing. The man who killed her —"

"Harold Ostenberg," I said.

"— he probably took the car."

"Can I go, Sergeant?" I asked.

"Detective Suggs is coming to pick you up," Dietrich said. "They wanted you to wait for him."

"Well, let me talk to Jewelle," I said. "She can go, right?"

"I guess."

JEWELLE DIDN'T WANT to leave me there but I told her that I had everything under control. I walked her to her car and apologized for swallowing her key.

"Don't worry, Easy," she replied. "You ain't never taken nuthin' from me that you ain't given back tenfold. Helpin' Jackson get his job means that he can finally lift up outta the street and make an honest woman outta me."

I was wondering if Jackson could make an honest man of himself but I didn't say it out loud. JJ drove off and white neighbors up and down the block stared at me as I made my way back to the crime scene. The man who had told the police about me ran to his door when I came near. He stood there at the entrance, shaking all over and slamming his right fist into his left palm. His deep consternation made me laugh. Here this guy didn't know me from the man in the moon but still he was beside himself with hatred for me just walking down the street.

SUGGS ARRIVED AT about eight-thirty. He wore a stained beige suit and brown brogans. He shook my hand in front of a dozen cop witnesses and then toured the crime scene with a hard eye.

By that time there were three plainclothes detectives on the scene. They seemed to know Suggs. They all talked for forty-five minutes or so.

"Jordan had Peter Rhone arrested as a material witness in the Payne murder," Suggs told me on the way to his car. "I had to give up his name."

"He didn't do it," I said.

"I know."

"Where we goin'?" I asked my new friend.

"That's up to you, Ezekiel," he said.

49

They found Miss Ostenberg's car on Fifty-fourth Place in an alley," Suggs told me as we headed back for South L.A. "They find him?"

Suggs shook his head while saying, "Hide nor hair."

We drove a little further.

I was tired by then. The wounds and drugs and company of death had weakened me. There would have been little I could do to subdue Harold even if he were standing in front of me. I doubted that I could have climbed out of my seat without help.

"You got any leads on the man, Rawlins?"

"No."

"Why would he kill his mother?"

"Same reason he killed all those other women. Because she preferred the company of a white man to him."

Suggs grimaced.

"Geneva Landry died this morning," he said.

"What? Who did it?"

"Nobody. The doctors think that she might have been allergic to an antibiotic that they gave her. They won't be sure until they do an autopsy."

"She just died in her bed?"

"I'm sorry, Ezekiel."

"Just died?" I said. "If you motherfuckers didn't put her in there she would have been fine. But you were so worried about yourselves you didn't even stop to find out about her."

Suggs drove the car, his big hands tight on the wheel.

"You killed her just as well as you killed all those other women," I continued.

"I didn't kill anybody," he said softly.

"No? Then who did? Who did? I told the people at the Seventy-seventh what I knew months ago. I told you just the other day."

"Nobody saw the pattern," he said, his voice getting fainter still.

"No," I said. "They didn't. But they heard Geneva yellin' about it. They sure enough threw her in a hospital and started shootin' her with drugs. They let her slip away right under their noses. Another woman dead and Gerald Jordan gets a party at the mayor's house."

Suggs said something else but it was too soft to hear over the car engine.

"What you say?" I asked him.

"Where are we going?"

"Take me to my office. Take me there and I will call you if I find out anything."

"We can't just let this go, Easy," Suggs said. "The man is a killer and Payne is innocent."

"I know that," I said. "So you go to the papers and tell them. Tell the *Examiner* and the *Times* and the *Los Angeles Sentinel.* Tell 'em that there's a Jack the Ripper goin' up and down the streets killin' black women. Give them Harold's full name. Put that picture I gave you on the news."

Melvin was already looking at the road but still it felt as if he were turning away from me.

"Mayor's office doesn't want any publicity," he whispered.

"Say what?"

Those two words were the last of our conversation. Suggs had a job. He saved banks from being robbed and protected innocent victims from predators in the night. He hid the truth about a killer for the betterment of people that had never been that murderer's victims. I was on the other side of the board. My queen and rooks and bishops were all gone. My pawns were exhausted, while he had a full complement of men. All I had left was a king behind a lazy pawn, flanked by a drunken man on a horse. He could have beaten me at any time he wanted to. And all I did was keep pushing ahead with no plan or hope.

If I were driving that car I might have run it into a wall.

SUGGS LET ME out in front of my building. I limped up the stairs and to my office. The door was open, I could see that and the damage that Harold's gun had done from ten feet away. The key to Jewelle's glove compartment was in my stomach and even if it weren't, she and her .45 were many miles away. I was unarmed and my door was open. I couldn't remember if

I had left it that way or if Harold had shot me before I'd unlocked it.

I couldn't run because of my wounds. I should have shuffled off but I didn't. Instead I jumped through the doorway and yelled.

Mouse looked up from my chair. He had his feet on the tabledesk, leaning back against the windowsill. He smiled when he saw me.

"Hey, Ease," he said. "How you doin'?"

I sighed but said nothing. I just walked to the visitor's chair and sat down with my wounded leg out straight in front of me.

"I saw Benita," Mouse said. "She was at the hospital with Bonnie and them."

I nodded and wondered where I could find Harold.

"She told me that she almost did herself in, that you busted down her door and took her to the hospital."

"Was my door open when you got here, Ray?"

"Naw. I jimmied it. I figured it didn't matter 'cause it was already fucked up from that gunfire."

"How long you been here?"

Raymond shook his head and pointed his gray eyes at the ceiling. "Couple'a hours. More."

"What you want?" I asked.

"You saved her life, Easy. Here I fucked around and almost got the girl killed but you showed up. There you were and now Benita got a new chance. That ain't half bad. I just wanted to tell you."

I noticed that Jackson's tape had moved. Between the desk and the back of my chair I was able to press myself into a standing position. I turned the arrow switch to "rewind" and then I switched it to "play."

"Easy, are you there?" Bonnie's worried voice asked. "The hospital called and said that you checked out without paying your bill. I'm calling everyone to find you. Raymond said that he'd look for you and if you called and had trouble, he said to leave a message with EttaMae."

"Where are you, Mr. Rawlins?" Juanda said then. "I been waitin' for you to call me. I wanna see you real bad."

Mouse's eyes lit up at Juanda's tone. He gave me a look that almost made me laugh but I was knee-deep in dead black women. From where I stood laughter was a sin.

"Mr. Rawlings? Are you there?" a timid woman's voice asked. If I didn't know better I would have said that it was a slender child talking. But I did know better.

"I need you to come over here, Mr. Rawlings. It's Honey May. I think you might wanna hear what I got to say."

Jackson left me a message and so did Jewelle. Both of them were thanking me.

I picked up the phone and called Bonnie.

"Hello," a musical male Spanish voice answered.

"Hey, Juice. How you doin', boy?"

"Daddy," he said.

That one word called up a deep emotion in me. Jesus hadn't called me daddy since we were alone with no Feather or Bonnie or nice house in West L.A. He was my baby boy again and it hurt me that I'd put him through so much pain.

"I'm okay, Juice. Just had to do a thing or two before getting to you."

"Where are you?"

"At the office with Raymond. He's gonna help me close out my business and then you and me and Bonnie and your sister are all going to San Francisco for a vacation like we used to do a long time ago."

"Okay," the boy said. "But you're okay?"

"Those bullets just stung."

Feather stayed on the phone with me for ten minutes asking about my leg and my arm and my fingers one at a time. She knew each wound and wanted to know what they looked like and how they felt.

Bonnie didn't speak many words. She was waiting for me. That's all I needed to know.

"Baby," she said. "Benita wants to say hi."

"Mr. Rawlins?" Benita said. She never called me Easy again. "I just wanted to say that I know you're busy and I'm sorry that you got shot. And thank you so much for takin' the time to help me get back on my feet. I told Raymond that you saved my life and he said that you were the only good man that he ever knew."

I looked up at my crazy friend then. He smiled and nodded as if he knew what she was saying.

"I'll see you later on, Miss Flag," I said. Then I hung up the phone and limped back to the chair.

"What's up, Ease?" Mouse asked just as if it was a normal day and we were sitting on the front porch watching the children playing with a water hose.

"You got a gun, Mouse?"

"Hell, yeah. I got two."

Finally something I could laugh about.

50

I wasn't too worried about Honey May. She wasn't the type to take a shot at you and she was too kindhearted to lie and bushwhack someone. Raymond and I went to the door and knocked.

"Who is it?"

"Easy Rawlins, Honey. Me and a friend."

"I didn't expect you to bring a party, Mr. Rawlins," the closed door said.

"It's all right, ma'am. He's family."

Honey pulled the door open and waved for us to hurry up into the small purple room.

I say purple instead of violet because the shades were pulled and the lighter color had taken a more sinister hue. This was accented by the corpse of Harold Ostenberg, which lay on the little couch that wasn't quite large enough to contain him.

One eye was open. There was dried foam on his lips. His jeans had been starched by street living and his shirt was a color that no manufacturer could duplicate. There was blood near the shoulder of his army surplus jacket. I pulled the fabric back to see the wound.

There was a glass next to him on a small table. It contained the dregs of a milky fluid. Next to the bed was a fancy pillow — probably from his mother's house.

"He died," Honey said.

Mouse nodded.

Someone had taken Harold's shoes off. His feet were chafed from too much weight and motion, the twin banes of a homeless man's life.

"Why did you call me, Honey?"

"I didn't know what to do."

I picked up the water glass and sniffed it.

"What do you want me to do?"

"Tell the police that he's dead," she said. She went to a chair and sat down heavily. "I don't know."

"How long has he been here?"

"Since late last night," she whimpered.

"When did he die?"

"'Bout daybreak, I suppose."

"Did he say anything before?" I didn't want to upset her but I had to know.

"Oh yeah. It was awful. Women he hunted and then killed and robbed. He said that his mama shot him and that he killed her to protect himself. I pretended to go down to the store and I called her house and the po-lice answered. I hung right up then.

"He killed women just like you said, Mr. Rawlings —"

"Hey, Easy," Mouse said.

He had pulled back Harold's coat, revealing a pistol, .22 caliber from the looks of it.

"Go on, Honey," I said.

"That's all really. He was scared from bein' shot. He said that his mama shot him. But when he talked about it I could tell that she shot him tryin' to save her life. It sounded like he done killed a dozen women."

"Did he name them?"

Honey just shook her head.

"So you decided that you would kill him," I said.

She looked up at me as if I had just discovered the secret of eternal life. There was no denial. How could there be? The sleeping powders were in the glass next to the couch.

"No," she said feebly.

"If I call the cops," I said, "they will come here and arrest you for homicide."

"You better believe that," Mouse crooned.

"What we have to do is to get this body out from here," I said. "If we don't, you'll just be another black woman on Harold's long list of names."

RAYMOND, EVER THE pragmatist, suggested that we cut Harold up but Honey wouldn't hear of it. She blamed it on her Christian beliefs but I believe that neither her nor my stomach could have dealt with the hacking or the blood.

Originally I thought that we could build a box around him and then move him at night down the stairs.

"You crazy, Easy?" Mouse said. "A coffin's a coffin. Any fool could see that. And somethin' that big we'd have to tie on the top'a your car. What you think the cops gonna say about that?"

Finally we decided to drop the body out of the window later that night. I went down to the driveway that Honey's window looked over and put the mattress from her bed down so that there wouldn't be too much noise.

At ten past two Raymond and Honey threw the body out of the window. Harold landed mostly on the mattress but his passage was not silent. I dragged the stiff corpse into the backseat before Mouse rushed down to help me. I had the engine turned over and was headed down the block before any alarms or sirens could be sounded.

WE LEFT HAROLD in the last empty lot that I knew he'd inhabited. He was a little beat up, and no detective would believe that he'd actually died there on that lot. Any coroner could have testified that he died of an overdose of phenobarbital and not the shot to his shoulder. All of that was true but I wasn't worried. What would matter was that his name was Ostenberg and that he had on his person the weapon that most probably was used on the bodies of Nola Payne, Jocelyn Ostenberg, and me.

The police would have their murderer, and all the witnesses were dead. They didn't even have to pay for a trial or execution. All they had to do was slap their hands together to knock off the graveyard dust.

51

They called me to Gerald Jordan's office three days later. The riots were dead by then. Vietnam and the space shuttle dominated the news. There was no coverage of the nearly forty funerals held in memory of those who had died.

It was just Jordan and me at the meeting. No Suggs, no uniforms, no elite cadre of police bodyguards.

"You've heard about the discovery of the body of the man you claim killed Nola Payne?" he asked after the preliminaries.

"Uh-huh."

"He had the gun on him that was used to shoot her," Jordan continued. "That lends credence to your story."

"I don't need any credence, Deputy Commissioner. Harold killed Nola and a dozen other women. You got men in jail right now today that were railroaded because your department don't give a damn about a black woman's death."

"So you say," he said with a smile. "Detective Suggs agrees with you. I've given him permission to reopen certain cases. If he can come up with something, my office will support him. I also had Peter Rhone released."

"Okay," I said. "That's it, I guess."

"The coroner says that Harold was poisoned, that he was killed somewhere else and brought to that lot on Grape."

"Really?"

Jordan's eyes were like the twin bodies of black widow spiders hovering in space, waiting for an opportunity.

"What would you like from me, Mr. Rawlins?"

"I already told you that this job was for Nola and Geneva. They both might be dead but at least they weren't forgotten."

"You don't like me," Gerald Jordan said. "I understand that. You and I are on opposite sides of the street. But that doesn't mean we don't have common interests."

I didn't like the drift of his conversation. It was as if he were trying to pull me into something, something dirty and rife with disease. I was reminded of a conversation I had with a white man named DeWitt Albright in 1948. Up until that moment, I had thought that Albright was the most morally corrupt man I had ever met. But Jordan beat him easily.

"The only thing we have in common is what we hate about each other," I said.

"I don't hate you, Rawlins. I like you. I like you so much that I recommended to the chief that we give you an investigator's license. So the next time you're out there hustling, nobody will be able to say you have no right to be there."

———

THERE WAS A small cemetery north of Inglewood where we laid Geneva and Nola to rest. Benita stayed home with Jesus and Feather. EttaMae came because she helped Bonnie with the service. I invited Peter Rhone because he was the only one I knew who truly loved Nola.

EttaMae's minister, Zachary Tellford, gave the eulogy under a hot sun.

"These women were taken from us, Lord," he said. "They were good women who worked hard and who loved each other so much that they come to you in one chariot. They are the best we have to offer, Lord. You may see millionaires and kings and queens this week. There may be saints and hardworking clergy at your door. But no one of them will shine brighter in your heaven. Our own lives will be less for their absence."

Peter started crying from the first words. He cried harder and harder until EttaMae had to hold him up.

The service was brief and the caskets were lowered side by side into the grave. I drove Peter's rented car to my house because he was too broken up to drive and EttaMae said that he could come home with her. His wife had thrown him out when he confessed his love for a dead black woman. He really had nowhere else to go.

THREE WEEKS LATER the riots were all but forgotten. Benita was still with us but she had a job and would move out soon. On the weekends she went sailing with Jesus. They both seemed to love the quietude and possibilities of being out on the Pacific.

Jackson bought five suits and worked eighty hours a week.

He dropped by now and then to bring over bottles of French wine in appreciation for my lies.

One Tuesday I called Juanda and asked her to meet me for lunch at Pepe's.

She was early and at the same banquette we sat at on our first date.

She wore a flouncy orange dress and white low-heeled shoes. When I came up to the table she stood and kissed me on the lips.

"Hi," she said.

I exhaled, thinking that she was the most beautiful woman I'd ever seen.

"I missed you," she told me.

"I wanted to call you every day," I said.

"You know, I don't care if you got a girlfriend," she said. "I mean, I want you all for myself but I need to see you sometime and I don't mind if that has to be when you say."

She had thought about it as much as I had. She'd made concessions in her own mind and offered them up to me. But I had other ideas. And where Juanda's thoughts were young and about the light of love, my deliberations were of a much darker cast. I'd been thinking about Nola and Geneva and the lucky one, Benita — the woman who survived. I was thinking about Honey, who killed a boy that she'd help to raise, and Jocelyn, who hated the skin she came in and the blood that spawned her.

"There's no way I could have you on the side, Juanda," I said. "I love you the way you are and I want you to do the best you can. I went to LACC the other day and they have a high school equivalency program there. You can get your diploma and then start taking college classes."

"I cain't afford that," she said.

I took out the envelope with the money Mouse had given me. That and the ring I handed to the young woman.

"I can't be with you the way we both want to be," I said. "But I'd like to help you get through this school thing and see you be what you want to be."

There was no moment of weakness with Juanda. No secret assignation, no one-time love in the dark. We talked for a long time about the envelope between us. I talked to her about the riots and the dead women and the hatred we have for ourselves.

When I finished she said, "You know, I love the way you talk, Mr. Rawlins. You done talked the dress off my back and then talked it back on my shoulders. I'll take your money if you promise to be my friend."

"You better watch out, girl," I said. "You might just make me into a happy man."

WALTER MOSLEY is the author of the ac-
claimed Easy Rawlins series of mysteries and
numerous other works of fiction and nonfiction.
He has received a Grammy Award and the
Anisfield-Wolf Award, among other honors. He
was born in Los Angeles and lives in New York.